A Player to Be Maimed Later

A LLOYD KEATON MYSTERY

A PLAYER TO BE MAIMED LATER

JOHN BILLHEIMER

FIVE STAR
A part of Gale, Cengage Learning

GALE
CENGAGE Learning·

Detroit • New York • San Francisco • New Haven, Conn • Waterville, Maine • London

GALE
CENGAGE Learning·

Copyright © 2013 by John Billheimer
Five Star™ Publishing, a part of Gale, Cengage Learning.

LIBRARY OF CONGRESS CATALOGING-IN-PUBLICATION DATA

Billheimer, John W.
    A player to be maimed later : a Lloyd Keaton mystery / John Billheimer. — First Edition.
        pages cm
    ISBN 978-1-4328-2719-9 (hardcover) — ISBN 1-4328-2719-7 (hardcover)
    1. Sportswriters—Fiction. 2. Baseball—Fiction. I. Title.
813'.54—dc23   2013008357

First Edition. First Printing: August 2013
Find us on Facebook– https://www.facebook.com/FiveStarCengage
Visit our website– http://www.gale.cengage.com/fivestar/
Contact Five Star™ Publishing at FiveStar@cengage.com

Printed in Mexico
1 2 3 4 5 6 7 17 16 15 14 13

For Jim Stapleton, whose gracious good nature had a lasting impact on my life and the lives of all who knew him

ACKNOWLEDGMENTS

Every work of fiction reflects some matters of fact. As always, I am indebted to a number of people who helped me get a few facts straight. These include Denis and Gail Boyer Hayes of the firm Hayes, Hayes, and Hayes for legal advice; Bob and Dale Lewis for pharmaceutical details; and Scott Warnasch and Howard Sussman for insights into pathology and the impact of water temperature on bodily decay. Any blame for misstatements in these matters belongs to the author.

In the interests of sharing the blame, I once again wish to acknowledge the contributions of the Wednesday Night Wine Tasting and Literary Society, whose members help to keep me upbeat, upstanding, and up-to-date. The West Coast contingent of this quasi-elite group includes Sheila Scobba Banning, Mark Coggins, and Ann Hillesland, while Sheila York contributes a sharp editorial eye from the East Coast.

Smart lad, to slip betimes away
From fields where glory does not stay
And early though the laurel grows
It withers quicker than the rose.

Eyes the shady night has shut
Cannot see the record cut,
And silence sounds no worse than cheers
After earth has stopped the ears:

Now you will not swell the rout
Of lads that wore their honours out,
Runners whom renown outran
And the name died before the man.

—A. E. HOUSMAN, *To an Athlete Dying Young*

CHAPTER ONE:
A DYING BUSINESS

CLEVELAND NEWS, **September 4**

BLAZE STENDER MISSING IN BOATING ACCIDENT

Former Cleveland Indians pitching ace Blaze Stender was reported missing early this morning after debris from his thirty-seven-foot pleasure boat, Three Strikes, *washed ashore in Cleveland Harbor. The boat apparently slammed into the harbor's west breakwater at a high rate of speed sometime during last evening's severe storms.*

Heavy waves persist at the breakwater, making the Coast Guard's search for survivors difficult. It is not known whether any passengers were aboard the boat with Stender when the storm hit. According to harbor personnel, Stender was a familiar figure in the Edgewater Marina and an experienced boat handler, although harbormaster Peter Nosler noted that "It wasn't like Blaze to ignore gale force wind advisories." Stender's craft was the third to crash against the breakwater this year.

Stender spent the first six years of his professional career in Cleveland, making the All-Star team in five of those years. After leaving the Indians as a free agent, he pitched for a variety of teams, including the Los Angeles Dodgers, New York Mets, Chicago Cubs, and New York Yankees, before retiring three years ago with two hundred and fifty-three regular-season wins and two Cy Young awards.

More details, photos on page 7.

(Two Weeks Earlier)

The weather was unseasonably hot for August, and the air-conditioning in the *Menckenburg Herald* office had been on the fritz for three days, causing Lloyd Keaton's shirt to stick to the back of his chair as he leaned forward to proof his next day's column. He'd just scrolled through the first paragraph when the squeaking of chairs in nearby cubicles and the growing murmur of voices in the aisle alerted him to an advancing procession.

The two-person parade stopped at the entrance to his cubicle. Jeannie, the newspaper's bosomy receptionist, swept her left hand in an arc as if she were a magician completing a trick. "Here he is, Mr. Stender."

Heads popped up over partition walls as a Hollywood-handsome figure with shoulders not quite as broad as a Humvee ducked past Jeannie's upraised arm and entered Keaton's cubicle.

Keaton's shirt pulled free of the chair back as he rose quickly and held out his hand. "Blaze. Blaze Stender. It's good to see you."

Stender shook Keaton's hand and waved the reporter back into his swivel chair. Looking impossibly cool in a blue blazer, he settled his athletic frame into the spare chair beside Keaton's file cabinet and stretched out his long legs. The two men nearly exceeded the capacity of Keaton's cubicle, so Jeannie stepped back into the aisle and asked, "Can I get you anything?"

Stender smiled. "Coffee'd be real nice, thanks."

"Iced tea would be nice too, but nobody asked me," Keaton called out as Jeannie swiveled her hips back through the honeycomb of cubicles. "That's a first. Usually a beverage request won't get you anything but a five-minute lecture on women's rights."

"She's just being hospitable. I gave her an autograph for her nephew."

"That's another first. She's an only child. Any nephew would have to appear in the Guinness Book of Records."

"I won't let on you told me."

"What brings you to Menckenburg? Retracing your glory years?"

"Something like that." Stender clasped both hands behind his head. "Got a proposition for you. I'd like you to write my life story."

"Your life story?" Keaton was surprised and flattered. "Your life's nowhere near over. You've only been out of baseball what? A couple of years?"

"Three, actually. And that's one of the reasons I'm here. Two more years and I'll be eligible for the Hall of Fame. Be nice to have a little publicity when my name comes up for a vote."

"You think a timely biography might swing some votes?"

"Couldn't hurt."

"Seems like your two hundred and fifty wins make a better argument."

Stender raised three fingers. "Two hundred and fifty-three wins. Might not be enough, though. There's pitchers with more wins who haven't made it in. Look at Tommy John. And Bert Blyleven barely made it on the last possible ballot."

"But there's pitchers who've won a lot fewer games and made it in."

"Guys who were real popular. Or died while still playing, like Addie Joss."

"Come on, Blaze. There's no need for you to die young. You were plenty popular. Cleveland fans nearly rioted when you left for free agency."

"Yeah. Leaving the Tribe was probably a mistake. After that I was just a hired gun with no real home. Seven teams in twelve years."

The receptionist returned with a mug of coffee, a carton of

cream, and assorted sweeteners on a silver platter. "I didn't know how you took it, so I brought all the fixings."

Stender smiled and lifted the mug. "Black's just fine, hon. Think you could find my friend here some iced tea?"

Jeannie returned the smile. "Of course." She sashayed back down the carpeted aisle.

"Talk about popular," Keaton said. "If you can get Jeannie to bring me tea, getting seventy-five percent of the baseball writers to vote for you should be a cinch."

"Takes a different kind of persuasion, I'm afraid. Most of the voters are male."

"Have Jeannie take them all coffee. Put your picture on the mugs." When Stender didn't smile, Keaton changed the subject. "You said there are other reasons you wanted your bio written."

Stender poked his head outside the cubicle, looked up and down the corridor, and then lowered his voice. "This is just between us, old friend, but I need the money."

"Come on. You cashed in on the free-agent market at least four times. They called you the ten-million-dollar man."

Stender shrugged. "Uncle Sam took a lot of that. A few bad investments and two stock-market crashes didn't help. And my investment advisor got me into a Ponzi scheme like Bernie Madoff's. Like he was doing me a favor."

"Good Lord, Blaze. I'm sorry. I didn't know."

Stender shrugged again. "It's not like I'm destitute. I've still got the boat and the place on Lake Erie. But it's a bad time to sell them, even if I wanted to. So every bit of income I can scratch together will help."

"Well, I've got to tell you, I doubt that a publisher's advance will come close to your pitching salary."

"I've already got two publishers bidding, and the action's up to four hundred grand. With you as part of the package, the bids might go even higher."

Keaton shook his head. "I don't think my name will mean much to a big-time publisher."

"Don't be so modest. Your name still gets a lot of recognition."

"Could be that's because it's my father's name too. And my grandfather's."

"But you're still doing the family tradition proud. Come on. I'll cut you in for a quarter of the deal."

The offer nearly matched Keaton's annual salary. Still, he wasn't sure. "I don't know, Blaze. In today's market, the kind of book you're pushing tends to be a puff piece, a hatchet job, or a steroid tell-all. I don't want to write a puff piece or a hatchet job, and so far as I know, you missed the steroid bandwagon."

Stender's palm pierced the air like an airplane taking off. "Passed me right by."

"They took those anonymous drug tests your last year in the bigs. Anything in those records likely to come back and bite you the way it did A-Rod?"

Stender stood and put both hands on his waist, parting his blazer to show off his slim frame. "Do I look bulked up?"

"You look fine to me," Jeannie said, returning with Keaton's iced tea.

As Keaton took the drink from Jeannie, Stender kept his hands on his waist, holding his pose like a statue. Keaton recognized the pose as one the ex-pitcher had struck while modeling underwear when he was heavily into endorsements. "What about your teammates? Were any of them juicers?"

Jeannie backed out of the cubicle and Stender sat down. "The last couple of years, I was just trying to hang on. I wasn't paying much attention to my teammates."

"So what is there to write about? Oklahoma country boy makes good?"

"What's wrong with that?" Stender hooked his thumbs in his

belt and affected an Okie twang. "There's lots of us good ol' country boys out there."

"Unfortunately, damn few of them buy books."

"Well, then, we'll just have to give the reader a lot of good solid insider baseball. Tight pennant races. I pitched in three World Series, you know."

"I'll grant you there's some exciting stuff there. But why come to me to write it?"

Stender leaned forward. "I've always liked you, Lloyd. Ever since we started out together in Cleveland. I'd just come up from a season here in Menckenburg and had a lot of rough edges. Some of the reporters and announcers worked me over pretty good. But not you."

"I was pretty green myself back then."

"You and Liz helped me and Barb over a lot of rough patches."

Keaton smiled at the thought of Stender's bright, lovely wife. "How is Barb?"

"Just fine. She encouraged me to bring you on board. Insisted I drive down here to ask you personally."

"We did have some good times." Keaton shook his head. "Kind of lost track after you left Cleveland, though."

"Well, you know how it is. I was in the National League for quite a while. I came back through Cleveland when I was with the Yankees, but you were gone by then."

"Pretty far gone." Keaton stared at his darkened computer screen. "I'm getting it back together, though. Cleaned up my debts. Joined Gamblers Anonymous."

"I know. Barb kept up through Liz. We were sorry to hear the two of you split up."

"Liz stayed here with Davy after the divorce." Keaton spread his arms in a gesture that took in his computer and his cubicle. "This is not a bad gig. Menckenburg's a good place to raise a kid. And Triple-A's the next best thing to the big leagues."

"It's not Cleveland though. And the *Herald* isn't the *Cleveland News*. And I'll let you in on a little secret. Neither of them is the *New York Times.*"

"That's not necessarily a bad thing."

"Oh, hell, Lloyd. You deserve better than this. That series you did on steroids and congressional grandstanding was Pulitzer Prize stuff. And I liked the way you stuck up for Dale Loren when he was being railroaded by Congress and the grand jury."

"That's right. You would have known Loren when he was with the Indians."

"He was the reason I got called up from Menckenburg. They needed another lefty starter when he lost his stuff."

"Bait MacFarland overworked him. Filled him with cortisone and blew his arm out."

"See, that's the kind of inside stuff you could put in the book. Show up some of those fakers in the old-boy network. Like MacFarland." Stender punched his left fist forward as if he'd just struck out a hitter. "Come on. What do you say? I know you can use the extra money."

"I've got a full-time job right here. I'd have to clear it with my editor."

"Want me to talk to him?"

"No. I'll talk to him. Give me a day to think about it. Get all my ducks in a row."

Stender laid on his Okie twang. "Get all them peckers pointed in the same di-rection."

"With talk like that, maybe you should be writing your own book."

Stender stood up. "Nope. This ol' country boy is willing to pay you city folks to keep talk like that out of the book."

"That could be a big mistake."

★ ★ ★ ★ ★

As soon as Stender had gone, Meri Atkins's red hair and green eyes appeared over the wall of Keaton's cubicle. "You're going to take the job, aren't you?"

Keaton was more amused than offended by his neighbor's eavesdropping. "You heard."

"Are you kidding? With our little Miss 'Drink Service Is Not, Like, In My Job Description' delivering cleavage and coffee and even going back for iced tea, I was waiting for a third miracle so we could start the canonization process."

Keaton shrugged. "I don't know about his offer. I've got a full-time job right here."

"How much time could it take? A book on Stender's life might be a little longer than an Amish phone book, but it's bound to be a lot shorter than the first chapter of *War and Peace*."

"You're not a fan of his?"

"Actually, he was my first real crush. But I never forgave him for selling out the Indians."

"It's the curse of small-market teams. They can't outbid the big boys when their best players file for free agency."

"I know that now. But as a teenager I took it personally."

"You mean you weren't always the worldly sophisticate I see kneeling on her desk to peek into my cubicle?"

"It took me years to develop this suave persona. I'm still a work in progress. Still growing. Any day now I expect to be able to spy on you without kneeling on my desk."

"Or putting your ear to the partition?"

"How else am I going to learn enough to take over your column? If God hadn't meant for us to eavesdrop, she wouldn't have made this wallboard so flimsy."

"So you're saying if you had my job and Blaze Stender's offer, you'd write his biography."

"Oh, yeah. And you should too. If I were you, I'd go see Eddie right now."

"I'll do that. If only to get out of earshot."

City Editor Eddie Oliver sat at his desk flanked by stacks of the most recent *Herald* editions and the day's copy sheets. A wiry, balding man just past sixty, he took an unlit pipe from his mouth when Keaton entered, pointed its stem at the reporter, and asked, "What was all that commotion out there?"

"Blaze Stender paid me a surprise visit."

"Blaze always could attract a crowd. What'd he want?"

"Wants me to write his life story."

"Strikes me that would be a pretty slim volume. Is there really that much of a story there?"

"For baseball fans there is. He's hoping to get it out in time to influence the Hall of Fame voters."

"Well, all the big politicians come out with biographies just before election day. Guess it was just a matter of time before baseball players caught on. Think my grandson ought to write his memoirs before he runs for sophomore class president?"

"Can't hurt."

"You gonna take Stender's offer?"

Keaton shrugged. "Mark me down as undecided. That's why I came to see you."

Oliver riffled the edges of the stack of newspapers on his desk. "Well, it's no secret this rag is on life support. We've been hemorrhaging red ink for three years. Subscriptions are down thirty percent and advertising revenue's down forty percent."

"Thinking about pulling the plug?"

"Not if I can help it. Bad enough we went from a two-newspaper town to a one-newspaper town. Don't want to think about living in a no-newspaper town. Brass wants me to cut staff."

"You going to do it?"

"Got to do something. We've already cut pages and dropped a lot of syndicated strips. I won't cut your job, but you're bound to be affected."

"Affected? How?"

"If I do cut staff, the survivors will have to do more work, pick up more assignments, just to take up the slack. Instead of that, I've been thinking about cutting everybody back to a thirty-six-hour week."

"So you wouldn't have to lay anybody off and we'd all do the same amount of work for less pay."

Oliver clamped his pipe between his teeth and nodded. "That's about the size of it."

"Sure glad I stopped in to see you."

Oliver laid his hand on the stack of *Herald*s. "Read the papers. We're a dying business."

"There's a contradiction in there somewhere."

"Never thought I'd see the day. Old-timers like your daddy and granddaddy wouldn't recognize the business."

"Sounds like you're telling me to moonlight for Stender."

"Beats moonlighting at the Colonel's chicken emporium."

"Stender started out here with the Mammoths. You were around then. What do you remember about him?"

"That was a while back, and he was only here for six months or so before Cleveland called him up." Oliver stared into the bowl of his pipe, then shook his head. "Don't remember much, really. Pretty steady guy. Fastball in the mid-nineties. Seemed to keep improving." Oliver looked up from his pipe. "The Mammoths had two young hotshots back then. Both out of Oklahoma State. Stender and this other kid, Lanny Morton. Hell, if you had to bet at the time, you would have picked Morton for the future Hall of Famer. He could hit a hundred miles per hour with his fastball. Went through Triple-A batters like a hot knife through butter. The two of them came here together, and Cleveland called them both up at the same time. But Morton got all the headlines. Started right out as the Tribe closer. Did just fine for a time, but never developed another pitch to go with his heater. He flamed out after a couple of years, but Stender just kept getting better and better."

Oliver returned his pipe to his mouth. "But hell, you know that part of it. You were in Cleveland then with the *News.*"

Keaton nodded. "But anything you could tell me about their time here in the minors would be a big help."

"Well, that's over twenty-five years ago. I can barely remember what I had for breakfast this morning. You can find the box scores on microfiche in the morgue. We gave both the young pitchers a lot of ink at the time. Seems to me there was talk of some DUI charges being fixed. Some kind of spring training high jinks. But I'm pretty sure those involved Morton, not Stender. Morton was wild on and off the diamond. He'd probably make better copy for a book. Stender was pretty much a straight arrow when he was here. Popular, though. Got on well with the press and the fans. Went on to marry a real honey. Wife's quite a looker. Wouldn't be much of a hardship to interview her."

"I'm looking forward to it. I knew her in Cleveland."

"Sounds like you've decided to take the job."

"Like you say, it beats moonlighting at Kentucky Fried Chicken. I still need to clear it with Liz, though."

"At least you two are still talking. I take that to be a good sign."

After work, Keaton detoured by the frame house where his ex-wife Liz lived with their teenage son Davy. He sat for a few moments in the driveway, remembering better times and listening to a succession of sharp *thocks* that meant Davy was practicing

21

fielding by bouncing a tennis ball off the back steps.

While he was still sitting in the driver's seat of his Ford Escort, Liz appeared in the doorway, holding a dish towel in one hand and patting a tendril of black hair back into her bun with the other. "Lloyd. I thought that sounded like you. Are you just going to sit there, or will you come in?"

Keaton opened the car door. "I'm coming in."

Liz held the screen door open as Keaton brushed by her, close enough to catch the scent of lilacs. "Stay for dinner?" she asked, leading him into the kitchen.

"I'd like to, but I can't. I've got to check in on Dad."

Liz draped the dish towel over the kitchen faucet. "How is he getting along?"

"No better. But I don't think he's any worse."

"Well, that's something."

"He's the reason I stopped by, really. Blaze Stender dropped in at the office today."

Liz brightened at the sound of Stender's name. "Blaze. My God. It's been years. What did he want?"

"He asked me to write his biography. It was quite a surprise."

"I don't know. You were such good friends when he was in Cleveland. Remember when we shaped our social life to fit the team's schedule? We'd go out to dinner on free days and rain-outs. You and me and Blaze and Barb."

"Blaze says you're still in touch with Barb."

"Christmas cards, mostly. You know how hard it is for me to let go of friends."

"Harder than letting go of husbands?"

Liz changed the subject. "When will you start on Blaze's book?"

"I haven't told him I'll take the job."

"Why not?"

"I wanted to talk to you first. There may be some travel

involved. For interviews."

"Oh, I see." Liz looked down. "There's your dad."

"He needs looking after. Not full time. Not yet. But a little every day."

"When and where would you be traveling?"

"I'm really not sure yet. Cleveland, certainly. Probably Oklahoma."

"Cleveland's not that far away. You might even take your dad. He could stay with your aunt Martha."

"Aunt Martha gave up on him. She shipped him south to me."

"Your aunt Martha's a saint. But she's getting on in years, and full-time care was just too much for her. I'll bet she'd love a few short visits from your dad. And you'd be there to help."

"There are bound to be places I can't take him." Keaton raised his hand as if he were going to reach out to Liz, then let it drop back into his side. "I was hoping you'd be able to help. He's fine living in the apartment down the hall from me. I look in before I go to work and when I get home. He's got his books and the TV. Most of the time he's no problem."

"Lloyd. There are times when he doesn't know who or where he is. Don't forget, I've seen him at those times."

"I'm looking into homes if he gets worse. The extra money from the book would be a big help if it comes to that." Keaton took a deep breath. "The money would help with Davy's college fund as well."

Liz's lower lip moved almost imperceptibly, and Keaton knew she was biting the inside of it to keep from pointing out that Davy's college fund had been raided and decimated twice to cover bets on sure things that never materialized. The second raid had cost them their marriage. Keaton had argued that divorce was "just another damn thing they couldn't afford," but Liz had insisted on the breakup.

Keaton winced at the memory. "If Dad's going to be a problem, maybe I shouldn't take the job."

Liz patted his arm. "Don't worry. We'll find a way. I think it's great that Blaze has asked you to do it. I can check on your dad when I finish up at the library. And Davy can help out too."

Davy burst through the kitchen door. "What can I help out with?" He raised his shortstop's glove, which still had a tennis ball clamped in its webbing. "Hey, Dad. What's up?"

"Blaze Stender has asked your dad to write his biography," Liz said.

"Wow. That's great. Can you get me his autograph?"

Keaton smiled. "I'm sure he'd be glad to sign a first edition."

"You can sign it too, can't you?" Davy said. "I mean, it won't be one of those ghostwritten things, will it?"

"Oh, no. My name will be on it too."

"Does that mean you'll have the final say on what goes into it?" Davy asked.

"We didn't talk about that," Keaton said. "I certainly hope so."

"You shouldn't have any problems with Blaze," Liz said. "But some authors can get into trouble even if their names aren't on the book. Wasn't there some Hollywood starlet who sued her ghostwriter on the grounds that her alleged autobiography damaged her career?"

"Blaze is much more levelheaded than that," Keaton said.

"I certainly hope so." Liz turned to Davy. "There will be some travel involved. You and I will have to help out with your grandfather when your dad is out of town."

"No problemo," Davy said. "I like Granddad. He tells great stories about his sports-writing days."

"Some of them are even true," Keaton said.

"I know, he makes stuff up," Davy said. "But he's pretty funny. Will you have to make stuff up about Blaze Stender?"

"His life should be interesting enough so that I don't have to make stuff up."

"What if there's something he doesn't want you to tell?"

"I guess we'll have to work that out."

"Cover it up, you mean?" Davy said. "Isn't that just as bad as making stuff up?"

"With any luck, we shouldn't have to do either one."

CHAPTER TWO:
THE TOMMY FUND

KEATON'S KORNER

This columnist received an unexpected but most welcome visit yesterday from Blaze Stender, who retired from baseball three years ago after amassing two hundred fifty-three wins with an ERA of 3.24. Since his retirement, Blaze has been working with Indians pitchers in spring training and spearheading the Tommy Fund, the charity he started for research into Down's syndrome.

Full Disclosure: After a pleasant conversation, yours truly agreed to collaborate with Blaze on an upcoming biography. Those of you who have been around as long as I have will remember that Blaze was a first-round draft pick who started his professional career right here in Menckenburg. Anyone who would like to share anecdotes or recollections of that phase of his career should contact me through my Web site, www.keatons korner.com.

Built-in bookcases holding trophies, plaques, and autographed baseballs lined one wall of the den in Blaze Stender's home in the Cleveland suburb of Shaker Heights. Two other walls displayed awards and photographs, including pictures of Stender with each president from Reagan to George W. Bush, along with four framed *Sports Illustrated* covers showing the pitcher in four different uniforms.

Keaton leaned forward in a chair whose vertical slats and legs had been formed from baseball bats while Stender roamed the room, pausing in front of a trophy and reciting his won-lost record for the year etched on its base, gripping an autographed ball across the seams and recalling the score of the game it commemorated, or polishing a plaque with his sleeve and reading the words engraved on the award.

They'd been at it for over an hour when Keaton held up his hand. "Whoa there, Blaze. This is all good background, but how about giving me something I can't get by Googling?"

Stender put the autographed ball he'd been gripping back on its stand. "Like what?"

"Well, like what was your proudest moment on the diamond?"

Stender tapped the framed *Sports Illustrated* cover with the familiar picture of his Cleveland catcher, Red Gilles, lifting him in a bear hug following his first no-hitter. "No-hitting the Yankees my second year up. That was when I first knew I really belonged in the bigs."

"What do you remember most about the game?"

"Getting Kemp on a called third strike to end it."

"Pitch looked like it might have been a little outside."

Stender smiled. "That's what Kemp thought. But the ump's opinion was the only one that counted."

Keaton flipped to a fresh page in his notebook and checked his tape recorder. "What's been your biggest disappointment?"

"Not winning the Cy Young award my last year with Cleveland. I won twenty-eight games against four losses and didn't get a single vote from the Boston writers."

"They were pissed that you coldcocked Bengie Daugherty."

"Daugherty came at me windmilling his arms. It was all over the TV at the time. Hell, you must have seen it. Benches emptied after I beaned Evans. Still plays on those sports countdowns once or twice a year."

"You stiff-armed him with your glove, then decked him with

27

a left hook."

Stender clenched and unclenched his left fist. "Little shit asked for it."

"He was a foot shorter than you and fifty years older."

"What can I tell you? He came after me. It was self-defense. Got me suspended for ten days." Stender tapped a silver plaque. "Without the Boston votes, I had to wait till I got to the National League to win the Cy Young."

"Think the Boston writers will still harbor a grudge when it comes to the Hall of Fame vote?"

"Most likely. It'll make it tougher to get the seventy-five percent I need." Stender pounded his left fist into his right hand. "It's hell, isn't it. You win two hundred and fifty-three games, but all one city remembers is that you flattened a seventy-year-old coach."

Keaton smiled. "It's like that old joke about the bridge builder."

"Don't think I know it."

"Guy's built fifty bridges, but when he looks back on his life, he says, 'Do they call me John the Bridge Builder?' He shakes his head and says, 'No, they don't.' Then he raises his index finger and says, 'But suck one cock . . .' "

Stender laughed. "So they call me Blaze the coldcocker. In Boston at least. What can I tell you? I wish I'd never swung at him."

"*Sports Illustrated* said it was the only time they'd ever seen you show any emotion on the mound."

"Yeah, well. You can't let 'em see you sweat."

"How do you feel about that reputation?"

"It was always good for business. Like it gave me an edge."

"But how did you feel about it yourself? Was it just a pose? Or were you really able to shut off your emotions?"

Stender smiled and shook his head. "I'm no good at this

touchy-feely stuff. Best thing for you might be to talk to folks who know me, then come to me for any details you need."

"I'd planned to talk to your teammates and a few opponents." Keaton flipped to a fresh page in his notebook. "Anybody in particular you think I should contact?"

"Start with my teammates. You talk to opposing hitters, you might not get very flattering reports." Stender pointed to the *Sports Illustrated* cover showing him in the clutches of his catcher after his first no-hitter. "You know who would be good to talk to? Red Gilles. He caught me all the time I was with Cleveland. And I still see a lot of him. We play poker the first Friday of every month."

Stender turned away from the wall of photographs. "Hell, you know what? Be good for you to talk to a lot of the guys in the poker group. There's Webb Bruna—he was an exec with the Tribe when I came up—my trainer Andy Younker, my neighbor and fishing buddy Dale Lewis, and a couple of others it wouldn't hurt you to meet. Just come on over Friday night. What I remember, playing poker was never a hardship for you."

Keaton smiled. "That was before my stint with Gamblers Anonymous."

"Well, come on over anyhow. You can meet the guys. Besides the ones I mentioned, there's Bob Kessler, the doc who's in charge of the Tommy Fund."

"The Tommy Fund. That's your version of Ted Williams's Jimmy Fund."

Stender masked his features with a stone-faced stare. "You make it sound like we stole it from Williams. No such thing. Our boy Tommy had Down's syndrome. We lost him when he was only four. First thing I did with my free-agent money was to set up a research foundation to look into causes and cures. Doc Kessler runs it for me."

Keaton was glad he'd never had to face Stender's cold stare

from the batter's box. "Sorry. I didn't mean to sound so casual. How can I find out more about the fund? And Tommy?"

"Kessler can fill you in on the fund. Or Barb. Barb can tell you more about Tommy. I'm sorry, but I don't like to talk about him."

"You never had any other children?"

"No. It's one of my big regrets. I wanted more, but after Tommy . . ." Stender shook his head. "Well, Barb just didn't." Another head shake, the kind he gave to catchers when he was unhappy with their signals, reemphasized that he didn't want to talk any more about his son.

"What about talking to Lanny Morton? You guys came up together."

Stender stroked his chin and stared off into the distance. Then his features froze into the impassive look Keaton recognized from TV close-ups. "We came up together, but he didn't last long. I haven't seen much of him lately."

"What can you tell me about the rest of your family? I know both your parents are dead."

"Dad was a mechanic. A real hell-raiser. Lived all his life in Oklahoma. Died not long after I cashed in on the free-agent market. Mom was a schoolteacher. She passed just last year."

"Brothers and sisters?"

"One of each. Doubt that they'll be much help to you. They sure weren't much help when Mom was fighting lung cancer." Stender nodded toward Keaton's notebook. "Think you've got enough to start with? Be lots of time later after you've had a chance to meet with other folks. Talk of Tommy has kind of put me off my feed."

Keaton closed his notebook. "Eventually, I'll want to ask you more about Tommy. And about your family."

"Sure. Sure. There'll be lots of time for that." Stender opened the door to let Keaton out. "This door is always open."

The outside door to Blaze Stender's den took Keaton to a hedge-lined walkway between the rear of Stender's brick home and two tennis courts. Keaton passed the two empty courts and turned the corner of the house, which was modest by the standards of the Medici, when he heard someone call his name. Stender's wife Barb knelt in a bed of petunias at the far corner of the concrete wall surrounding the property.

Barb stuck her trowel in the petunia bed and stood, dusting off her jeans and then stripping off her gardening gloves as she started up the winding stone pathway toward Keaton. The afternoon sun highlighted her blonde hair as she transferred her gloves to her left hand and held out her right. "Lloyd. It's wonderful to see you again. It's been much too long."

Keaton took the extended hand. "Fifteen years, give or take. But you haven't aged a bit."

"It's nice of you to pretend not to notice."

"Absolutely no pretense involved."

"It's good of you to take on Blaze's biography too. I was really pleased to hear you'd agreed to help with it."

"It's a welcome relief from watching the newspaper flounder. Besides, I'm happy for the chance to catch up with the two of you."

"It'll be good for us too. Like old times." She reached out and touched Keaton's arm. "I was so sorry to hear that you and Liz split up."

"My fault, really. I managed to let gambling screw up everything in my life. Except Davy. I've managed not to screw him up. So far at least."

"That's good. Children can be such a blessing."

"Blaze talked a little about losing your boy Tommy. I'm sorry."

Barb shielded her blue eyes against the sun. "Losing isn't exactly the way I'd put it."

"He didn't want to go into the details."

"I imagine not." Barb sighed and shook her head. "Let's get out of this damn sun." She took Keaton's hand and led him to a stone bench built into a shaded alcove in the wall around the estate.

Barb sat and played with the fingers of her gardening glove. "We weren't prepared for Tommy. We were first-time parents. We didn't know what to expect. There were tantrums. We kept waiting for him to talk. To show signs of ordinary development. By the time Tommy turned three, Blaze was in pretty deep denial. We both were, I guess.

"I loved Tommy all the same, but Blaze seemed to turn away. It was one of those years when he changed teams in mid-season, so he was on the road all the time. He kept making excuses to stay away."

Barb twisted the gardening gloves as if she wanted to wring them dry. "When the season ended, Blaze wanted the three of us to visit his father and mother in Oklahoma. I didn't want to go, but Blaze insisted. His father was in failing health, and his sister had organized a family reunion.

"Well, we went for a week, and it was awful. Blaze's father was an ignorant Okie who made fun of Tommy's stammering attempts to talk. Can you imagine that? His own grandfather actually called him a reject. And Tommy's cousins followed Grandpa's lead and teased him mercilessly."

Barb shook her head. "Children can be so cruel. One afternoon, I'd gone shopping with Blaze's mom and his sister, and Blaze put Tommy down for a nap in his parents' bed. Well, Tommy woke up. He found some sleeping pills in his grandmother's nightstand and must have thought they were candy. By the time I got back from shopping, it was too late."

Barb's shoulders slumped and the gloves hung limply in her hands. "Blaze had never looked in on Tommy. Not once. Well, he says he cracked the door open and peeked in a couple of times, but Tommy seemed to be resting peacefully. Peacefully. Imagine that. Tommy napped his life away for three hours and no one thought a thing about it."

Keaton reached out and covered the hands that were still clutching the gardening gloves. "I'm so sorry. After what you went through, I can see why you wouldn't want to have more children."

Barb pulled her hands away. "Oh, I wanted to have another child. And another after that. As quickly as possible. But Blaze didn't want any. Said he was too broken up. Broken up. So he started the Tommy Fund and has dumped God knows how much money and time into it. When, if he'd just taken the time to look in on our son's nap . . . really look in, I mean . . . well, we might have had a real family."

Keaton looked down at his empty hands. "I'm sorry. I didn't know."

"How could you? By that time we'd left Cleveland for greener pastures." She brushed at a wisp of hair that had fallen across her forehead. "I'm sorry. I didn't mean to sound morose. But if you're going to do your job, really do it, you'll need to know all about us, won't you? How can I help you with that job?"

"Well, you've known Blaze better and longer than anyone else I'm likely to talk to."

Barb smiled and looked down at her gardening gloves. "High-school sweethearts. Married not long after I graduated from college. But you know all that." She brushed the empty gloves against Keaton's arm. "Tell you what. I kept a journal and scrapbooks all those years Blaze was playing. Give me a couple of days to pull the clippings together and flag the most useful parts of the journal and we can go through it together."

"Sounds great. Who else should I be talking to?"

"Who did Blaze suggest?"

"Mostly his poker buddies. Bait MacFarland of course"

"Well, that's a start. There's his brother and sister as well."

"Were there any teammates he was particularly close to?"

"Red Gilles. But he's in the poker group. After we left Cleveland we moved around so much, it was hard to form friendships. For me at least. We were always the new kids on the block."

"What about Lanny Morton?"

"Lanny was in college with Blaze, and they started out in Menckenburg and went up to the big club together. They were pretty tight for a while, but things didn't seem to be the same after Lanny was sent down."

"Think he was jealous of Blaze's success?"

"I didn't see enough of him to form an opinion." Barb stood up. "I'll call you as soon as I've got the scrapbooks organized. In the meantime, just call me if you have any questions. I really am glad you're working on Blaze's story."

Keaton stood and held out his hand. Barb ignored it. "What the hell," she said. "We're old friends, aren't we? Give me a real hug."

Barb pressed against him with such force that Keaton took a step backward to steady himself. When she finally released the clinch, she slid back slowly and he caught her by both elbows. His face must have betrayed some uncertainty, because she asked, "What is it?"

"I don't know. There's something different about you."

"Well, of course. It's been fifteen years. A gal loses her looks over time."

"It's not that, and you know it. You're as beautiful as ever." Keaton released her arm. "It's your accent. You've lost your Okie twang."

Barb smiled. "Traveling around the big cities can do that for you. I can still reclaim it when I go home to visit my mom."

"I remember meeting your mom in Cleveland. How is she?"

"She says she's in good shape for the shape she's in. What about your folks?"

"My mom died. My dad moved down here from Cleveland a year ago. We're not sure how much longer he'll be able to live alone."

"He was a sportswriter like you, wasn't he?"

"Yes. Sports are pretty much all he lives for now."

"Well, at least he has something. Remember me to him."

"I'll do that."

Barb stepped forward and hugged Keaton again, more quickly this time. "It's been great seeing you again." As she backed off toward her corner garden, she added, "I'll call as soon as I get things organized. It'll be fun. You'll see."

Keaton watched Barb retreat until she knelt again in her petunia bed. From that distance, she looked like the same pert Southern girl he remembered from their days in Cleveland. He waved and started back toward his car.

CHAPTER THREE:
THE HALL OF SHAME

KEATON'S KORNER

A few days ago in this column, I asked readers to share their memories of Blaze Stender when he stopped here in Mencken-burg for a year on his way to the major leagues and two hundred and fifty-three wins. Since that time my in-box has been flooded with stories and memories of that time over twenty-five years ago when Stender was on the mound for the Mammoths.

The e-mails and letters cramming my in-box recall Blaze's exploits on the field—his six shutouts, his strikeout record, and his win in the AAA All-Star game. But just as many focus on his deeds off the diamond. Blaze "never refused an autograph," "donated equipment to our boys' club," "visited our hospital ward," and "always gave one hundred percent, on the field and off."

More than a few of my correspondents claim they foresaw future greatness in Blaze in those early years. When their predictions came true, they felt they owned a part of his success. And Blaze, always ready to acknowledge his debt to his loyal fans here in Menckenburg, was more than happy to share it with them.

Lanny Morton's home in the Cleveland suburb of University Heights was nearly as large as Blaze Stender's, but there were no trophies in the den. The only reminders of Morton's short career were the baseball coasters on the bar and a large oil painting of Morton in an Indians uniform finishing his follow-through. The engraved title on the frame displayed Morton's nickname, SUPERCHIEF, in large block letters.

The current version of Lanny Morton looked nothing like the painting. Stocky and swarthy, he wore his graying hair in a ponytail and the outsized buckle on his belt was nearly hidden by his protruding gut as he handed Keaton a can of Budweiser from the bar refrigerator. After pouring himself a stiff scotch, he waved Keaton toward a seat at the bar and asked, "So who suggested you talk to me about Blaze?"

"My editor. He remembered the two of you came up together and spent almost a year in Menckenburg before Cleveland called you up."

"Oh, we come up together all right. Pitched together for almost five years, counting two in college, one in Menckenburg, and two in the bigs before I got sent down."

"So you must know Blaze pretty well."

"Oh, yeah. I can tell you more than you want to know about my old buddy Blaze."

Keaton made a show of unclipping his pen and holding it over a fresh notebook page. "I'm ready anytime."

"Where do you want me to start?"

"My editor said he remembered some problem with your first spring-training trip."

"That's what he called it? A problem?"

"He wasn't too sure of the details."

"Well, let me tell you the details." Morton swallowed a slug of scotch. "Blaze and me were going to drive from Oklahoma to spring training in Tucson. Some of our college buddies got together to give us a little send-off and it got to be pretty late before we started out."

"How late?"

Morton shrugged. "Nine, ten o'clock maybe."

"Been drinking?"

"Some." Morton smirked. "But not enough to affect our driving. We were young. We could handle it. Anyhow, we took off in Blaze's brand-new Mustang. Cherry red. Bought it with his bonus money. He went a couple of rounds higher in the draft than I did and had bonus money to spare."

Morton shook his head. "Never could figure that. I had a better record in college, but he went higher in the draft. Not the first time us injuns were beat out by you white folks."

"You really think race was the reason? I remember when Cleveland brought you up. The club made a big thing about your Native American heritage. First Indian on the Tribe since Sockalexis in the eighteen nineties."

"Yeah. There haven't been a lot of us. They make room for all the other minorities, but not us. It's all right to name teams after us and draw cartoons of us and make tomahawk chops, but when it comes to signing us up, they turn a blind eye."

Keaton could think of several Native Americans who had had successful big-league careers. Rather than argue with Morton, though, he tried to steer the conversation back to the topic of spring training. "But Cleveland did sign you. And you got a pretty late start on what must have been a long drive to Arizona."

Morton shook his glass, winced at the tinkle of the ice cubes, and poured in more scotch. "Yeah, well. A little over an hour after we start out, a huge storm comes up. Rains like a son of a bitch. Can't see beyond your hood ornament. But we're late, so Blaze keeps on driving until he spins off the left side of the road and wraps his new car around a telephone pole."

"You were lucky there was no oncoming traffic."

"No one else was crazy enough to be driving in that weather. Anyhow, the pole stove in the left-hand side of the car behind the driver's door and sprung the door open so it wouldn't shut, but it didn't hurt the running of the car none. Didn't hurt me nor Blaze neither. If anything, it sobered us up. So we used a couple of leather belts to tie the driver's door shut and got back on the road."

Morton gulped down more scotch. "I'm driving now, see, and we get about thirty miles down the road in the rain when this cop pulls us over. Well, he'd seen the car door flapping in the wind and wanted to know what happened. We figured he thought we'd hit somebody or something important, so we tell him the truth. We hit a telephone pole."

Morton raised his glass in a shaky gesture, and the scotch sloshed close to the brim. "Know what the cop asks us? Was the telephone pole hurt? I tell you, I couldn't believe it. I said I didn't know for certain about the pole, but it was still standing when we left, and it sure got the best of us. Well, the cop stares at me through the rain and I can see he's one of them Okies who grew up watching John Wayne shooting the nasty redskins every Saturday. So he sizes me up and says, 'Let's go back and take a look.' "

Morton shook his head and stared into his glass. " 'Let's go back and take a look.' Can you believe that? So we drive thirty miles back in the frigging rain to find the telephone pole. All them damn things look the same, you know. Like pussy. But even in the rain we could see our skid marks, so we found the pole we'd hit. Like I told the cop, it was still standing, but he pointed out we'd splintered it a little.

"So the cop says we've got to follow him back down the road to his station house. We plead with him, saying we've got to get to spring training, but he don't believe us. Or maybe he just don't care."

Morton brought the full glass to his lips gingerly, as if he were afraid it might spill over. "The cop just assumes I was driving when we hit the pole. Fits his image of the useless redskin, I guess. On the way back to the station, Blaze and I agree to let him go on thinking that. They've already got me for speeding, and if they break out the breathalyzers, there's no point in both of us going down.

"Back in the station house, the cop threatens to charge us with hit-and-run for leaving the scene of an accident. That's when Blaze did the first smart thing he'd done that night. He asked to make a phone call and woke up the Mammoths' general manager, Webb Bruna, the guy who recruited us.

"Well, Webb asked to talk to the cop. After he'd done that, he got Blaze back on the line and told him everything was going to be all right. He was sending a lawyer, and the worst that might happen was that we'd have to spend the night in jail."

Morton set his glass on the bar, fetched a fresh bottle of scotch from the sideboard, set it beside his glass, and settled back onto his bar stool. "After Webb hung up, the cop sets us down and lectures us about the need to report accidents right away and the penalties for hit-and-run. Hit-and-run. Can you believe it? I'm telling you it never would have come to that if Blaze had been driving alone. Him being white and all. But the cop saw a chance to get back at this injun to avenge the Little Big Horn.

"Anyhow, the cop drones on for an hour and then says, 'Well, boys, being as how you're on your way to spring training, I'm going to give you a break. I'm not going to hold you for hit-and-run.' "

Morton stood up from the bar stool. "So I stand up, thinking, 'Hallelujah, we're on the road again,' when the cop says, 'Instead, I'm going to hold you for being left of the center line.' He explains that left-of-center is a lesser offense, but Blaze and me still have to spend the night in jail. Next morning, we go before the magistrate and plead guilty to the lesser offense. By that time, the Mammoths have sent a lawyer to help us plead out and Mr. Webb Bruna has come hisself to see that there's no more nonsense. So the judge fines us a hundred bucks, which the Mammoths pay, and sends us on our way."

Morton drained half of his glass with a single gulp and wiped his mouth with the back of a frayed shirt cuff. "Now the way the brass behaved, I've always suspected there were a few more payoffs than the one recorded in the court log."

"How's that?"

"Well, Webb Bruna was there hisself. And the charge was a pissant one, with a pissant fine we could have paid ourselves. But we was lucky they never hooked us up to a breathalyzer. I'm thinking maybe the Mammoths paid for that luck."

"So that was the end of it?"

"Except that the big club branded me as a bad apple right off the bat and brought it up every time I got into a little trouble after that. I'm thinking they might have cut me more slack if I'd of been somebody else."

"Somebody else?"

"Somebody white. Like Blaze, for example. It was him hit the pole, after all."

"But he was never charged?"

"Nope. Got off scot-free. The left-of-center offense went on my record. About a year later, though, know what I got in the mail? A bill for the phone pole. Five hundred bucks for splintering an Okie telephone pole. Well, I took the bill to Blaze and he paid it. And that was the end of that."

Keaton flipped to a fresh page in his notebook. "So it didn't end too badly."

"Except for me. Like I say, I was a marked man from then on. Anything bad happened, they looked to me. They cut me no slack at all. Not like Blaze. They made him a starter and gave him time to develop. His first year he lost as many games as he won. Me, they put in the bullpen and expect results right from the get-go.

41

"Looky here. Let me show you something." He rolled up his sleeves and showed Keaton tattoos on both his upper arms. The left arm bore the cartoon face of Chief Wahoo, the Indians' symbol, while the right arm displayed a bow and arrow. "They even gave me hell for getting these tats. Said it was bad for the team image. Hell, nowadays every teenage girl has more tattoos than this." Morton grimaced and rubbed his right arm under the bow and arrow. "Then that bastard Bait MacFarland worked me so hard I threw my arm out."

"That was his reputation. You weren't the only one."

"Som bitch is still managing in the minors. Can you beat that? He must have something on somebody high up in the organization." Morton rolled his sleeves back down. "Anyhow, back then nobody worried about pitch counts or giving your closer a day off. Need a strikeout? Bring in the Superchief. Two years of that, and my arm gave out."

Keaton looked around the room, taking in its plush leather furnishings, high ceiling, and stained-glass windows. "Doesn't look like you're doing too badly now."

"I made a few good investments. Not near enough to cover two alimony settlements, though. Two years in the bigs won't near cover that. What did Blaze put in? Fifteen, twenty years? Now if I'd had a career like that, I'd really be sitting in the cat-bird seat. When they sent me down, I asked Blaze to put in a good word for me. Think he'd do that? Hell, no. Instead, know what he did? He put his pecker in my wife."

Keaton stopped writing and looked up from his notepad.

"Yeah. That's right. You heard me right." Morton extended his right arm toward Keaton's notebook and flipped his hand up and down as if he were trying to dry his nails. "Go ahead and write it down. I know it won't make your book, 'cause it would sully the image of Mr. Nice Guy, but I want to see you write it down anyhow."

Keaton shrugged and wrote the word "unfaithful" at the top of a page, followed by a question mark. "Tell me about it."

"Day after I got the word I was sent down, the team had a day off. I drove by Blaze's place to say good-bye, ask him to put in a good word for me with MacFarland. What do I see but my wife's car, parked right in front of his house. Well, I pull in a couple of houses down and wait. After about fifteen minutes the door opens and there's my wife Annie, clinging to Blaze and kissing him. Weren't no sisterly kiss, I can tell you that."

"Any chance you misinterpreted what you saw?"

"Misinterpreted? Hell, she was cleaning his tonsils with her tongue."

"What'd you do?"

"Well, I was pretty shook up. I mean, I'd just been sent down, and my wife's kissing a guy I thought was my friend. I wait about five minutes, trying to settle down, and then I knock on Blaze's door. I can tell he's surprised to see me, but he invites me in. First thing I do is ask him if he's seen my wife."

Morton paused to take another slug of scotch. "Blaze says, no, he hasn't seen her. So I call him a lying sack of shit and deck him. Laid him out flat with one punch, right there in his living room."

"Then what happened?" Keaton asked.

"Then I drove back to my apartment to have a showdown with my soon-to-be ex-wife."

"Was she there?"

"No. Our bags were all packed for Menckenburg, but she's not there. So I wait. Have a couple of drinks and wait. Finally she comes in, all cheery and 'Hi, honey.' Well, I start right in. Tell her I seen her with Blaze. And she goes from cheery to teary. Denies everything. Claims she was just saying good-bye to him. Like I don't know what I seen."

Morton stopped and shook his head. His right hand moved

in jerks and starts as if it were out of his control. Finally he slapped it against his thigh and said, "I don't remember what happened then. In the divorce, Annie said I slapped her around. I don't remember. Can't say I did. Can't say I didn't."

Morton cocked his right arm and tried to make a fist, but had trouble bringing his fingers together. "Next thing I know for sure, I've got my suitcases in the car, driving to Menckenburg. Alone. Anne didn't come with me. Got a lawyer and filed for divorce. Any wonder I couldn't get my act together in Menckenburg? Got knocked around every time I took the mound. Lost my job and my wife while that son of a bitch was in Cleveland, making a big name for hisself. Man wouldn't lift a finger to help me. Too busy fingering my wife."

Morton stood unsteadily and set his glass on the bar. "Put that in your book, why don't you? But you won't, will you? Nothing bad ever sticks to Blaze Stender. Man could walk naked through a shit storm and come out fresh as a newborn babe."

Morton walked gingerly over to Keaton and put his hand over the reporter's notebook. "That's enough for now. I'm losing my focus."

On the way to the door, Morton said, "I could tell you more about the Golden Boy, you know. Man wants to be in the Hall of Fame? Shit. What I know would put him in the Hall of Shame. Locked away with no time off for good behavior."

Keaton stopped and took out his notebook. "Sounds like something I ought to hear."

Morton pushed the notebook back against Keaton's chest. "Not now. A little too soon." He put his hand to his mouth and looked as if he were about to deposit his scotches in the entryway. Sweating, he shook his head and said, "Call me in a week." He opened the large oak door and waited while Keaton stepped through it. Just before he closed the door, he added, "Hall of Shame. That's where Blaze belongs."

CHAPTER FOUR:
NICK AT NIGHT

KEATON'S KORNER

On Friday, this column will be joined by a once-weekly syndicated column on poker. What's the world coming to? On any day, I can find more poker games than baseball games on my TV. But poker was never meant to be a spectator sport. It's a blood sport. You sit at a table with five to ten other people who want to take your money. Internet poker isn't poker. Neither are those casino slot machines that masquerade as dealers. They are to real poker what phone sex is to lovemaking. Poker requires the live, immediate presence of other human beings.

And God help anyone who tries to learn poker by watching those TV tournaments where six guys in sunglasses and backward baseball hats sit around trying not to twitch. Winning poker requires a mixture of aggression, skill, luck, and patience. The TV shows edit out the dull hands, so all you see is Doyle Brunson raking in a pot after bluffing everyone out with a low pair. They don't show you the twelve hands Brunson folded before the one they televised. The TV viewer learns the lesson of aggression, but not of patience, and expects to play and win every hand. It's like forming one's expectations of intercourse by counting the climaxes in a porn movie.

Keaton arrived a half hour early for Blaze Stender's Friday night poker game, hoping to get a quick rundown on the other guests before the games began. He also wanted to remind Blaze

45

that his membership in Gamblers Anonymous would confine him to the role of observer. Even though he'd arrived early, one player had beaten him there. Red Gilles, Stender's catcher when he was with the Indians and Cleveland's current bench coach, sat in a corner of Stender's trophy-lined den, autographing a box of baseballs with the host. A squat figure with a walrus mustache and a protruding paunch, Gilles rose when Keaton entered and waved off Stender's attempt at an introduction.

"Hell, I remember you from your days at the *News*," Gilles said, holding out his hand. "Good to see you again."

Gilles sat back down and retrieved a baseball from the box on the edge of the poker table. " 'Scuse me while I finish signing these."

"They're for a charity dinner for the Boys and Girls Clubs." Stender held up the ball he'd just signed. "The wives of the Cleveland players make up a nice display backed by the *Sports Illustrated* cover of Red here giving me a bear hug after my first no-hitter and sell the balls at a silent auction."

"Be surprised what they bring," Gilles said. "Top bid last year was five hundred big ones."

"Nice." Keaton ran his hand over the polished wooden edge of the octagonal poker table in the center of the room. "This is nice too."

"Bird's-eye maple," Stender said. "Designed it myself. With nice deep troughs around the edge to hold your drinks and all the chips you rake in."

Keaton buffed the shiny blond wood with his shirt cuff and ran his fingers over the green felt surface at the center of the octagon. "Even nicer."

The outside door opened and a short curly-haired man wearing a green eyeshade and carrying a six-pack of Amstel Light entered. Stender looked up from the baseball in his hand and said, "Lloyd Keaton, meet my accountant, Dennis Youngman."

Youngman nodded, crossed the room, and put his six-pack in the refrigerator under the wet bar. Then he opened the cabinet next to the refrigerator, took out an antique wooden poker-chip holder, and started counting chips into stacks on the table.

"Can I help?" Keaton asked.

"Each player gets five blues, eight reds, and ten whites to start," Youngman said. "Blues are ten dollars, reds are fives, and whites are ones. There's a hundred-dollar buy-in."

Keaton took a column of blue chips from the holder and let them cascade from his left hand to his right and back again before splitting them into stacks of five chips each. *Would it really be so bad if I played?* he wondered as his fingers caressed the beveled edges of the last fifty-dollar stack.

Youngman nodded toward the box of baseballs on the other side of the table. "Auction time again, huh? Don't forget to claim those on your taxes."

"The Indians are donating the balls," Gilles said.

"But it's your signatures that make them valuable. You're entitled to claim whatever they bring at auction as a charitable deduction." Youngman looked up from his chip counting. "Less the cost of the donated balls, of course."

Two more men entered the room. The first, a buff, muscular man wearing a black leather jacket over a black T-shirt, Stender introduced as his trainer, Andy Younker. The second, a balding, birdlike man in jeans and a navy-blue blazer, was his agent, Steve Parnell. The two newcomers each picked up the stacks of the red, white, and blue chips that Keaton and Youngman had prepared and took their places at the poker table.

"Hey, guys, those chips aren't free," Youngman said, tapping the antique chip holder.

Younker took five twenties from a bulging but tattered wallet, while Parnell peeled two crisp fifties from a money clip. Both men handed their bills across to Youngman, who rolled them around his finger and inserted them into one of the empty cylinders in the chip holder.

Keaton immediately recognized the next player to enter the room. The tall, distinguished man with wavy gray hair was Webb Bruna, the former general manager of the Mammoths, Indians, and Pirates. With the Indians, Bruna had succeeded a parade of old-school GMs who'd plunged the team into three decades of obscurity by trading talented young players for a series of aging stars well past their prime. Bruna had reversed this trend by revamping the scouting system and signing rising young stars like Blaze Stender to long-term contracts. This strategy had taken the Tribe to the top of their division, until the contracts of the young stars expired and they were bid away from Cleveland by big-market teams like New York and Boston that had more money to spend.

Bruna smiled when he saw Keaton and extended his hand. "Why Lloyd, what a nice surprise. I don't think I've seen you since you left the *News*. Still read a lot of your columns, though. Pretty good stuff."

"Thank you."

"How's your dad? I used to see quite a bit of him at the ballpark after we'd both retired, but he hasn't been around lately."

"He's failing, I'm afraid," Keaton said. "He moved down to Menckenburg so we could keep a closer eye on him. We still get up to Cleveland for a game now and then, though."

"Well, give him my regards. I miss the crusty old coot."

"We here to chitchat or play cards?" Youngman said. "Let's shut up and deal."

"We're still waiting for Lewis," Stender said.

"Christ," Youngman said. "Guy lives closer than any of us and he's always late."

The door opened and a balding man with an infectious grin entered. "Thought I'd wait until I saw all your cars in the driveway and make a grand entrance."

"About damn time," Youngman said.

"Lloyd, this is my neighbor and fishing buddy Dale Lewis." Stender pointed across the table to Keaton. "Now you've all met Lloyd Keaton here. I invited him tonight because we're working together on my biography. I thought it would be good if he met some of my friends. Any questions?"

"Yeah." Lewis smiled. "Why's he wasting time with us? Why doesn't he go out and see if he can find anyone who'll admit to being your friend?"

"Very funny," Stender said. "He'll probably be contacting each of you in the next couple of weeks." He started dealing cards face up to each man at the table. "Let's get started. Dealer's choice. First jack wins the first deal."

Keaton held up his hand. "If it's all right, I'll just watch."

"Sure, that's fine," Stender said, dealing around Keaton. "Just give ten dollars every other hand to Big Bucks Bruna over there. That's about what the rest of us contribute."

"No charge for the first-time watcher," Bruna said. "Just be careful not to learn too much."

Red Gilles won the first deal, anted a ten-dollar chip, and shuffled the cards for a game of Texas Hold 'Em.

Keaton's hands clenched and unclenched as he watched the red-backed cards fall on the green felt. Listening to the rat-a-tat of the riffle shuffle, he wanted to do more than watch. He wanted in the game. He told himself he'd stay out of trouble and learn more by watching, but he felt like a recovering alcoholic at a moonshiner's wake.

The game fell into an easy rhythm of banter building to suspense as each hand played itself out. It didn't take Keaton long to identify the pigeon at the table. Stender's trainer, Andy Younker, was in over his head, playing for stakes out of his reach. He compensated by staying in every hand, whether or not his cards warranted it, hoping for a miracle with the next card dealt. But the evening was short on miracles, and he had to buy another hundred dollars' worth of chips from the bank within the first half hour of play.

The best player at the table was Webb Bruna. Affable and unflappable, he knew the odds on each hand and bet accordingly, building the pot when he held winning cards and bluffing just enough to keep his opponents off balance. The stack of chips in front of him grew steadily as the evening advanced.

Stender's accountant, Dennis Youngman, was easily the tightest player at the table. He folded most hands early, called only when he had prime cards, raised only when he felt he had a sure thing, and never seemed to bluff at all. His stack of chips grew at a much smaller rate than Bruna's but it did grow, even though the other players tended to fold when he bet heavily.

Most of the men chose to play Texas Hold 'Em when the deal passed to them, an aftereffect of the poker tournaments cluttering the cable channels every night. The two exceptions were Webb Bruna, who dealt a variety of high-low stud games, and Dennis Youngman, who dealt a five-card high-low stud game called Little Squeeze. The "squeeze" occurred after five cards had been dealt and players were asked in turn if they would like to replace one of their cards. In the version Youngman dealt, the dealer was the last to choose, giving him a distinct advantage. In his playing days, Keaton had been in several groups where Little Squeeze was outlawed, and he was surprised Stender and his friends allowed Youngman to deal the game. The dealer's advantage was so great that the only way to offset it was to have everyone deal the same game or to randomize the order in which replacement cards were dealt so that the dealer didn't always get the last choice.

Stender's agent, Steve Parnell, kept up a steady line of patter throughout the game. His comments ranged from the politically incorrect ("Question: What has five balls and fucks Okies? Answer: Lotto.") to some familiar poker standbys ("Just put your money in—we'll tell you when you win.") The only time Parnell stopped chattering was when he held a good hand, a fact that Keaton assumed the other players at the table must have noticed by now.

The other players at the table were no better than average. Stender himself wasn't a bad player, but he bet rashly just enough to keep his stack of chips from growing at the rate of Bruna's.

"I could take these guys," Keaton thought. *"What the hell am I doing watching? I've won in much tougher games than this."* The trouble was, he knew, that he'd also lost in much tougher games than this. Lost much more than he could afford, including his job, his home, and his wife. He forced himself just to watch the play closely, intuiting each player's holdings from their betting patterns and imagining how he might use that knowledge. If he were playing, that is.

In the game of seven-card stud he was watching, three players remained in the pot with one card yet to come. Three of Bruna's four up cards were hearts, including the ace. From his heavy betting, Keaton assumed Bruna had already made his flush and was making the other two players pay dearly to see their last card. One of the remaining players, Red Gilles, showed four cards to a straight and couldn't bring himself to fold it, hoping against hope that Bruna was either bluffing or hadn't yet filled his flush. The other remaining player, no surprise, was Andy Younker. His up cards included two tens, but he evidently hadn't noticed that other players had already folded the two remaining tens, so that there were none left to be dealt to him, and certainly none among his two hole cards. Keaton put him on two pair, drawing for an unlikely full house.

Both Younker and Gilles called Bruna's raise, putting two

hundred dollars in the pot. When each player received his final card, Younker sneaked a peek at his, made a face like someone trying not to make a face, and began fingering his chips.

Uh-oh, Keaton thought. Looks like Younker got the card he was hoping for. He bet forty dollars, the last of his stack, and Gilles called his bet. Bad decision. Gilles's straight was bound to be beaten two ways. Bruna, the last to bet, said, "Looks like you hit your draw." He shrugged and tossed forty dollars into the pot. "Well, show it to us."

Younker turned over three queens to make a winning full house with his two tens. He'd caught the third queen, the only remaining card that could have helped him, on the last card dealt.

Gilles mucked his cards and sighed, "Well suck my dick and call me shorty."

Younker smiled and leaned across the table to rake in the chips. "This pot makes me well again. The cream always rises to the top."

"So do turds in a toilet," Gilles said.

Bruna just smiled and turned over his cards. Sitting next to him, Keaton gathered up his discards to pass down to the next dealer when he noticed a small nick along the bottom edge of the last card Bruna had turned over, the ace of hearts. He squared up the seven cards, feeling along the edges for other nicks, before he passed them along to be shuffled back into the deck.

None of the other cards he'd passed down appeared to be nicked. The ace of hearts could be an accident, the result of normal wear and tear, but Keaton didn't really believe it. Two decks of bicycle cards were in play, one with red backs and one with blue backs. Neither had been opened fresh that night. The nicked ace of hearts was a part of the red deck, which Dale Lewis was shuffling as Red Gilles dealt a hand of Texas Hold

'Em using the blue cards.

Keaton leaned forward and watched as Gilles dealt two cards face down to each player. Nothing obvious, although most of the players squared up their hole cards after checking them so that only the top card was visible.

After a round of betting, Gilles set aside one card and dealt three common cards, the flop, face up in the center of the table. The middle card of the flop was the king of clubs. Looking closely, Keaton could see a small nick about halfway down the long side of the king, right next to the hilt of his sword. No doubt about it: someone at the table was marking selected cards.

But who? The biggest stacks of chips at the table belonged to Webb Bruna, who was obviously an accomplished player, and Dennis Youngman, who played his own hands so tightly and predictably he didn't appear to pay attention to the cards anyone else was holding.

What the hell, Keaton told himself, he wasn't going to learn much more by just sitting and watching. He got up from the table, walked to the cabinet where Stender had stored the poker chips, and found what he wanted. A fresh deck of red playing cards.

He returned to the table, waited until the Hold 'Em hand ended, and said, "I think I'd like to play after all."

"You sure, Lloyd?" The concern in Bruna's voice reminded Keaton that the former Tribe general manager knew all about his struggles with gambling in Cleveland.

"The more the merrier," Steve Parnell said. "Just don't sit in Blaze's lucky seat, make fun of Denny's green eyeshade, or wear sunglasses indoors like those creeps on TV."

"I can handle that. I do have a superstition of my own, though." Keaton held up the fresh deck of cards. "New player, new deck."

"Fair enough." Blaze Stender took the fresh deck, slit the cellophane wrapper with his thumbnail, discarded the jokers, and began shuffling. "Let's have another game of Texas Hold 'Em."

When the marked blue deck was in play, Keaton managed to identify at least three other cards besides the king of clubs with signature marks. They were the ace of spades, the ace of diamonds, and the king of spades. Whenever he was dealt one of the nicked cards face down, he quickly covered the nick with his hand or another card. So far as he could tell, none of the other players were taking this precaution, suggesting that the only person who knew the cards were marked was the one doing the marking.

When the deal passed to Keaton, he felt such a rush just holding and shuffling the deck that he decided to include a small tutorial with his choice of games. "Let's play Dennis Youngman's game of Little Squeeze," he said, handing the blue deck to Youngman to cut. "With one slight variation. I'll deal five card high-low stud with an optional sixth card, but instead of offering the optional card in order, so that the dealer always goes last, I'll offer the first option to the highest hand showing on the board, and then go around the table in order."

"Why do it that way?" Andy Younker asked.

"If the dealer always has the last option, he has an enormous advantage," Keaton said. "Everyone else has drawn his last card and his hand is pretty much exposed. The dealer can see this and may not have to risk taking the optional card. It's like the blackjack dealer who doesn't have to risk taking a card and busting his hand if everyone busts ahead of him."

Youngman cut the cards. "It's not that big an advantage."

"Las Vegas has built big casinos on smaller advantages," Keaton said.

"Lloyd's right, Dennis," Bruna said. "We've been letting you get away with dealing your version much too long. Let's try it his way."

Keaton dealt the hand. Three players remained after five cards and four rounds of betting. On Keaton's left, Andy Younker showed a king, two, three, and four in different suits. On his right, Webb Bruna showed the ace, three, and four of hearts and the queen of clubs. Keaton himself showed the ten of clubs with the six, four, and three of diamonds up and the ace of diamonds in the hole.

Keaton continued the tutorial for Younker's benefit. "It's time to take a replacement card if you want one. The way Dennis played the game, the dealer would go last and have the benefit of seeing what happened to everyone else before making his decision. Because Webb has the highest hand showing, though, he'll get the first chance at a replacement card, I'll go second, and Andy will have the advantage of going last."

"I like this game," Andy said.

Webb Bruna discarded the queen of clubs, and Keaton replaced it with the two of spades, giving Bruna an ace, two, three, and four showing. A possible straight or a very good low. But Keaton knew Bruna had neither of these potential winning hands. His hole card was nicked about halfway down the long side, the mark of the king of clubs.

"Possible straight or a very good low hand," Keaton announced. "Dealer goes next." He threw away his ten of clubs, hoping to hit a diamond flush or a good low hand. Unfortunately, he replaced the ten of clubs with the ten of spades.

"No apparent help," he announced, drawing laughs from Parnell and Youngman. "What about you, Andy?"

Andy Younker threw away his king, hoping to complete a low hand, but Keaton replaced the king with the queen of hearts.

"Shit," Andy said. "I don't like this game anymore."

"Bet your ace," Keaton said to Bruna.

Bruna threw ten blue chips into the pot. "A hundred dollars on the possible straight."

Under normal circumstances, Keaton would have folded. Bruna was the only player who appeared to have improved his hand with the optional final card and, on the face of it, his hand could be either high or low. Because of the nicked hole card, however, Keaton knew Bruna was bluffing. He shifted a stack of blue chips from hand to hand, relishing the rush of being in control, then stifled the impulse to reraise and just called the hundred dollars.

"Too rich for my blood," Andy Younker said. "I fold. I'm not going to make the same mistake twice."

No, Keaton thought. *You don't make the same mistake twice. You make it over and over and over.*

Both Keaton and Bruna declared low, and Keaton's ten beat out Bruna's king for best low hand.

Bruna was aghast. "How can you stay and go low with that shitty ten? I've got a much better hand showing."

Keaton shrugged as he raked in the pot. "I read you for a straight or a bluff. Just lucky, I guess." *Lucky someone had marked your hole card,* he thought.

Bruna tossed his king and the ace, two, three, and four into the discard pile. "Well, kiss my ace."

The next deals progressed quickly. Keaton folded early twice, won a small Hold 'Em pot and lost a larger pot to Bruna in a game of seven-card stud. *Too bad whoever's marking the cards didn't nick every one,* he thought, *or I'd be a consistent winner. But then so would the card marker.*

On the next hand, Keaton was dealt two red cards face down to start a game of Hold 'Em. The long edge of his second card, the king of hearts, had been nicked about halfway down. Someone was already hard at work marking the fresh deck.

Keaton hadn't seen anything suspicious, and couldn't recall a recent hand where the king of hearts had figured prominently in the betting. He looked around the table, but didn't see any nicks on the other red cards that had been dealt. He stayed in the hand long enough to see the flop, which didn't help him, and then folded so he could concentrate on the other players. He tried to watch those people who weren't immediately involved in the betting, but saw nothing suspicious. No one except Andy Younker even touched their hole cards, but Andy kept checking and rechecking his as if he were afraid the spots might change in mid-deal.

When the deal passed to Dennis Youngman, he anted ten dollars and announced the game of Little Squeeze.

"Big surprise," said Steve Parnell.

"Denny," Webb Bruna said. "Let me suggest you deal Lloyd's variation, so that the last-card option doesn't necessarily fall to the dealer and the playing field is a little more level."

Youngman shook his head. "No. I'm going to deal it the way I've always dealt it. This game is called dealer's choice, and that's what I choose to do." He dealt one card down and one card up to each player. Keaton's up card was the ace of spades.

"Ace bets," Youngman said to Keaton.

Keaton turned his ace face down. "I fold."

"An ace is a pretty good card," Youngman said. "There's been no bet so far. You can just check and bet or fold later if you want."

"I know that," Keaton said. "It's a player's choice, and I choose to fold."

Sitting on Keaton's left, Red Gilles turned over his up card, the two of hearts, and said, "I fold too."

Each of the other players folded in turn. Even Andy Younker caught on and folded the king of hearts.

"Everyone's folded around to you, Denny," Blaze said. "You won your ante. Now pass the deal."

"What the fuck." Youngman retrieved his blue chip from the center of the table and stood up. "Well, if you guys aren't going to play my game, I'm sure as shit not going to play yours. Cash me out."

"Cash yourself out," Blaze said. "You're the bank."

Youngman counted his chips, took one hundred thirty dollars from the antique chip holder, and stormed out of the room.

"Sorry, fellows," Keaton said. "I didn't mean to raise a fuss."

"You were right to do it," Webb Bruna said. "We'd been letting him take advantage of the dealer's position way too long."

"Position is everything in life," Blaze said.

Steve Parnell smiled. "You say that to all the girls."

"It's not midnight yet," Andy Younker said. "The rest of us can still play, can't we?"

"Of course we can." Blaze Stender pulled the chip holder full of money across the table to rest in front of him. "I'll take over as banker."

After Youngman left, the game proceeded without incident until it broke up at midnight. Keaton spotted two more marked cards in the newly opened red deck, but was unable to spot the person doing the marking. He finished the evening with two hundred fifty dollars more than he'd started with and a craving to find more poker games. He hadn't realized how much he missed the game, and two hundred fifty dollars wasn't a bad profit for a couple of hours of pure excitement.

After the others had gone, Blaze Stender handed Keaton an Amstel Light and started sorting the poker chips back into the holder. "What do you think? Great bunch of guys, huh? Denny got a little bent out of shape, but I liked the way you showed him up."

Keaton set aside his beer and fanned out the blue deck of cards face down near the center of the poker table. "Let me show you something." Examining the backs of the cards, he pointed to one near the center of the pack and said, "King of clubs." Then he turned over the card to show it was the king of clubs.

"What is that, some kind of parlor trick?" Stender asked.

Keaton pointed to another card near the end of the deck. "Ace of spades." He turned the card over to show the ace.

"What the hell?" Stender said.

Keaton held up his hand. "Wait. There's more." He fanned out the red deck face down and pulled a card free of the pack. "King of diamonds." He picked up the card and handed it to Stender. "See that tiny nick along the side? Somebody's been marking your cards."

"Son of a bitch. That red deck was fresh this evening." Stender picked up two red cards and ran his fingers along the edges, then shrugged his shoulders. "I can't feel anything. How are they marked?"

"You don't have to mark every card to give yourself a mighty big advantage. So far I've only found three or four markers in each deck. But I took a big pot from Webb Bruna because I knew he had that marked king of clubs for his hole card."

Stender sat down. "Son of a bitch." He pounded the table so hard the remaining stacks of chips all tumbled. "All right. Who's doing it?"

Keaton shrugged. "I don't know that. I wasn't able to catch anyone in the act."

"But why? None of the guys need money that badly."

"Your trainer Andy Younker seemed to be in over his head."

"Andy?" Stender snorted. "If he's marking the cards, he's an even worse player than he looks. He hasn't won anything to speak of in at least six months."

"Who are the big winners?"

"Well, Webb, of course. And Denny. But Denny's been doing it with tight play and that shitty dealer-advantage Little Squeeze game."

"Doesn't mean he can't be marking the cards as well. If I'm not mistaken, though, at least one of the red cards was marked after he left tonight. I don't think it's Webb, either."

"Why not?"

"He's too good a player to have to cheat, for one thing. For another, he left that nick on the king of clubs exposed so I could take advantage of it. I don't think he knew it was there."

"But he wouldn't expect anyone else to know his code."

"Still, it's not prudent. I know I managed to cover up the nick every time I got a marked card face down."

"But you knew there was someone else at the table who could read the markings. How do we find out who that is?"

"When's the next game?"

"A month from tonight."

"Where?"

"Here. It's always here."

"Invite me back. We'll ring in two fresh decks and each pick a couple of players to watch. With both of us watching closely, we ought to be able to figure it out." Keaton looked around the room. "Maybe we could even hide a video camera somewhere. Just like a Vegas casino."

Stender shook his head. "I can't believe it."

"Don't worry. We'll catch him." Keaton felt alive, energized by the game, ready to take on anything. "Listen. I've run into some questions regarding your book. Do you have time to talk?"

Stender slumped in his chair. "Not now, man. It's after midnight and I'm wacked out." He picked up the nicked king of clubs and waved it at Keaton. "And there's all this to think about. Can it wait until tomorrow?"

Keaton shrugged. "Sure. What time?"

"Let's do it first thing in the morning. Why don't you stay over in the guest room? I'll take you out on my boat. Give us a little privacy."

CHAPTER FIVE:
STORM WARNINGS

KEATON'S KORNER

Mammoth center fielder Travis Brown, one of the highest-rated players in the Tribe's farm system, returns to action tonight against the Pawtucket Red Sox following a fifty-game suspension for using a banned substance, human growth hormone (HGH).

Brown's suspension is unique in that it did not result from testing but rather from an anonymous phone tip to a hotline established at the recommendation of the congressional committee chaired by Representative James Bloodworth. The hotline call resulted in a management grilling and (allegedly) a confession from Brown.

It goes without saying that a system that relies on anonymous tips is ripe for misuse. Brown, who by all reports did not get along well with his teammates, could have been ratted out by a jealous rival, a jilted girlfriend, or a neighbor who doesn't like the way Brown mows his lawn. We have no way of knowing, which is one major problem with the current system. The Mammoths' promising center fielder has been denied the chance of facing his accuser and punished for (allegedly) using an undetectable substance which (also allegedly) is ineffective as a performance-enhancing drug.

Before his suspension, Brown was among the league leaders in batting average and runs batted in. The Mammoths have managed to remain in playoff contention during his absence, and it will be interesting to see how his return affects both local fan reaction and the tail end of the International League pennant race.

Keaton and Blaze Stender left the Whiskey Island Marina at 8:30 Saturday morning in Stender's cabin cruiser, the *Three Strikes*. As soon as they passed the West Pierhead Lighthouse on the edge of the breakwater protecting Cleveland Harbor, they encountered a light chop.

The up-and-down motion of the boat made Keaton grimace.

"You look a little queasy," Stender said. "I've got some seasick tablets if you want them."

"Won't do any good," Keaton said. "My stomach's fine. I've just never been comfortable on the water."

"How can that be? You grew up here. I grew up in Oklahoma with just a few muddy rivers, and I love it on this lake."

"I guess it's because I never learned to swim."

"No kidding?"

"No. My folks sent me to the local Y to learn. The pool there was sixty feet long. In order to be a tadpole, or whatever their first step was called, you had to jump in and swim the sixty feet."

"Doesn't sound too tough."

"Well, I learned to do it, all right. But I never went on to the next stage. Minnow or whatever. To this day I can only swim sixty feet."

"What happens at sixty-one feet?"

"I sink like a rock."

"That's real goal orientation. Why didn't you go back?"

"Don't know. Didn't really enjoy it." Keaton could still recall his unease standing naked at the edge of the pool with twenty other six-year-old boys.

Stender slowed the cruiser, lifted the top of one of the bench seats that lined the cabin, and pulled out an orange life vest.

"Better take this, then."

Keaton slipped his arms into the vest. "Thanks."

"You shouldn't need it. There's a storm warning for this afternoon, but we should be back in the marina before it hits. Especially since you're not comfortable on the water."

Keaton shielded his eyes against the glare of the morning sun. "I'll be fine." He ran his hand along the shiny blond wood that lined the forward half of the cabin and housed the instrument panel. "Bird's-eye maple. Just like your poker table."

"I like the random pattern of the wood."

Keaton put his face close to the paneling. "I can almost see my reflection in it."

"I just hope I can hang onto it."

"You think you might have to sell it?"

"I hope not. Denny Youngman is trying to sort through my finances and come up with a few options."

"I'm afraid I was a little hard on Youngman last night."

"He'll get over it. What I can't get over is the fact that somebody in the game has been cheating." Stender shook his head. "I still can't believe it."

"We'll catch him next time out."

Stender cut the engines. "Let's just drift a while. You said you wanted to talk." He opened the tiny refrigerator under the cabin sink. "Want a drink?"

"Way too early for me. You go ahead, though."

"I never drink alcohol while I'm sailing. Got some soft drinks, orange juice, and a few mixes if you want something."

"I'll have some Bloody Mary mix if you've got it."

Stender rummaged through the refrigerator, poured himself a glass of orange juice, and then filled Keaton's order. "One Virgin Mary, coming up." He swiveled his pilot chair sideways so it faced Keaton, handed him his drink, and leaned forward to clink glasses. "So what's on your mind?"

"I wanted to check out a few facts." Keaton turned on his pocket recorder. "I had a long talk with Lanny Morton."

Stender looked out over the horizon. Dark storm clouds were forming in the distance. "Why'd you want to do that?"

"The two of you started out together. I thought it would be good background."

Stender kept his eyes on the cloud formation. "What did he tell you?"

"He talked about your car trip to spring training your first year in pro ball."

Stender's face darkened to match the approaching clouds. "What did he say about that?"

"That you'd been drinking and had an accident when you were driving."

Stender pounded the pilot wheel so hard the boat lurched to the starboard. "That son of a bitch."

Keaton was surprised by Stender's reaction. "Why don't you tell me about it?"

"It wasn't that big a deal. I was driving in the rain, skidded, and hit a telephone pole. That's about it."

"Morton said he got blamed for it."

"He was driving when the cops stopped us farther down the road. They assumed he was driving when we hit the pole, and neither of us corrected them. We were both scared of a breathalyzer test."

"That's pretty much the way Morton told it. But the Mammoths bailed you both out, so nothing appeared on either of your driving records. No harm, no foul."

Stender took the wheel and steadied the boat. "That's true. But Lanny always claimed that taking the rap for me got him off on the wrong foot with management. He had an excuse for everything."

Lightning flashed over the lake, followed closely by a loud

thunderclap. "That storm's going to hit a lot earlier than they predicted," Stender said.

"So you're saying I shouldn't trust Morton?"

"No farther than you could throw a dead horse."

"Because he said some other things."

"I'm sure he did." The boat began to rock. Stender revved up the engines. "We better start back."

"He said you had an affair with his wife."

"Oh, for Christ's sake. Is he still on that kick? That's the original old wives' tale."

Rain began to pelt the cabin's windows.

"He claims he caught the two of you together," Keaton said.

Stender swung the boat around in a tight arc. "This would be the day he was sent down to the minors?"

"That's what he said."

"His wife Annie came to see me that day. For advice, that's all. Their marriage was in trouble. She didn't know whether to break it off clean or follow him to the minors. There were tomcats more faithful than Lanny, and she knew it. Hell, he'd fuck the crack of doom."

Stender gave the boat full throttle, trying to outrun the pelting rain. The boat bounced along the swells, with the peaks and troughs coming quicker and quicker. Keaton gripped the edge of the bench seat, but the ups and downs didn't seem to bother Stender.

Keaton shouted to make himself heard over the storm and the revving engine. "He said he saw you two kissing."

"He saw a good-bye hug. In the doorway. In front of God and everybody."

The boat lurched and hit the trough of a wave hard, bottoming out. Both drink glasses bounced onto the deck and rolled toward the bow.

Stender peered into the slashing rain. It was impossible to see more than ten feet ahead of them. He cut back on the throttle and grabbed a life jacket from the nearest bench seat.

"Oh, shit," Keaton said. "It's bad, isn't it?"

"Just a little bouncing around. Nothing the boat can't handle."

"What can I do to help?"

"The ride will smooth itself out if we can get back past the breakwater that protects the harbor. Keep an eye out for that lighthouse we passed on the way out."

Keaton looked out into the pounding rain. "Lighthouse? I can't even see the prow of the boat."

"We should be coming on it pretty soon. We need to keep it on our starboard side."

Lightning flashed and outlined a dark vertical shape ahead of them. "That looks like the lighthouse." Keaton pointed. "On the right."

"Just where it should be." Stender pushed the throttle forward and the boat lurched ahead, bouncing on the swells. As the boat crashed forward, the lighthouse materialized as a disembodied glow thirty feet high, changing from red to white and back again every five seconds.

Once they passed the lighthouse, the boat's bouncing subsided to a steadier bobbing. Stender steered to starboard and eased back on the throttle. "The breakwater will protect us from the worst of the swells. I'm just going to hug it until the storm lets up. No point in trying to dock until we can see the marina."

"That was some ride," Keaton said. "Is that typical?"

Stender shook his head. "Not really. Usually we have better lead times on storm warnings and can avoid the worst of them."

Rain still pelted the cabin, but the boat bobbed peacefully inside the protected harbor. "What were we talking about when the storm hit?" Stender asked.

"You were saying there was no truth to Morton's claim that you were having an affair with his wife."

"None at all. Lanny carried his brains between his legs and figured everybody else did too. Not that there was enough weight there to rupture anything."

"Suppose I track down Annie and talk to her?"

"Why would you do that? She wasn't entirely blameless in their breakup. She had affairs too. From what I heard, she was about as hard to get as junk mail."

"Then you shouldn't mind if I talk to her."

Stender's voice rose above the pounding rain. "What are you trying to do? Crucify me?"

"I just want to get at the truth. You're telling me one thing. Morton has another story."

"You better fucking believe me."

"I told you I didn't sign on to do a puff piece. If you want me to do this, you've got to let me do it my way."

"I don't expect a puff piece. But I don't expect a smear job either."

"What makes you think I'd be part of a smear job?"

"You're listening to Lanny Morton. He's had it in for me ever since he washed out of baseball."

"I want to hear all sides of the Blaze Stender story. I may not use all of them, and I won't print unsubstantiated crap, but I need to hear as much as I can if I'm going to do my job."

Stender shook his head. "This isn't going to work, is it?"

"Not if you want to control whom I talk to and what I write."

"Maybe I'd be better off doing it myself. Writing my own autobiography."

"Fine with me. That's why they call it an autobiography."

The rain stopped as suddenly as it started and sunlight filled the boat's cabin.

"What'll it take to buy you out of your contract?" Stender said.

"Just say the word and I'm gone."

"No. You've already put some time in. You ought to be paid for that. I'll talk to my lawyer on Monday."

Keaton fought to control his hurt and anger. "There's no need for that. I took two hundred fifty dollars out of your poker game last night. Just get me to dry land and we'll call it even."

The storm system hung on for days, with cold rains blanketing central and northern Ohio throughout the weekend. The Menckenburg Mammoths postponed two straight games, but the forecast predicted the weather would clear in time to allow the Tuesday night game with the Pawtucket Red Sox to be played as scheduled.

The tarp still covered the infield when Keaton arrived at the Mammoths' ballpark with his son Davy and his own father. The prospect of rain had delayed the start of the game and discouraged enough fans so that the stands were half empty and there was room for all three generations of Keatons in the press box. The three Keatons had distinctly different builds, with Keaton taller than his wiry father, but just a little shorter than his teenage son, who was still filling out a firm, athletic body. Still, the family resemblance was evident to anyone who looked closely at the deep-set brown eyes and the easy, identical smiles of men comfortable with one another.

The smell of rain hung in the air, and the ground crew waited until the last possible minute to line up along the edge of the green tarp and haul it off the infield. When the crew finally made its appearance, Grace Hanson, who claimed to be the Mammoths' oldest fan, rattled her cowbell in the center-field bleachers.

Keaton's dad laughed and said, "Good old Gracie." The cowbell was answered by an ooga horn manned by former mayor Tony DiCenzo, and he and Grace entertained the crowd with a "dueling banjos" act until the tarp was stowed away and the public address system announced the starting lineups.

Keaton entered the names of the home and visitor lineups on his scorecard. Sitting on his right, his father did the same. On his left, though, his son shook his head and laughed. "Couple of dinosaurs, using pencil and paper to keep score. Can't be more than ten people in the park doing it that way."

Davy pulled his iPhone out of his pocket and tapped it. "Anytime I want to know what happened tonight, I can download the play-by-play from the Internet. Any game, anytime."

Keaton riffled the pages of his program. "Yeah, but you won't have all these player photos and alluring ads to remind you of the evening."

"Oh, I can get those too." Davy moved his thumb over his iPhone and held it up to show his father and grandfather a close-up of Pawtucket's leadoff hitter. It was the same photo currently displayed on the jumbo-tron in center field.

"Show off," Keaton said.

"When I was starting out as a sports reporter, they had artists drawing pictures of all the players," Keaton's father said. "There weren't any photos on the scoreboards. And you had to learn Morse code just to get the out-of-town scores."

"I thought they used carrier pigeons, Granddad," Davy said.

Keaton's father laughed. "You know, they actually did use carrier pigeons once or twice. In Chicago in the nineteen oh-seven World Series. They used pigeons to carry the play-by-play results out to the suburbs at the end of each inning. That was before they broadcast the games on radio. Even before your great-grandfather's time."

"I never know when you're kidding, Granddad."

"You could look it up. Nineteen oh-seven Series. Cubs swept the Tigers."

The plate umpire called, "Play ball!" and the first Pawtucket hitter took a practice swing as he approached the batter's box. Keaton settled back in his chair. The press box at the Mammoths' home park was cantilevered under the second deck right behind home plate. Close enough to smell the wet grass and hear the infield chatter. Keaton couldn't imagine any place he'd rather be. Or any two people he'd rather be with.

Pawtucket went down in order in the top of the first inning. In the bottom of the first, Menckenburg's number-three hitter walked with two men out, bringing cleanup hitter Travis Brown to the plate.

"Brown's fresh from a fifty-game suspension for using a banned substance," Keaton said. "Be interesting to see what kind of a welcome he gets."

Grace Hanson's cowbell and Tony DiCenzo's ooga horn led the cheers as Brown advanced to the plate, but the applause was matched by an equal number of boos from the sparse crowd.

"If the fans boo him here at home, he'll be in for a real roasting on the road," Keaton said.

"I hear he's not a very nice guy to be around," Davy said.

"Could be that's why somebody snitched on him," Keaton said. "As one of the Mammoths' top prospects, he's too valuable to care much about being nice. He's still young, though. All that could change."

Brown lined a double into the left-center-field gap, scoring the Mammoth runner from first base. As he stood on second base dusting himself off, the crowd rose and cheered.

"Best way to quiet the boo birds," Keaton said, recording the double on his scorecard. "Just produce at the plate. Might even make him more popular with his teammates."

"You know, Davy," Keaton's father said. "You don't have to

be a nice guy to be a great ballplayer."

"Got somebody in mind, Dad?" Keaton asked.

"Well, there's Ty Cobb, of course. He always slid spikes high and once went into the stands to beat up a one-armed heckler. But that was back in the days when my dad was reporting."

"What about in your day, Granddad?" Davy asked.

"When I first started reporting, Early Wynn was pitching for the Indians. Won three hundred games and went to the Hall of Fame, but he deliberately threw at a lot of hitters' heads. Claimed he'd bean his mother if she crowded the plate."

"And did he?" Keaton asked.

"I don't know about his mother, but Roger Kahn saw him throw at his son once."

Keaton nudged Davy. "Remember that. The lesson there is respect for your elders."

"You couldn't hit me if you did throw at me," Davy said.

"Of course, some great players have been real gentlemen." Keaton's father raised his pencil to make a point. "There was Lou Gehrig in my dad's day, and Stan Musial in mine." He tilted the pencil so it pointed at Keaton. "And your man Blaze Stender has the reputation of being a great guy."

"He's not my man anymore," Keaton said. "We parted ways. Creative differences."

"Maybe he's not such a great guy, then?" Keaton's father turned the statement into a question.

Keaton shrugged. "Don't know. Didn't get far enough into his life to make that call."

The two teams traded scores and went into the seventh inning tied at two-all. As soon as the Pawtucket cleanup hitter made the last out in the top of the seventh inning, Keaton turned to his father and said, "Shall you do the honors?"

Keaton's dad smiled, stood, and shouted, "All right, everybody up!"

Keaton nudged his son. "Now watch." And they watched as all the spectators rose to their feet. "See, it's magic."

Davy smiled. "Yeah, you pulled that stunt on me the first game you ever took me to see. I thought it was magic. Then I learned about the seventh-inning stretch."

"You were sharper than me. It took me five games with your granddad before I figured it out."

"Didn't take me nearly that long," Keaton's father said. "Some killjoy in the press box at League Park explained it to me the second time my dad tried it."

"So what we've got here is three generations of gullible kids," Keaton said.

"No, I'd say it's three generations of pretty sharp baseball fans," his father said.

Keaton touched his father's empty beer can and his son's half-empty coke bottle with his own plastic beer cup. "I'll drink to that."

The Mammoths failed to score in the bottom of the seventh. As Keaton flipped his scorebook to the visitors' page, his father said, "When is Yastrzemski coming to bat?"

Keaton thought he must have heard wrong. "Excuse me?" He looked over at his father, who had a blank, confused look on his face.

"When's Yaz due up?" his father said.

"Dad, Yastrzemski retired in the early eighties. These are the Pawtucket Red Sox, not the Boston Red Sox."

"They've got to be careful when Yaz comes up."

Keaton looked down at his father's scorecard. For the first six innings, the outcome of each at bat had been recorded in neat, precise notations. The column for the home-team half of the seventh inning, though, was filled with a series of meaningless loops and squiggles.

"Davy," Keaton said, "get your grandfather a glass of water."

"Are you all right, Granddad?" Davy asked.

His grandfather seemed to be considering an answer, but no words came.

"Just get him some water," Keaton said.

As Davy left, Keaton rubbed his father's back and said, "It's all right, Dad. You're going to be all right."

"Why are the stands so empty? We're playing the Red Sox, aren't we?"

Keaton continued to rub his father's back. "It's been raining, Dad. The rain kept lots of people away."

Keaton had never seen his father like this. His aunt had said his father had become forgetful at times. That was why they brought him down to Menckenburg. But this was more than forgetful. Forgetful was when you misplaced your keys. His father had just misplaced thirty years.

"They've got to be careful with Yaz, or they'll never win the game," his father said.

"You're right, Dad." Keaton continued the massage. It was all he could think of to do.

Davy returned with a plastic cup filled with water and handed it to his grandfather.

Keaton's father took a sip from the cup. "Thank you, Lloyd."

"I'm Davy, Granddad."

Keaton's father looked quizzically at his grandson. "Of course you are." He glanced down at his scorebook, saw the squiggles on the home-team page, and quickly flipped the book so that the visitors' page was face up.

"You all right, Dad?" Keaton asked.

"Of course I am. Why wouldn't I be?"

"You seemed a little out of it there for a minute."

His father looked into the plastic cup. "Why isn't this beer?"

"They stopped serving beer in the seventh inning."

"This never happened at the old Municipal Stadium."

"I'll have a beer with you when we get home," Keaton said.

The game was still tied at the end of nine innings, but Keaton wasn't paying much attention to the baseball diamond. He was watching his father, who was keeping score as if nothing had happened.

When they'd moved his father down from Cleveland, Keaton had found him an apartment in his own building, thinking he could keep an eye on him. It was obvious now, though, that one eye wouldn't be enough. His father would require live-in care, maybe even round-the-clock care.

The Mammoths won the game in the bottom of the twelfth, when Travis Brown singled, stole second, and scored on a broken-bat flare to right field.

While Grace Hanson clanged her cowbell and the die-hard fans who had stuck it out to the game's end stood and applauded, Keaton took his father by the elbow. "Come on, Dad. We'll go get that beer."

With the early rain delay and the extra innings, it was nearly eleven o'clock when Keaton pulled up in front of his ex-wife's house to drop Davy off. As his son climbed out of the rear seat of the Ford Escort, Keaton turned to his father, who had pushed himself back against the passenger door. "I need to see Liz for a minute. Want to come in and say hello?"

"No thanks. I'll just wait here."

Keaton thought his dad had the look of a freshly caged animal who suddenly found himself under observation.

Keaton followed Davy up the walk to the front porch of his former home. His ex-wife Liz opened the door to meet them. In the glare of the porch light, he could see the concerned, accusing look he'd seen too many times in their years together. When the bank shut down their credit, when the repo men came for the family car and when she'd caught Davy using steroids.

"I'm sorry," he said as soon as he reached the top porch step.

"The game ran long."

Liz just shook her head and stood aside to let him in the house. "You better see this," she said, nodding toward the TV in the living room.

The TV screen was filled with dark images of men in black and yellow slickers moving about in a heavy rain, ducking under a yellow crime-scene tape. A police flasher glowed red in the foreground, while in the distance a high, disembodied light blinked red, then white, then red again. At the bottom of the screen, red letters spelled out the news in a slow crawl: FORMER MAJOR-LEAGUE PITCHER BLAZE STENDER MISSING FOLLOWING CLEVELAND HARBOR BOAT-ING ACCIDENT.

CHAPTER SIX:
NOT A HOPE IN HELL

KEATON'S KORNER

I got the news from Cleveland last night on my way home from a baseball game. Blaze Stender was dead in a boating accident. It was hard to believe and harder to accept. Less than three years ago he was on the mound, notching his two hundred fifty-third victory and setting his sights on Cooperstown.

A few weeks ago he was in my office, asking me to help him write his biography. When I reported that request in my column, I asked readers who remembered his time with the Mammoths to share their thoughts about Blaze as a player and man. The results were astonishing. I got over a thousand letters and e-mails filled with praise for Blaze and recalling something he had done to inspire them or enrich their lives. Not one person had anything negative to say.

Blaze Stender was one of the most popular and respected baseball players in an age when too many professional athletes have feet made of clay, arms pumped with steroids, or heads filled with dollar signs. He went out and did his job superbly, start after start, for twenty years, with no scandals, no steroids, and no showboating.

He was the epitome of class on and off the diamond. Married twenty-two years to his childhood sweetheart, he founded and supported the Tommy Fund, which sponsors research into Down's syndrome, to commemorate the tragic death of their only child.

Blaze was a steady professional who excelled in big games. Crowds never fazed him. Large or small, he gave them his best effort. Last night, crowds gathered on the stormy shores of Lake Erie hoping he would emerge unscathed from the wreck of his boat. It was the first time he ever failed them.

Keaton dropped his father off at his apartment and drove straight to Cleveland, making the best time he could in the pelting rain. Police had blocked off the road leading to the Whiskey Island Marina, so he parked on a gravel berm next to a railroad siding and slogged through streaming rivulets back to the police cordon.

Strips of torn crime-scene tape whipped like manic pennants from light poles on either side of the marina road. At the end of the road, sawhorses blocked the entrance to the boat pier and marina office. It had been three hours since Keaton had seen the news of the crash on his ex-wife's TV, but a small crowd of umbrella-clutching onlookers still milled around the sawhorse perimeter.

A security guard in a yellow slicker stood hunched over in the meager shelter of overhanging eaves where the sawhorse barrier butted against the marina office. Keaton worked his way along the barrier and shouted to the guard. "I'd like to get through. I'm a friend of the family."

"Family sure has a lot of friends." The guard waved his hand toward the wind-whipped umbrellas on the other side of the barrier. "That's what all these folks say. My orders are not to let anyone through."

Keaton reached in his hip pocket for his wallet and his press card. "I'm a friend and a reporter. Does that help?"

The guard shook his head. "Not with me, it doesn't. My boss said nobody gets through."

Keaton pointed out a white TV van in the marina parking lot. "You let those reporters through."

"That was before I got here."

The door to the TV van opened, and Keaton recognized the man ducking out into the rain. It was Dale Lewis, Stender's neighbor and part owner of the marina. Keaton waved and yelled, "Dale! Over here, Dale."

Lewis squinted into the rain and walked over to Keaton and the security guard.

Keaton held out his hand. "I'm Lloyd Keaton, we met . . ."

Lewis cut Keaton off and nodded, his face drawn. "Let this man through, George."

The guard pulled back a sawhorse just far enough to let Keaton edge through. "Have they found him yet?"

Lewis shook his head. "Still no sign." He led Keaton around the office to the edge of the marina and shouted over the noise of the crashing waves. "There are divers out there beyond the breakwater, but there's no point in keeping them out there much longer. It's just too rough."

Keaton shielded his eyes against the cold rain and stared out at the lake. He could barely make out the blinking red-and-green light that marked the edge of the channel.

Lewis pointed in the direction of the blinking light. "He hit the breakwater just west of the lighthouse. Going full speed. Damn near sheared off half the boat."

"That doesn't make sense," Keaton said. "I was out with him only a couple of days ago. He seemed to be a super-cautious skipper."

"And he knew these waters like the back of his hand."

"And he said he never drank when he took his boat out." Lightning silhouetted the lighthouse. "But then, he also said he always tried to avoid stormy weather."

"That's all true." Lewis sighed.

"You think he could have done this on purpose?"

"There was talk. He had money troubles. Really bad money troubles."

Keaton wiped the streaming rain from his eyes with the back of his hand and started for the lighted office door. "Maybe so. But suicide? We both saw him Friday night, and I was with him on Saturday. Did he look like a suicide to you?"

"Who knows what a suicide looks like?" Lewis grabbed Keaton's arm. "Before you go in, you should know Barb's in there with a couple of friends. She thinks because the divers haven't found Blaze's body he might still be alive. Between you and me, there's not a hope in hell he survived that wreck. But no one in there is saying so. And I'm not going to be the first."

Keaton paused with his hand on the doorknob. "Okay, I get it." He opened the office door and rain followed the two men into a room littered with wet slickers and dripping umbrellas. Barb sat in a corner of the waiting room wearing a yellow cardigan, soaked blue jeans, and wading boots that looked a couple of sizes too large for her. Dennis Youngman, the Stenders' accountant, leaned on the service counter with a glass in his hand and a bottle of scotch near his elbow. A man Keaton didn't recognize sat in a chair next to Barb.

Keaton went straight to Barb, who stood and threw her arms around him. She smelled of wet wool and whiskey.

"Oh, Lloyd. Thank you so much for coming." She held him a while longer, then turned to the black-haired man he hadn't recognized. "This is Jim Stapleton, our lawyer." As Keaton shook Stapleton's hand, Barb tugged at his free arm and pointed to Dennis Youngman. "And this is our accountant, Dennis Youngman."

"I know Dennis," Keaton said. "We played poker together last Friday night."

Youngman lifted his glass just enough for the gesture to pass as a salute.

"I came as soon as I heard," Keaton said to Barb. "How are you holding up?"

Barb shrugged and sat down. "As well as can be expected."

"Does anyone know what happened?" Keaton asked.

"Blaze hit the breakwater," Youngman said. "Going pretty fast. Happens three or four times a year in that channel. Usually in weather like this. Usually after the pilot's had too much to drink."

"Blaze wouldn't have been drinking," Lewis said.

Youngman took a sip of scotch. "I didn't say he was."

"You implied it," Barb said. "Blaze was always careful on the water. That boat was his pride and joy."

"I kept telling him to sell it," Youngman said. "He couldn't afford to keep it."

Barb sighed. "Then things must have been much worse than he let on."

Youngman looked down into his scotch glass. "Evidently."

"You'll have to explain that to me," Barb said. "Very carefully."

"Whenever you'd like," Youngman said.

"Tomorrow, then." She closed her eyes and shook her head. "Which I guess is really today. In the afternoon. After we've all had some sleep."

"All right," Youngman said.

"And I'd like these two gentlemen to hear what you have to say then." Barb took in Keaton and her lawyer with her eyes.

"Wouldn't you rather keep the matter private?" Youngman said.

"I have a short attention span when it comes to money matters," Barb said. "I'd like to have a couple of extra pairs of eyes and ears on hand. Jim is our lawyer and Lloyd is an old friend. And Blaze's biographer. Can you do that, Jim? Lloyd?"

"I'll clear my schedule," Stapleton said.

"I'm happy to do it," Keaton said. "But you should know that Blaze fired me."

"I'll rehire you. The publisher will still want the book." Barb looked out at the storm. "Maybe even more now. And it looks as if I could use the money."

Youngman frowned. "But if Blaze didn't want Keaton writing his life story . . . ?"

Barb cut him off. "I'd discussed it with Blaze and he fully intended to rehire Lloyd."

The office phone rang. The room was suddenly silent as Dale Lewis answered the second ring. Grim faced, Lewis listened for a short time, then said, "I see." After a longer silence, he said, "I completely understand." Another silence, then, "I do understand, John. Please thank your men for me."

Lewis hung up the phone. All eyes were on him as he said, "That was the officer in charge of the rescue team. He's sending the divers home. They'll come back when the storm breaks."

Barb put her hand to her throat. "They're giving up?"

"It's too dangerous out there," Lewis said. "The storm is bashing the divers and their boats against the breakwater."

"But they're giving up." Resignation swamped Barb's voice.

"They've been at it over four hours. They've searched every inch of the breakwater above the surface and most of what's below it. Helicopters have been scanning the lake farther out."

"But we can barely see the helicopters. How can they hope to see anything as small as a man in this weather?" Barb said.

"They'll be back as soon as the weather clears." Lewis buttoned his raincoat. "We should all go home and get some rest."

"They're giving up because there's no hope." Barb stood and picked up a black slicker that had been draped over the edge of the counter. "The police brought me. Can you drive me home, Lloyd?"

"Of course."

She pulled on the slicker and paused in the doorway. "I want to thank you all for being here tonight. You've been good friends to Blaze."

As the door closed behind them and rain pelted their faces, Keaton remembered where he had parked. "Listen," he yelled over the storm. "I had to park four blocks away. Why don't you go back inside and wait while I bring the car around?"

"That's all right. I'd rather walk."

"Even in this rain?"

"Especially in this rain."

The onlookers had evidently departed when the rescue teams left, and the sawhorses no longer blocked the road. The storm made conversation difficult during the walk to the car, and Barb was quiet for most of the trip home. When they passed the sign welcoming them to Shaker Heights, she sighed and said, "Those men tonight. My husband's friends. They kept dancing around the obvious, not wanting to say it out loud."

She shifted in the passenger seat, facing Keaton. "Blaze is dead. I know he's dead. He must be. I saw his boat. But there's no body. So long as there's no body, there's hope. And so long as there's hope, I've got to cling to it. Anything else would be . . . I don't know, disloyal. But I know in my heart he's dead. Does that make any sense?"

"As much sense as Blaze running full speed into that breakwater."

"That's the other thing his friends kept dancing around. Blaze was too good a sailor to do that. Too careful. It couldn't have been an accident. He must have done it on purpose, don't you think?"

The rain flooding the windshield threatened to overwhelm the car's wipers, and Keaton slowed the car. "Seems hard to believe. Blaze was always so positive. Nothing ever seemed to faze him. I'm no expert on suicide, but there are easier, surer ways to kill yourself than crashing your favorite plaything into a retaining wall."

As Keaton turned onto the long driveway leading to the Stenders' home, Barb reached over and touched his sleeve. "Listen. It's awfully late, and you promised to be here tomorrow when Dennis Youngman stops by. Why don't you come in and spend what's left of the night? It's a long drive back to Menckenburg, and I don't particularly want to be alone in the house."

"I don't want to be any trouble."

"Good heavens, you're no trouble. You're a blessing. And you know where the guest room is. You used it last Friday night."

Keaton parked in front of the three-car garage and turned off the engine. "Friday night seems like a long time ago, but I guess I can still find my way to the guest room."

Inside the house, Barb sat down on a hall chair. "I'm going to get out of these borrowed cop boots and into a glass of wine. Will you join me?"

"Sounds good to me."

She kicked aside the boots and stood up. In her bare feet, with her blonde hair plastered against her forehead and her jeans soaked, she looked tiny and vulnerable.

She saw him staring and said, "I must look terrible."

"You look just fine. For someone who's just had a terrible load dropped on her."

"I'm not sure that's a compliment, but right now I don't give a damn. Follow me into the kitchen."

The Stenders' kitchen could have accommodated a tennis court with ample room for spectators. A long, granite-topped island where the net would have been cut the room in half. Barb stood at one end of the island, poured them each a glass of cabernet, clinked glasses with Keaton, and said, "Here's to old friends."

"To old friends," Keaton repeated.

"Thank you for coming. And staying. And for agreeing to meet with Dennis."

"Sounds like you don't trust him."

"I don't know whether I do or not. Blaze was so secretive about money. I need to have a fresh set of ears listening to Dennis. Someone I know I can trust. And I don't have that many friends."

"That can't be true."

Barb nodded. "When we first moved to Cleveland, there were some people we were close to. You. And Liz. And a few others we could both name. But that was a long time ago. We moved around a lot. I was always the new kid on the block. It never bothered Blaze. He was the center of attention. And he made friends easily. Those men tonight were all friends of his. Not mine."

"What about neighbors?"

Barb drained her wineglass. "We're not so much neighbors as the local celebrities." She set her glass down on the granite top. "I need a hot shower and some cool sheets. I have a feeling tomorrow is going to be another tough day."

Keaton nodded. "Wouldn't surprise me."

She rose on tiptoes and kissed Keaton's cheek. "Anyhow, Mr. Keaton, I thank you for being here."

Keaton was startled by the sudden intimacy. "All part of the service."

"I'll let you finish your wine and find your own way to bed. Sleep as long as you like." Barb walked to the doorway, turned, and said, "Good night. And thanks again."

"Good night," Keaton said. He looked down at his wineglass. It was trembling in his hands.

Keaton woke at his usual time of 7:30 the next morning. He'd just gotten out of the shower when Barb knocked on his door.

"Lloyd. You decent?"

"Give me a couple of minutes."

"I need your car keys."

Keaton pulled on his trousers and T-shirt and opened the bedroom door. "Are you going somewhere?"

Barb came into the room. She was wearing black slacks and a white blouse underneath a short black jacket. "There's a TV van in the driveway. Taking whatever footage they can get and waiting for a statement. 'How did you like the play, Mrs. Lincoln?' That kind of thing. We left your car in front of the garage."

"My ultrasensitive colleagues from the fourth estate." Keaton gave Barb his keys. "What do you want to do about the car?"

"My gardener is working outside. I'll have him move it into the garage. With luck, anyone watching will assume it's his car. In the meantime, you'd better stay out of sight. We don't want to set cameras rolling and tongues wagging."

"I'll call the office and lie low here working on tomorrow's column."

"You can use Blaze's laptop. I'll get it for you." She left and returned with an Apple MacBook Pro, which she set on the bedside stand. "The password should be 'jiggs.' With two g's. Let me know if you have any trouble with it."

Barb backed off as far as the doorway. "The sheriff called. Now that the weather's cleared, the divers will go back out. I don't think I want to go back to the marina and wait, though. Not with all those eyes on me. I'll hear right away as soon as anyone knows anything."

"Anything I can do?"

"No. You've been a big help already. Just get your column written and be ready to listen to Dennis talk about my finances this afternoon."

After Barb left, Keaton called his office to tell them he was in

Cleveland following the story of Blaze Stender's accident. Then he took his pocket notebook and began composing a eulogy. When Barb had brought in Blaze's laptop, he'd been embarrassed to admit that he still composed his column in longhand, but the computer would come in handy for transmitting the final copy to the paper once he'd written it and typed it up.

He was polishing a paragraph praising Blaze's popularity when Barb came into the room with a file box full of scrapbooks and set it on the floor. "I promised these to you, and here they are."

"You don't have to worry about me. You've got enough on your mind today."

"That's exactly why I wanted to pull this stuff together. It keeps my mind off other things." She knelt and pulled one red scrapbook out of the file box. "There are three books here with Indians clippings and one for each of his other teams."

She opened the scrapbook to show clippings neatly cut and arranged under glassine protectors. "There's another box in my room filled with clippings I never found time to file. I always felt a little guilty about it. That seems so silly now." She stood up. "I'll go get that box too."

"Let me go with you," Keaton said. "I'll carry the newsprint. After all, I am a professional journalist."

The bedroom looked like an expensive hotel room after a maid had visited. Impersonal, but in exquisite taste. Dresses hung neatly in the walk-in closet where she retrieved the file box full of unsorted clippings. As Keaton carried the box out, she said, "You know, Blaze has a scrapbook of his own. Some duplicates, and clippings he never passed along to me. It's in his room. I'll go get it." She disappeared into a room across the hall. Separate bedrooms, Keaton thought. Even when their marriage had hit bottom, he and Liz had shared the same bedroom.

Of course, their house wasn't big enough to offer many alternatives.

Barb returned with a large brown scrapbook under her arm. While the scrapbook she showed Keaton earlier had been neatly organized, this one bulged at the seams, with folded newspapers and whole magazines protruding from the edges.

Keaton managed an exaggerated wince at the volume of material. "Looks like I'll be earning my pay."

"Oh yes. Your pay. I called Blaze's publisher this morning. They're more than happy to have you continue with the book." She frowned and shook her head. "I got the impression they think there'll be more interest in Blaze dead than if he were still alive."

"I'm sorry."

"It's not your fault. Anyhow, Blaze evidently never bothered to tell them he fired you, so that's not an issue."

"Well, thanks for taking care of it."

"Not a problem. I told you, I've been creating jobs to keep my mind off what's really happening here." She nodded toward the box of clippings in Keaton's hands. "Let me know if you need any help sorting through that stuff. I still feel a little guilty that I never got it organized."

When Barb called Keaton to come down for lunch, the entryway was filled with flowers, large arrangements that spilled over into the living quarters and threatened to turn the downstairs into a rain forest. The smell of lilies clogged the air.

"It's amazing, isn't it?" Barb said. "They just keep coming. There's one from the Players Association, and every team Blaze played with has sent a wreath. Except the Yankees. But most of the flowers are from ordinary fans. They loved Blaze."

They were just finishing sandwiches in a flower-free zone in the kitchen when Dennis Youngman arrived carrying two thick packets of paper under his arm. They adjourned to Blaze's trophy room, where they were joined by Jim Stapleton.

The poker table was still standing from Friday night's game. Keaton and Stapleton took seats on either side of Barb Stender across the green felt table from Youngman.

Youngman took a thick rubber band from one of the packets and passed it across to Barb, keeping the other for himself.

"Just one copy for the three of us?" Barb asked.

Youngman grunted as if the question annoyed him.

"Never mind," she said. "We'll share."

Youngman held up a pamphlet whose cover featured sketches of a bat and ball integrated in the title, "Major-League Baseball Players Pension Plan." "To begin with," he said, "Blaze's benefits as a veteran with over ten years of service are quite generous. When he turned sixty-seven, he would have been eligible to receive around one hundred and fifty thousand dollars a year."

"But he'll never turn sixty-seven," Barb said.

"As his widow, you're eligible for all the benefits he would have received. Because Blaze needed money right away, he'd filled out papers to allow him to start taking a lesser amount next year, when he'd turn forty-five."

"How much is the lesser amount?" Barb asked.

Youngman consulted his notes. "Around fifteen hundred a month."

"That won't cover our property taxes," Barb said.

"Blaze never filed his request for early payment, so you can still elect to wait and qualify for the full benefit amount," Youngman said.

"What about life insurance?" Keaton asked.

"Five hundred thousand in term insurance. He had a couple of full life policies when he was playing, but he let those lapse after he retired and the money tightened."

Hardly the action of a man contemplating suicide, Keaton thought.

"Well, that's something, anyhow," Barb said. "But what I really want to know is how we got into such a desperate state that Blaze let some of his insurance lapse and wanted to draw his pension early."

Youngman tapped the stack of papers in front of him. "The details are all right here."

"Before you go into them, can you give us a quick overview?" Barb said.

Youngman adjusted his glasses. "I'm afraid it's not a very pretty overview."

"Then the details aren't likely to make it any prettier," Barb said.

"The year Blaze stopped pitching, you had about forty million dollars in various accounts. Mutual funds, mostly, aggressively invested in growth issues. The first year after he retired, your investments returned a little over three million. More than enough to live on without touching the principal, even with Blaze donating over one million to the Tommy Fund. Then the market took its big dip. You lost half your principal."

"That would still leave us with twenty million," Barb said.

Youngman nodded. "That's correct, but it wasn't enough to suit Blaze. Once the IRS took its cut of your earnings, he didn't have enough left to give a million a year to the Tommy Fund without eating into your principal."

"Couldn't he cut back on his donations to the fund?" Barb asked.

"He didn't want to. He felt an obligation to maintain that level of funding." Youngman took a sip of water. "Blaze let me and his investment advisor know he was looking for opportunities that would bring in enough to cover his donations and your lifestyle."

"*My* lifestyle?" Barb said.

"I mean the two of you together. This house. The boat. The cottage on the lake. The place in Vail."

Barb waved her hand. "All right. All right."

"Blaze fired the advisor. I had a client who was getting a steady return on his money from an investment group in New York. Ten, eleven percent. Year after year, even when the market tanked. I told Blaze about it and he wanted in. So I placed the balance of your holdings with them." Youngman shrugged. "They turned out to be investing in a Ponzi scheme like Bernie Madoff's."

"How much did we lose?" Barb asked.

Youngman looked down at the papers in front of him. "Nearly all of it. There's around two or three hundred thousand left."

"So you managed to turn forty million dollars into two hundred thousand in just three years," Barb said.

Youngman wiped his glasses. "Look, I'm just an accountant."

"And Rasputin was just a spiritual advisor," Barb said.

"That's not fair. Blaze signed off on all the investment decisions." Youngman tapped the papers in front of him. "They may not have been good decisions, but I can account for every penny."

"That's like taking the dimensions of the vault after Jesse James has cleaned it out," Keaton said.

The phone rang. The three men turned to look at it, but Barb just closed her eyes and said, "Dear God, that's all I need."

Keaton picked up the phone and said, "Stender residence." Then he handed the receiver to Barb. "It's the sheriff's office."

Barb took the phone. She stared fixedly at the center of the poker table, repeated "I see" three times, then said, "Of course I'll be there," and hung up.

She faced the three men. "The divers have found a body. They want me to come down to the morgue and identify it.

Him, I mean." Turning to Keaton and Stapleton, she asked, "Can you two come with me, please?" pointedly excluding Youngman from the invitation.

"Of course," Keaton said.

Stapleton apologized, saying he had appointments he had to keep with clients.

"I don't mind coming," Youngman said.

"If it's all the same to you, Dennis, I'd rather not see your face any more today," Barb said.

"But Blaze was my friend."

"I'm sorry," Barb said. "But friends don't let friends lose forty million dollars."

The Cuyahoga County Morgue was on Cedar Avenue, just a short stretcher ride from the Cleveland Clinic. The county sheriff, a short round man wearing a Sam Browne belt and a forest ranger's hat, met Barb and Keaton in the vestibule.

He took off his hat and addressed Barb. "Thank you for coming. I should warn you, though, that the sight you'll see downstairs is not pretty, even though the body was in the water less than twenty-four hours."

Barb took a step backward, as if she were dodging a blow.

"Look," Keaton said, "there's no need for both of us to identify the body, is there? Why don't you wait upstairs here, Barb, and I'll go downstairs with the sheriff."

"All right," Barb said. "I thought I could handle this, but now I'm not so sure."

"If you're not sure, you shouldn't go." The sheriff turned to Keaton. "I assume you knew him well enough to perform the identification."

Keaton nodded and said to Barb, "It might help if I had some idea what Blaze was wearing."

"I wasn't in the house when he left," Barb said. "I really have no idea."

Keaton followed the sheriff downstairs through a pair of double doors that opened on a sterile room lined with outsized storage lockers. Four steel stretchers, two bearing sheet-covered bodies, stood side by side in the center of the room. A white-coated attendant waited at the head of the first stretcher.

The smell of ammonia and modeling clay hung in the air. The room was not so cold as Keaton had expected, but he shivered anyhow.

The sheriff nodded to the attendant, who walked over to a steel locker halfway up the wall farthest from the double doors. When Keaton and the sheriff joined him, he opened the locker, slid out a corpse, and unzipped the top half of the body bag.

Keaton shuddered involuntarily. The face of the corpse was wrinkled and bloated, with shards of flesh dangling where something had nibbled on it. It was hard to look at the face and even harder to identify it. But the body bag had been opened far enough for Keaton to see the right shoulder of the corpse and the bow-and-arrow tattoo that Lanny Morton had gotten when he pitched for the Cleveland Indians.

CHAPTER SEVEN:
THE PATHS OF GLORY

KEATON'S KORNER

The photo at the top of today's column says it all. Two friends, fresh out of college, in their first major-league spring-training camp. Leaning forward, side-by-side, holding baseballs straight out in front of them, smiling at their futures. One left-handed, one right-handed. The glory of their times.

The right-hander had more promise, but flamed out early. The left-hander was steadier and improved with time, putting together what could be a Hall of Fame career.

They started together, Blaze Stender and Lanny Morton, and last Tuesday night they ended together, smashed against a Lake Erie breakwater. Their once-promising futures behind them, facing an even greater journey, reminders of the stern words of Thomas Gray:

> *The boast of heraldry, the pomp of power,*
> *And all that beauty, all that wealth e'er gave,*
> *Awaits alike th' inevitable hour:*
> *The paths of glory lead but to the grave.*

Barb's voice was a high-pitched buzz saw. "How could they make a mistake like that?" she asked the sheriff after he and Keaton had come back upstairs to the coroner's office. "Lanny Morton doesn't look anything like my husband."

"They could have been twins back when they were both pitching," the sheriff said.

93

"Lanny hadn't pitched for over fifteen years," Keaton said. "He was paunchy and out of shape."

"His face was pretty messed up," the sheriff said. "And, to be fair, the deputy on duty was fresh out of the academy. One of those modern kids who gets his sports from video games. He'd never heard of Blaze Stender."

"Blaze's picture was all over the newspapers," Keaton said. "Are you telling me the kid doesn't read either?"

"Probably doesn't read newspapers," the sheriff said. "And even if he'd seen Mr. Stender's picture, it wouldn't have done much good. Excuse me, ma'am, but a person couldn't tell who he was from his face."

Barb closed her eyes and shuddered.

The sheriff went on. "But there was more than just it being Mr. Stender's boat to make us think it was his body." He held up a plastic bag containing a silver wristwatch. "Dead man was wearing a watch inscribed to Blaze Stender."

Barb gasped. "That's Blaze's Rolex. I gave it to him on our twentieth anniversary."

"Then you'd recognize the inscription," the sheriff said.

"Of course. It reads 'To Blaze. The love of my life.' "

The sheriff laid the plastic bag on top of the desk. "That's it all right. It's his watch."

"But how did it get on Morton's wrist?" Keaton asked.

The sheriff shrugged. "When did you last see your husband wearing it?"

Barb closed her eyes. "At the Whiskey Island Black and White Ball. I remember watching him put it on with his tux. That was about a month ago."

"But you hadn't seen him wearing it since then?" the sheriff said.

"I don't know. But I think I would have noticed if it was missing from his wrist."

"But the last time you remember seeing it was a month ago?"

"What earthly difference does it make? There's no conceivable reason why Blaze would have willingly given the watch to Lanny Morton. Morton must have taken it." Barb paused, then clutched Keaton's arm. "Maybe Morton robbed Blaze and took the boat. Maybe Blaze was never at the helm. He was much too good a sailor to hit that breakwater at full speed."

The sheriff shook his head. "I'm afraid there's no doubt Blaze was at the helm. At least on the way out. His neighbor, Mr. Lewis, saw him leave the dock, and he waved at two fishermen on the point when he passed the lighthouse."

"There's no doubt it was Blaze?"

"No doubt at all."

"It could have happened the way you suggest, though," Keaton said. "Maybe the two of them had an argument and Morton overpowered Blaze and tried to bring the *Three Strikes* back alone in the storm. That would explain the watch and the crash."

"But it doesn't make things look any brighter for Blaze," Barb said.

"No, it surely doesn't," the sheriff said.

On the way back to Barb's house, the grim silence in the car was broken by the ringtone of Keaton's cell. He fumbled for the phone and heard the voice of his ex-wife.

"Lloyd, it's Liz. You've got to come home. The police found your father wandering alone in Germantown. He didn't seem to know who or where he was."

"Where is he now?"

"I just picked him up at the police station. They found both our cards in his wallet and contacted me."

"How is he?"

"He seems to be recovering his memory, but I can't keep watch over him."

In the background, Keaton heard his father say, "Don't need anyone to watch over me."

"All right," Keaton said. "I'm with Barb Stender right now. I'll drop her off and get home as soon as I can."

There was a long silence. Keaton could hear his father grumbling in the background. Then Liz said, "Just hurry. Please."

Keaton ended the call, stared at his cell phone, and deposited it in the cup holder.

"Bad news?" Barb asked.

"My father. He had a senior moment. More like a senior hour, actually. Police found him wandering a couple of miles from home. I've got to get back to Menckenburg."

Barb touched his sleeve. "Is there anything I can do?"

Keaton patted her hand. "I'd say you've got more than enough on your mind right now. Thanks for the offer, though."

They pulled into Barb's driveway to find the TV van still parked in front of the house.

"Oh, God," Barb said. "I can't stay here alone."

"Can I drop you somewhere?"

"No. I'll grab some clothes and check into a hotel." She picked up his cell and made some quick movements on the keypad. "Now you've got my phone number." She punched another button. "And I've got yours. I'll let you know if I hear anything about Blaze. You let me know when you get back up here."

She jumped out of his car and ran up the steps to her home, just beating a TV cameraman to her door.

Keaton stood in Liz's hall, with one hand on his father's arm and the other on the knob of the front door. Liz and Davy flanked his father to make sure he didn't retreat into the house.

"I just went for a little walk," John Keaton said. "It was no big deal."

"Dad," Keaton said. "No one could find you."

"The cops could. They solved the mystery pretty quick."

"Dad. Liz and Davy were worried."

"No need to be worried." John Keaton ran a hand through his disheveled gray hair. "Not on my account."

"I'm sorry, Lloyd," Liz said. "I can't watch him around the clock."

"I can spend some time with him between now and when school starts," Davy said.

John Keaton rapped sharply on the door. "Hey. I'm right here. Quit talking about me like I'm not."

"Okay, you're here," Keaton said. "But not for long. I'm taking you home to your apartment."

"Then what? Gonna chain me to the bedpost?"

"That's one idea," Keaton said. "I thought duct taping you to the TV chair might be more humane. You could still work the remote."

"A real smart ass." Keaton's father said. "I can't believe you're my own flesh and blood."

Keaton yanked the front door open. "That's what Mom always said. Let's get you into the car."

Keaton had barely started his Ford Escort when his father said, "I don't want to be shut up in a home."

"We'll find a place that doesn't shut you up."

"I'm okay in my apartment."

"Dad, you can't stay there by yourself. We just want what's best for you."

"That's what Martha said when she closed my house and sent me down here."

"Aunt Martha was doing what she thought best."

"Best for who? Not for me."

"Dad, you were wandering in the streets. You didn't know who you were or where you were."

"It worked out all right. And I'm all right now. I'm all right most of the time."

"We've got to find someone who's sure to be around when you're not all right."

"But you and Liz think that's a full-time job." John Keaton slumped against the passenger door. "You want to put me someplace where I'll be watched around the clock."

"Nobody's going to be looking over your shoulder. You won't even know they're there."

"I'll bet that's what jailers tell new inmates about prison bars."

Keaton couldn't think of anything more to say, and they rode in silence the rest of the way to their apartment building. As his father put the key into his door, Keaton said, "Want to come over and watch some TV? Games on the West Coast should be about to start."

John Keaton swung his door open. "No thanks. It's been a tough day. I think I'll just hit the sack. Got to start enjoying my freedom while I still can. Besides, you've got to go out and get some duct tape."

Keaton said, "Good night, Dad" into the closing door.

As soon as Keaton finished dressing the next morning, he knocked on his father's door. His father answered dressed in slacks and a wrinkled polo shirt. His eyes were bloodshot, and a gray stubble covered his chin.

"Why don't you come over and join me for breakfast?" Keaton said. "Then I thought maybe you could come to work with me."

"What's the matter? Couldn't you find any duct tape?"

"Just thought you might like some company."

"I've had breakfast, and I retired from the newspaper business twenty years ago."

"Then it's time you saw what a modern newspaper office looks like."

Keaton's dad gave a short, sharp laugh. "All right. Just wait a bit. I'll need to get a clean shirt and a fresh shave."

Keaton and his father had barely stepped inside the newsroom when his father shrugged and said, "What's the big deal? Doesn't look like things have changed much since I retired. Cubicles are still too small. Computers look a little slimmer. So do the young ladies."

"Yeah, well. At least one thing's changed," Keaton said. "You can call the computers slimmer, but you can't make that kind of a remark about young ladies without having a sexual harassment suit on your hands."

"Guess I retired just in time."

Keaton turned into his own cubicle and stepped aside to let his father enter.

"My God," his father said. "Is that my dad's old typewriter?"

"Sure is. I keep it around for inspiration."

"Funny. That's exactly what I did." Keaton's dad slid the carriage return as far as it would go and smiled at the satisfying "ding." Then he sat down, slipped a fresh sheet of paper under the roller, and started typing.

Meri Atkins's voice came from the next cubicle. "Hey, cut out that racket. This is no time to try to communicate with Ring Lardner." Her red hair and green eyes appeared over the top of the partition. "Why, it's Ring Lardner himself."

Keaton smiled. "Meri, this is my dad, John Keaton. Dad, meet Meredith Atkins."

Keaton's dad lifted his right hand off the typewriter keys and wiggled his fingers. "Pleased to meet you."

"Same here," Meri said. "Sorry about the Ring Lardner crack."

"That's okay," Keaton's dad said. "Actually, Ring Lardner was a generation ahead of me. He and my dad were good friends. So good that my middle name is Lardner."

"Did you know the man?"

"Not really. I was only seven when he died. I knew his son John though."

"What did his son do?"

"He was a sportswriter. Like his old man. One of the best. Shy, though. Walt Kelly said, 'To be alone with John Lardner was to enjoy solitude in the best of company.' "

Meri's eyebrows drooped. "Who's Walt Kelly?"

"Who's Walt Kelly? Woman, turn in your journalist credentials. Walt Kelly was only the premier newspaper cartoonist of the twentieth century."

"Give her a break, Dad," Keaton said. "Meri wasn't even born when Walt Kelly died."

"She wasn't born when Ring Lardner died, but she knew his name." Keaton's dad stood up so he could see across the cubicle wall. "Walt Kelly was the creator of Pogo the Possum, Albert the Alligator, and lots of other creatures in the Okefenokee swamp."

"Oh, that Walt Kelly."

"Even if you don't recognize his name, you must have heard his words," Keaton's father said. " 'We have met the enemy and he is us.' Or how about, 'Little did is little done, tho' little did'll do.' "

Keaton held up his hand. "Enough! That'll do, Dad. I'm sure Meri can rattle off the names of three or four bloggers that you won't recognize, and I don't care to hear her quote them."

He turned to his computer and downloaded the day's e-mail. "I've got a summons here to see the boss. Meri, can you keep my dad company until I get back?"

"Sure. Maybe he can tell me about the days when they chipped newspapers out of stone tablets. Must have made it tough on your paper route, huh, John Lardner?"

When Keaton entered the editor's office, Eddie Oliver said, "The wandering boy returns." Then he took his empty pipe from his mouth and pointed it at the stack of newspapers on his desk. "Just in time to take credit for the current surge in sales."

"Didn't know there was a surge. But I'm happy to take credit for it."

"Newsstand sales are up forty percent. When I ask myself what's changed, the only answer is your coverage of this mess in Cleveland." Oliver returned the pipe to his mouth. "And now there's another body to make a bona fide mystery out of it. So I have to ask myself, what the hell are you doing back here in Menckenburg?"

"My dad's been having some problems. He forgets things."

"That why you brought him in today? Hell, we all forget things."

"But he forgets things like where he is and who he is."

"Oh, shit. I'm sorry."

Keaton shrugged. "It's not your problem."

"If it affects your work, it's my problem. Anyhow, now that it looks like Stender's dead, where do you stand as his biographer?"

"His wife wants me to stay on and write the book. She's cleared it with the publisher."

"So you're tight with her?"

"Depends on what you mean by tight."

"No need to be coy. I want you to stay on the story. Get back up to Cleveland. We can take care of your duties here. And Meri Atkins has been drooling for the chance to cover the Mammoths."

"It's not that easy to take off right now. My dad needs to be watched."

"Maybe we can help with that. Find a caretaker, for example. It's not that far to Cleveland. Take your dad with you. We can spring expense money for hotel stays. Maybe even hire an expert or two."

"An expert? What for?"

"Find out whether there was anything fishy about that boat wreck. Stender was the skipper and he's still missing."

"Probably not for much longer. Lake's shallow around the Cleveland harbor. Most bodies surface pretty quickly."

"See? That's the kind of inside information you need in your stories. And you need to be there with the grieving widow when the body surfaces."

"There's no guarantee it will happen quickly."

"There is something that will happen quickly, though. There's a memorial service for Lanny Morton Friday morning. You ought to be there for that as well."

Keaton shook his head. "I've still got my dad to think about."

"Take him with you. From what I know about Morton, there'll be plenty of empty seats available." Oliver pointed his pipe stem at Keaton. "You need to stay on top of this. Both boys have ties to the local community. They both started out here. It's a big damn story. And you're out in front of the *Plain Dealer*, the bloggers, and the TV news. See that you stay that way."

Keaton returned to his cubicle to find his father snoring peacefully in his chair. Meri Atkins appeared at Keaton's elbow. "He was doing fine, telling war stories about newspaper life in the fifties, but then he just conked out."

"He had a tough night." Keaton shook his father's shoulder gently. "Dad. Now is the time for all good men to come to."

"Clever," Meri said.

"Not my invention," Keaton said. "Credit Walt Kelly again."

"Oh, yeah. Walt Kelly. I knew that."

Keaton's father snorted once, then jerked upright. "Oh, gosh. I must have faded." He peered at Meri. "I remember you. You were good fun. Lloyd, you ought to invite her over for dinner sometime."

"The newspaper has rules against fraternizing, Dad."

"Then I'll invite her."

Meri smiled. "I'd like that."

"Careful what you wish for," Keaton said. "The boss may formalize that assignment."

"What did he want?"

"Wants me to stay on the Stender case. Said you could cover the Mammoths while I'm in Cleveland."

"That's great," Meri said.

"If I know the way his mind works, though, the carrot may come with a stick. We'll need to find a caretaker for my dad while I'm in Cleveland."

"That's not so great," Meri said. "No offense, John Lardner."

"None taken."

"When is this likely to happen?" Meri asked.

"I need to be at a memorial service for Lanny Morton in Cleveland Friday morning."

"Cleveland?" Keaton's father said. "Hell, I could go to Cleveland."

"I bet you could," Keaton said.

"I won't get in your way."

"Even if you do," Keaton said, "Aunt Martha would probably enjoy spending a little time with you."

The memorial service for Lanny Morton was held in the Pilgrim Congregational Church in downtown Cleveland. Housed behind a traditional stone facade, the interior was bright and modern, with mahogany pews arranged in a semicircle around an altar set in a recessed archway. A center aisle and two side aisles cut the semicircle into four segments.

The assembled mourners didn't come close to filling the large chapel. Still, there were more attendees than Keaton would have expected. The front pews were occupied by six pallbearers in black suits and four women Keaton didn't recognize. In the back of the church, small clusters of people in casual clothes murmured to one another. Sensation seekers, Keaton decided, attracted by the headlines. He couldn't be too hard on them. He was there for headlines as well, looking for any connections he could find with the Stender story.

Keaton spotted Webb Bruna, the one-time general manager of the Mammoths and Indians, sitting alone in a pew in the middle of the church and led his father up the center aisle to join him. Keaton and his father slid into the pew beside him.

"The Keatons, father and son," Bruna whispered. "Now there's a pair to draw to."

While they waited for the service to start, Keaton nodded toward the two front rows and asked Bruna, "Who are those people?"

"I only know one of the pallbearers, Red Gilles. You know him from the poker game."

"Oh, yes," Keaton said. "What about the women?"

"The woman just to the right of the casket is Morton's current wife Brandy. They were getting a divorce, but she organized this memorial service. I'm guessing she expects to put herself in the way of a windfall from Morton's estate."

"So there's an estate worth talking about?"

"So I'm told. The woman with the dark headband to Brandy's right is Morton's mother. She's a full-blooded Cherokee. I'm not sure who that is sitting next to her." Bruna gestured toward the other side of the main aisle. "The woman to the left of the casket is Morton's first wife, Anne."

Keaton tried to envision Blaze Stender having an affair with the blowsy, heavyset woman in black, but his imagination failed him. First he'd have to reimagine her as the slim, attractive twenty-something he vaguely remembered from his days on the *News*.

A striking blonde wearing a black pantsuit strode down the center aisle and slid into an empty pew across the aisle from Webb Bruna and the two Keatons. Keaton nudged Bruna and raised his eyebrows, trying to look nonchalant. Bruna smiled and whispered, "Rosemary Spinetti. She worked with the team's traveling secretary for a short time before she married money. Broke a lot of hearts."

"I can see where she would," Keaton said.

As the large pipe organ to the right of the altar sounded out "Nearer, My God to Thee," Barb Stender came down the center aisle, nodded to Keaton and Bruna, and took a pew two rows in front of them.

Shortly after Barb was seated, a balding minister wearing black vestments took his place at the podium and cleared his throat before reading a prepared homily. The homily and the remainder of the service were mercifully short. When the minister asked members of the congregation to share their memories of the deceased, the only person to respond was Morton's estranged wife, who spoke tearfully of their courtship and honeymoon, omitting any mention of their impending divorce.

When the service ended, the pallbearers led the way out of the church, carrying the casket, with the crowd filing out behind them. Webb Bruna walked ahead with Keaton's father and Barb Stender slipped her arm through Keaton's to accompany him.

"You must have felt right at home with the minister's homily," Barb said. "He cribbed most of it from your column on

Blaze and Lanny."

"Well, I cribbed a lot from Thomas Gray, so I'm hardly in a position to sue."

Barb smiled. "I'm thinking of arranging a memorial service for Blaze next week, and I'm hoping you could say a few words."

"Of course. Has there been an official declaration of Blaze's death?"

"No." Barb bit her lower lip. "The sheriff tells me there's enough evidence to support a declaration of death *in absentia*, but I've been avoiding the paperwork. It just seems so final."

As they were about to leave the church, a tall gaunt man in an ill-fitting black suit nodded to Keaton. The nod sent a chill up his spine. He blinked his eyes against the sunlight as they exited and asked Barb, "Did you know that man, the one who nodded at us?"

"No. He was hard to miss, though. He looked like the Grim Reaper without his scythe."

Keaton looked back over his shoulder. The man was gone.

Outside the church, they caught up with Webb Bruna and Keaton's father. While Barb reintroduced herself to Keaton's dad, Keaton asked Bruna about the gaunt man. "He's gone now, but he was standing by the baptismal font. Did you see him?"

Bruna shook his head. "No. Why?"

"He seemed to know me. But I couldn't place him."

Bruna shrugged. "Can't help you, I'm afraid."

"You can help me in another way, actually. I'm staying over tonight and I'd like to talk to you a little about Stender's days in Cleveland. And a little about Morton too. Will you have some time tomorrow?"

Bruna handed Keaton his card. "I'm free all day. Give me a call."

★ ★ ★ ★ ★

Keaton had arranged for him and his father to stay at his aunt Martha's house in University Heights. Aunt Martha was a short, no-nonsense woman with black strands in her steel-gray hair. Three years older than Keaton's father, she had helped look after John Keaton when he was a child and Keaton's grandfather was covering out-of-town sports events.

Although stooped with age, Uncle Clem was still three inches taller than Keaton's six feet, and at least a foot taller than his wife. Where Aunt Martha was quick and decisive, Uncle Clem was slow and accepting. When he was a child, Keaton had called Uncle Clem "Big Guy" and still referred to him that way. The couple were a pleasure to visit, and Keaton understood now what he should have realized earlier: If Aunt Martha and Uncle Clem had sent his father south because they couldn't deal with him, the problem was deeper and more serious than he had allowed himself to believe.

After dinner, the four of them sat down to play bridge. Keaton was paired with his father, who played his cards well but bid as if he were playing poker and considered each bid as a chance to bluff rather than a chance to exchange information. Uncle Clem was just the opposite of John Keaton. Years of playing bridge with Martha had led to an unspoken understanding of each other's bids, but Clem lacked the card sense his wife and her brother exercised in playing the hands once the bidding was over.

The riffle and splat of his aunt's dovetail shuffle reminded Keaton how much he missed playing poker. As was his habit, he picked up the first five cards dealt to him and sorted them as a poker hand, letting the rest of his bridge hand accumulate in front of him. It was as close as he allowed himself to come to holding and betting a poker hand.

As soon as he fanned out his five-card poker hand, Keaton

remembered where he had seen the gaunt man who had nodded to him at Lanny Morton's memorial service. The man was a poker dealer and house shill at Little Bill Ellison's casino in East Wheeling, West Virginia, the casino where Keaton had gambled away his home, his job, and his marriage. No wonder he'd felt a chill when the man nodded to him.

Chapter Eight:
Casper the Friendly Ghostwriter

KEATON'S KORNER

In the last week, sports shows, newspapers, and blogs have been filled with the on-field exploits of Blaze Stender. But ever since I asked for local anecdotes about Stender in this column, I've received scores of stories of his exploits off the diamond. Each day brings an outpouring of positive remembrances about the man who was lost in Tuesday's boating accident.

The remembrances start with the Tommy Fund, the charity Blaze began to fund research into Down's syndrome. Named in honor of Blaze's late son, Tommy, the fund has raised over $200 million for this worthy cause since its inception. Blaze was not only the fund's founder, he was its chief supporter, speaking on its behalf at Little League games, American Legion banquets, churches, synagogues, shopping malls, libraries, and local museums like the Rock and Roll Hall of Fame.

The e-mails and letters I receive share a number of common themes. In an era of inflated egos, whining superstars, and pill-popping performers, Blaze was "a hero on the field and off," "an athlete you could look up to," and one who "personified the word class." He knew class when he saw it, and he saw it in his mirror every morning.

Webb Bruna's last posting as a general manager had been with the Pittsburgh Pirates. He'd been retired from that position for over four years, and now maintained an office in downtown

Cleveland, where he served as a freelance consultant to teams desiring his expertise. He sat in a swivel chair squeezed between a large oak table and four two-drawer file cabinets that lined the rear wall of his office. The remaining walls of the windowless cube were filled with framed photos of Bruna shaking hands with politicians and smiling at players as they signed professional contracts.

"You had bigger digs than this back when you were still just a gofer in Municipal Stadium," John Keaton said as he and Lloyd took folding chairs across the table from Bruna.

"Everything about Municipal Stadium was bigger," Bruna said. "But the new park is much better designed for baseball. And this office gives me a place to hang out during the day."

"For a while, the team was playing better baseball in the new park as well," John Keaton said.

Bruna smiled. "That's right. They had a pretty dismal record when you were with the *News.*"

"You can't blame all that on me. I was around in fifty-four when they set a record for wins."

"But then they lost four straight to the Giants in the World Series," Bruna said.

"After that it was all downhill. The Curse of Rocky Colavito took hold," John Keaton said. "Frank Lane never should have traded Rocky away."

Bruna nodded. "As I recall, you said that at the time in your columns."

"Lane would have traded his own mother for a headline. He wrecked the team, traded managers with Detroit, and ran out on his contract before anyone could fire him." John Keaton leaned forward, obviously enjoying the conversation. "Any team can have a bad year, but Lane and his buddies left us with three bad decades in a row. Those good players they didn't trade away, they lost to free agency."

"The Indians are still losing players when they get to be free agents," Bruna said. "They just can't outbid the big boys."

"They got nothing when they traded Maris away," Keaton's dad said. "Same with Eckersley. And they lost Blaze Stender to free agency."

Keaton loved seeing his father animated, discussing a topic he enjoyed with someone who matched his knowledge and enthusiasm. But the mention of Blaze Stender gave him a chance to steer the conversation to the purpose of their visit. "It's Blaze we came to talk about, Webb," Keaton said. "What can you tell us about his time in Menckenburg and Cleveland?"

"What do you want to know?"

"Let's start at the beginning. Something happened on his first trip to spring training with Lanny Morton."

"Oh, yeah." Bruna frowned as if the memory was unpleasant. "They hit a telephone pole with Blaze's brand-new Mustang and ran afoul of a cop in a speed trap near Red Rock."

"Morton said they got you involved," Keaton said.

"Yeah. I was a jack-of-all-trades in Menckenburg then. Troubleshooter. Fixer. Whatever you want to call it. Got a call from Blaze about two in the morning. He put the Red Rock cop on the line."

Bruna shook his head and smiled. "Cop was a real piece of work. Said he had two of our rookie pitchers in custody. They'd damaged public property and appeared to be drunk as skunks. Cop said they could hook their breathalyzer up to a moonshiner's still and get a lower reading than they'd get from either Lanny or Blaze."

"Who was driving?" Keaton asked.

"Lanny was driving when the cop pulled them over." Bruna cocked his head and frowned. "I've always suspected Blaze was driving when they hit the pole."

"That's what Lanny told me. What happened with the cop?"

"It was pretty straightforward. For ten grand he'd forget to administer a breathalyzer test and hold them on a lesser charge. Left-of-center. Something like that."

"So you paid?"

"Damn right I paid. He had two of our top draft picks behind bars. I got to Red Rock right away with a lawyer in tow."

"And the charges went away?"

Bruna nodded. "No record of anything but the left-of-center charge."

"Do you recall the cop's name?" Keaton asked.

"Called himself Radar." Bruna smiled. "Appropriate. Don't recall his last name. We didn't exactly write a check. He insisted on cash. I got the distinct impression it wasn't his first shakedown."

Bruna pulled out a file drawer. "It was some time ago, but it made my personal files. I had to keep records like that off the books. Why do you want his name?"

"Something happened on that trip to cause a rift between Blaze and Lanny. But nothing seems to have wound up on their driving records. I'd like to know more about what happened between the two of them."

Bruna pulled a sheet of paper from a manila folder. "Here it is. Radar's real name was Cletis Raptor." He replaced the sheet and closed the file drawer. "You want to know what caused an upset between Blaze and Lanny, though, don't look to Radar Raptor. Look to Annie Cummings."

"Who's Annie Cummings?"

"Married name's Anne Morton. Lanny's first wife. She was at the memorial service."

"Hard to imagine that woman upsetting anything but a canoe."

"She may not look it now," Bruna said, "but she was a knockout twenty-five years ago. Both Blaze and Lanny went for her in a big way."

"But Lanny won out."

"Let's just say she latched onto the most promising prospect. Their rookie year in the majors, both Blaze and Lanny had women chasing them in every city in the league. Annie lived here in Cleveland, so she had the home-field advantage. And it looked for a while as if Lanny was going to be a lot bigger star than Blaze."

"So she married Lanny. How did Blaze take it?"

Bruna shrugged. "Pretty hard at first. But he got over it. Concentrated on his pitching. Started going with Rosemary Spinetti."

"The woman across the aisle at Morton's memorial service?"

Bruna nodded. "She worked in our traveling secretary's office. Several steps up in class from Annie Cummings. Had men swarming around her like drones in a hive. Blaze was the first one I ever saw her get serious about."

"How serious?"

"They got engaged toward the end of Blaze's second season in Cleveland."

"Where did Barb come in?"

"Blaze went home to Oklahoma after the season. Showed up at spring training married with a pregnant wife in tow."

"What became of Rosemary? She wasn't around when I started working for the *News*. I'd have remembered her."

"She left the team when Blaze announced his wedding. Went to work for a brokerage firm in New York. I kept up through Christmas cards and an occasional phone call. Rosemary did quite well for herself. Worked her way up the system, then married a rich bond trader. Had a couple of kids. Seemed really happy the few times our paths crossed. Nice to see." The smile left Bruna's face. "Husband was killed in a car accident a couple of years ago."

"Did she remarry?" Keaton asked.

"Not so far."

"What happened with Lanny Morton and Annie?"

Bruna shook his head. "Lanny never stopped tomcatting. Still had at least one honey in every American League city. And the American League hitters started catching up with him."

"Was it his late-night carousing?"

"No. He just never developed another pitch to go with his fastball."

"What happened with Annie?"

"By the end of the boys' third year in the bigs, it was pretty clear she'd backed the wrong horse. She started mooning around Blaze."

"Even though he was married?"

"And an expectant father. Didn't faze Annie. She was pretty open about it."

"Anything come of it?"

"I'm reasonably sure nothing did."

"Lanny didn't think so."

Bruna smiled. "He wouldn't. But I'd be willing to bet Blaze never strayed from Barbara. I was watching pretty closely. I didn't want another Eckersley situation on our hands."

"Eckersley?" Keaton said. "What did Eckersley have to do with it?"

"It was a little before your time." Bruna turned to Keaton's father. "You remember, though, don't you, John?"

"Eckersley," John Keaton said. It wasn't clear whether he was remembering or just echoing Bruna.

"Dennis Eckersley and Rick Manning came up to the Tribe together in nineteen seventy-five," Bruna continued. "Our hope for the future. They'd been roommates in the minors, and it didn't take long for them to have an impact. Eckersley pitched a no-hitter and Manning won a gold glove in center field. It looked like the team was finally coming out of its twenty-year slump. Then Eckersley's wife, Denise, fell in love with Rick Manning."

"In love with Rick Manning," John Keaton said.

Bruna paused and looked at Keaton's father, expecting him to continue. When he said nothing, Bruna went on with the story. "It was an explosive situation. We felt like we had to trade one of them, so we dealt Eckersley to Boston. It didn't seem like a bad decision at the time. Eckersley had that awkward side-winding delivery, and we didn't think his arm would hold up. And even if it did, we wouldn't be able to outbid the big guys when he became a free agent. Besides, Manning had just hurt his back and wouldn't bring much in trade till he healed."

Bruna shook his head. "Turns out we traded the wrong guy."

"Traded the wrong guy," John Keaton said almost before Bruna had finished the sentence.

Keaton was alarmed by his father's behavior. He seemed to be parroting Bruna's words instead of processing his own thoughts. He reached across and put his hand on his father's arm. "I'll say you traded the wrong guy," Keaton said. "Eckersley went on to make the Hall of Fame."

"And Manning never lived up to his promise after he hurt his back. But Denise stuck with him after Eck went to Boston." Bruna raised his right hand, palm outward, and Keaton noticed it was trembling slightly. "Well, I didn't want to make that same mistake with Stender and Morton. Fortunately, that choice was pretty clear-cut. Blaze was starting to mature as a pitcher, and, like I said, the hitters were catching up with Lanny's fastball. We sent Lanny down to the minors."

Bruna shrugged. "Might have kept him around a little longer if Annie hadn't been stalking Blaze, but we hoped the trip down would help straighten out both Lanny and Annie."

"Instead, it ended his career," Keaton said.

"And his marriage. They split up and he never made it back to the bigs."

"Never made it back to the bigs," John Keaton stared straight ahead, expressionless.

"That was it for Lanny." Webb Bruna rose and took a book down from the shelves behind John Keaton's chair. As he squeezed behind the chair to return to his desk, he paused, looked down at Keaton's father, and shot Keaton a worried glance.

Anxious and puzzled, Keaton could only shrug.

Bruna sat behind his desk and held up the book. "*The Curse of Rocky Colavito,* written by Terry Pluto. Tells all about the Eckersley/Manning affair."

John Keaton unleashed a short, sharp laugh. "Pluto. Hah."

"I'm more interested in Stender and Morton," Keaton said, "but I'll pick up a copy of the book."

Bruna handed the book across the desk to Keaton. "Take mine."

"Pluto's a dog," John Keaton said.

"It's a different Pluto, Dad," Keaton said. He was worried about his father, but he also wanted to get as much information as he could from Webb Bruna. He asked Bruna, "What happened to Stender after Morton went down?"

"Stender just kept getting better and better. Got to be so good we couldn't afford him when he reached free agency. Three teams outbid us, and he went to the Dodgers."

"Cartoon dogs don't write books," John Keaton said. "Must have had a ghostwriter. Maybe Casper the friendly ghost. Get it?"

Bruna forced a laugh. "A cartoon ghostwriter for a cartoon dog. Good to see you haven't lost your touch, John."

"Lost my touch," John Keaton echoed.

Keaton stood. "We've taken up enough of your time." He put

his hand on his father's shoulder. "Let's go, Dad."

"Lost my touch," John Keaton said. "Got to find my touch before we go."

Keaton tugged on his father's arm. "I'm sure Mr. Bruna will get it to us if he finds it."

John Keaton stood up. "What's the matter? You used to have a sense of humor."

"Your humor is just too subtle for the average listener, Dad."

Keaton and his father were in the corridor and almost to the elevator when Webb Bruna came out of his office and called, "Lloyd. Come back here a minute. I just thought of another book."

Keaton left his father at the elevator door and walked back to Bruna.

Bruna handed Keaton a book with a Cleveland Indians cap on the dust jacket. "It's another book by Pluto. A history of the Indians through the late nineties. Covers the time Stender was with the team."

Keaton hefted the books in his hand. "Thanks. I'll get these back to you."

"No hurry." Bruna lowered his voice. "How long has your dad been like that?"

"My aunt sent him down to Menckenburg four months ago. He's lucid most of the time. But then he fades in and out. Well, you saw."

"It's a shame. His mind was razor sharp when he was writing here. Anything I can do?"

"I don't think so. You've been a big help already. You could see he really enjoyed talking to you."

"For a time." Bruna patted Keaton's shoulder. "Well, take care of him. And come back to see me when you get further along with your book. I can help with that, at least."

"Thanks, I will." Keaton raised the books in his hand as a

half salute, then turned and trudged down the corridor to his father and the waiting elevator.

Keaton left his father with his aunt Martha and went to meet with Lanny Morton's first wife, Anne, in her apartment on the outskirts of Cleveland. Both the apartment and its occupant had seen better days. The living room stank of stale cigarette smoke and was filled to bursting with the kind of Danish modern furniture that had been popular over thirty years ago. The furniture was scarred from one too many moves, and Keaton guessed that it had once graced a much larger room.

Anne Morton was also bursting at the seams. The middle button on her white blouse was missing, and when she sat down, the other buttons strained to keep from joining their missing comrade, allowing her bare skin to peek through an opening the size of a half dollar.

She tossed her short blonde hair in what might once have been a flirtatious gesture but now served only to reveal graying roots at her temple and said, "So you've got a big New York publisher paying you to write Blaze's story."

"That's right," Keaton said.

"Think they might be interested in paying for Lanny's story as well? It's got a lot more sex."

"You'll have to ask them."

Anne Morton smiled through smeared lipstick. "I could supply some pretty lurid photos to spice up the text. Think that might be worth something?"

"Photos?"

"Polaroids, videotapes. Lanny and me in bed. Mostly just the two of us, but from time to time we had company."

Keaton fought back the image of his overweight hostess coupling with the bloated, tattooed body of Lanny Morton. "Right now, I need to concentrate on Blaze Stender."

Anne shook her head. "No photos of Blaze, I'm afraid. He was strictly a lights out, shades drawn, missionary position kind of guy."

Keaton laughed. "That's more information than I was expecting."

"Nothing bashful about me. Blaze and I hit it off pretty good when he first came to Cleveland. I could have married him, but Lanny asked me first."

"How did Blaze take that?"

"He was plenty broke up. But he got over it. Started going with that Miss Priss from the front office."

"Rosemary Spinetti?"

"Yeah, Rosemary. The ice queen. But Blaze must have thawed her out some, 'cause they were talking marriage."

"What happened?"

Anne stubbed her cigarette out in the overflowing ashtray on the low coffee table. "Blaze went home in the off-season and his little Okie sweetheart got herself pregnant."

"Did you go on seeing Blaze after he was married?"

"See him? Of course. We still had feelings for each other."

"Did you act on those feelings?"

Anne lit another cigarette, sat back on the couch, and squinted through the smoke. "If that's your polite way of asking did we still fuck, the answer is no. I took my marriage vows seriously. Which is more than I can say for Lanny. He even brought a few of his whores home from time to time and insisted I join them. Now that he's dead in that accident, you think videos of our threesomes might be worth something to a publisher?"

Keaton shrugged. "Depends on the publisher. How long did you and Lanny stay married?"

"Three years."

"Just about as long as his pitching career lasted."

"Seemed like half my lifetime. He wasn't the same man after

119

the Indians sent him down. He couldn't control himself or his pitches. He barely lasted a year in the minors, and then he was out of baseball."

"What did he do for a living then?"

"Lots of ex-jock stuff. Card shows. Fantasy camps. Opened a bar near Municipal Stadium. That turned out to be a financial black hole. He hoped players would hang out there after the games, but then the Indians built that new park downtown. He lost his Chief Wahoo shirt."

"He had a pretty nice home. Where'd the money come from?"

Anne shrugged. "Don't know. He always seemed to have plenty. Never missed an alimony payment, long as they lasted. And he gambled big-time."

Keaton remembered the gaunt man at the memorial service. "Did he win?"

"Can't say for sure. Seems like he was all the time bragging up his wins. But that was his way. Still, he must have done okay. He lived pretty high on the hog."

"Blaze and Lanny started out as friends but wound up at each other's throats. Any idea what split them up?"

Anne smiled and slapped her thigh. "I'm sittin' on it. I was banging 'em both back when they were single. Lanny knew about Blaze, but Blaze didn't know about Lanny. Not until me and Lanny got engaged. Like I said, Blaze took it pretty hard."

"That explains what Blaze had against Lanny. What did Lanny have against Blaze?"

"Plain jealous, I guess. Blaze had the career Lanny wanted. Lanny was all the time badmouthing Blaze. Accused me of having an affair with him while we was still married."

"But there was nothing to that?"

"Nothing." Anne exhaled and blinked her eyes against a stream of cigarette smoke. "Wish it had been true. Pictures of me and Blaze'd be worth a lot more than pictures of me and Lanny."

"As far as you know, though, Blaze and Lanny never got together after Lanny busted out of baseball."

Anne shook her head. "Not while I was around."

"What do you suppose brought them together on Blaze's boat? Seems strange. Two former friends fall out. Don't see each other for years, then wind up dying together in a boating accident."

"It's a mystery to me."

Keaton stood to leave and handed Anne his card. "If you figure it out, give me a call."

"Think it might be worth something if I figure it out? Even if there aren't any pictures?"

"Could be," Keaton said. "It's worth a shot, anyhow."

Keaton's father appeared to be his old self when Keaton caught up with him at his aunt Martha's. After dinner and a rubber of bridge, Keaton excused himself, saying he had to work on his column.

He retired to his room, opened his laptop, and brought up his e-mails. Ever since he'd written his column inviting readers to share their memories of Blaze Stender, he'd gotten at least ten e-mails a day praising Blaze and recounting positive stories about his days in Cleveland and Menckenburg. The first e-mail he opened this evening broke that pattern. It read, "If you want to know about the real Blaze Stender, contact Rosemary Spinetti." It was signed, "A true fan."

Chapter Nine:
Doc Holiday

KEATON'S KORNER

Several readers have e-mailed me to ask about Blaze Stender's eligibility for baseball's Hall of Fame. Normally, former major leaguers who have spent a minimum of ten seasons in the big leagues become eligible for the Hall of Fame five years after they retire. In the event of the death of an eligible candidate, however, the five-year waiting period is reduced to six months. This has happened three times: Lou Gehrig in 1939, Roberto Clemente in 1973, and Thurman Munson in 1979. Gehrig and Clemente were both admitted to the Hall of Fame in the first election for which they were eligible.

In the light of Blaze Stender's recent boating accident, his death would make him eligible for the Hall of Fame in the election to be held next January. According to the Hall of Fame guidelines, "Voting is based on the individual's record, ability, integrity, sportsmanship, character, and contribution to the game of baseball." Given Blaze's two hundred and fifty-three wins, his popularity with the fans, and his leadership of the Tommy Fund, I can think of no more fitting memorial to his name than election to the Hall of Fame next January.

On the phone, Rosemary Spinetti's voice was crisp and businesslike, but much softer than Keaton would have expected from someone who had excelled in the financial world of Wall Street. He'd reached her New York office through his cell phone, and between the spotty reception and Rosemary's soft, clipped responses, he had to strain to accomplish the interview.

"We've never met," he said, "but I saw you at Lanny Morton's memorial service. I was sitting across the aisle with Webb Bruna."

"Yes, I remember you. I recognized your father. He was with the *News* when I worked for the Indians."

"Did you know Lanny well?"

"Not really. But Blaze Stender was a good friend. It was his accident that brought me back to Cleveland. I'm afraid I used Lanny's memorial service to catch up with some old friends."

"Webb Bruna, for instance?"

"Especially Webb."

"Webb had good things to say about your time in Cleveland. He suggested I call you to get some help with my biography of Blaze Stender. How well did you know Blaze?"

"If you talked with Webb, then you know Blaze broke my heart."

In his notebook, Keaton wrote, "Blaze broke my heart," surrounded by quotation marks. "But you stayed in touch with him?"

"Off and on over the years. We'd have dinner sometimes when he came through New York. Talk on the phone occasionally. In the last couple of years we stayed in touch through e-mails."

"Isn't that a bit unusual? To stay in close touch with a man who broke your heart?"

"Blaze was an unusual man. We were friends. Good friends. He was my first love. We stayed good friends, even after we both were married."

Keaton wrote "FIRST LOVE" in capital letters. "Webb said your husband died around two years ago."

"Yes. In an auto accident. Three years ago, actually."

"Have you seen Blaze Stender since that time?"

"No more than before my husband died. What are you getting at?"

"Well, Blaze retired around that time. I wondered if you'd seen him since he left . . ."

Her sharp response cut Keaton off. "Blaze retired from baseball, but he was still married. So the situation was the same as when I left Cleveland for New York."

"I'm sorry. I didn't mean to imply . . ."

"Look, Mr. Keaton. I'm happy to talk to you about Blaze, up to a point. You just passed that point. Don't misunderstand. I want to see you do a good job on his biography. I'm more than happy to serve as a sounding board or corroborate facts. If you like, I'll even review your manuscript before it goes to press."

The voice on the phone froze over and lost all its softness. "But I won't collaborate on a bunch of *Cosmo* clichés that cast me as the quote other woman unquote. Blaze and I were friends. Good friends. That's all. Are we clear on that?"

"Quite clear."

"Do you have any other questions?"

"How would you characterize the relationship between Blaze and Lanny Morton?"

"They were as different as night and day. They were both born in Oklahoma, both went to OSU, and were both drafted in the same year. But that's where the similarities end. Blaze was a true gentleman, in every sense of the word. And Lanny, well, he was just the opposite. Whatever the opposite of gentleman is."

Keaton tried the first words that popped into his head. "Cad? Bounder?"

"If you're working a crossword puzzle, maybe. I hope you're not intending to use those words in Blaze's biography."

"How would you characterize Lanny?"

The line went silent for a while. Then Rosemary's crisp voice said, "Asshole."

Keaton wrote LANNY = ASSHOLE, then said, "The publishers probably won't let me use that word either."

"That's the best I can do. Is there anything else?"

Keaton scanned the list of questions he'd prepared. The next ones on the list dealt with the relationship of Blaze and Barb. It was pretty clear those wouldn't be well received. "I don't have any more to ask right now. I'd like to call back after I've gotten deeper into Blaze's life and have more specific questions."

"Feel free to call back anytime. So long as those more specific questions are free of gossip and innuendo."

"Oh, they will be."

Keaton hung up and stared at his phone, half expecting to find it dripping icicles. He scanned his notes, wondering what had triggered the woman's outburst. She'd been quite frank about her relationship with Blaze when he was a young pitcher, calling him her first love and admitting to a broken heart.

But she bridled at the suggestion that she might have seen Blaze in the three years since her husband died and Blaze left baseball. Keaton thought he'd framed an innocent question, since Rosemary had already said she and Blaze had kept up with one another through the years. On reflection, though, he had to admit the question was open to a wide range of misinterpretation.

Keaton tried to relate Rosemary's continued relationship with Blaze to his own experience. His first love was his ex-wife Liz, and it seemed clear to him that he would want to know her whereabouts for as long as they lived, even if they didn't have a son in common. The thought of Liz made it easier for Keaton to understand Rosemary's longstanding connection with Stender, but it still didn't explain why she'd been so touchy about the last three years.

He'd have time to pursue the issue with Rosemary Spinetti later. After he'd had a chance to talk to people who might know why she would be so sensitive about her recent contacts with Blaze. And figure out who might have had a reason for sending the anonymous e-mail suggesting that Rosemary was the key to "the real Blaze Stender."

He stopped staring at his phone and punched in a familiar number. Too familiar, he thought, as he heard Little Bill Ellison's raspy "Hello" at the other end of the line. Little Bill owned and operated the casino in East Wheeling, West Virginia, that had been the scene of Keaton's wildest ups and downs as a gambler.

When Keaton identified himself, Ellison said, "I usually don't speak to reporters, but since you've been a regular customer in the past, I'll make an exception in your case."

Keaton could picture Ellison on the other end of the line, distributing his bulk over two barstools, with a red oxygen canister slung over his shoulder like an arrow quiver.

"On second thought," Ellison rasped, "I don't really know why I should make an exception in your case. The last time we had dealings, you nearly broke me. And cost me my best man."

"That barely made us even," Keaton said. "Before that, you nearly ruined me and cost me my wife."

"Those wounds were largely self-inflicted," Ellison said.

"But you helped. Anyhow, you seem to have survived your problems. You're still doing business at the same stand."

"Just barely. We've got competition from the state lotteries, Indian tribes, and any fool with a computer and a gambling itch. But you probably didn't call to talk about my business problems."

"No. I'm trying to get a line on an employee of yours for a piece I'm doing on Blaze Stender and Lanny Morton."

"Too bad about those two."

"This employee was at Lanny's memorial service. Tall, thin,

looked a little like the Grim Reaper without his hood and scythe."

Ellison loosed something between a laugh and a cough. "That would have to be Gentle Ben Brennan. We assigned him to host Morton during his visits here. Guess he got a little attached. Happens sometimes."

"Was Morton such a high roller he rated a host?"

"Not so much a high roller as a regular roller. Sure as sunrise, he showed up four times a year with a roll of bills ripe for plucking."

"And you provided the shearing service."

"Hey. That's the business we're in. But he got as good as he gave. He won a little. Enjoyed himself. Had to be a satisfied customer, the way he kept coming back for more."

"Can I talk to this Brennan?"

"He comes on at three. Why don't you drive on over?"

"It's a little out of my way, Bill. Couldn't you just have him call me at the *Herald?*"

"Come on by. We haven't seen you in a while. I'll give Ben some time off to talk to you, set you up in a private room, and comp you both a dinner."

Keaton sighed audibly.

"You're not worried we'd be a mite inhospitable on account of that business with Bull Harding?" Ellison said. "That's all blood under the bridge. Far as I'm concerned, we're all square, starting out with a fresh tab."

"I can't afford to run another tab with you, Bill."

"It was just a figure of speech. You want to talk to Ben, I'll make him available, provide a little food and liquor. All you have to do is show up. Anytime after three o'clock."

"All right. I'll be there."

★ ★ ★ ★ ★

The room Little Bill Ellison provided for Keaton to meet with Gentle Ben Brennan was on the second floor of his casino in the center of a cluster of rooms devoted to poker and blackjack. The riffle of cards and the laughter of players came through the thin walls as he waited for Brennan to appear, and he realized the selection of the room was Little Bill's less-than-subtle bid to lure him back to the world of gambling.

Keaton opened an Amstel Light from the minibar and took a seat at the empty poker table. He was dealing himself random hands of five-card draw when Brennan's gaunt face appeared in the doorway. A black sport coat hung loosely over his stooped shoulders, matching his black shirt and jeans.

Brennan reached down with long tapered fingers and scooped up the cards Keaton had been dealing. "Little Bill says you're a poker player. Want to deal a few hands while we talk?" The voice, a high, thin tenor, didn't match the Grim Reaper image.

"No thanks. I need to keep my mind on the interview."

Brennan squared the cards with a quick overhand shuffle and set them aside. "Bill said I should tell you anything you want to know. How can I help?"

"I'm working on profiles of Blaze Stender and Lanny Morton for my newspaper." Keaton pushed his handheld recorder forward and raised both eyebrows. When Brennan responded with a shrug, he turned on the recorder. "I saw you at Lanny Morton's memorial service and understand you escorted him around the casino here. What can you tell me about his gambling? How often did he come here? What games did he play? How did he do? Did you get to know him personally? Any insights you can give me would be helpful."

"I only saw Morton four times a year. That's how often he came, regular as clockwork, New Year's, Easter, Memorial Day, and Labor Day. Four big holidays. Always wore cowboy boots, a bright red vest, and a Stetson with a long feather in the band. On account of all that we called him Doc Holiday."

"What did he play?"

"Little bit of everything. Mostly craps and blackjack. Bet the sports book during baseball season."

"Did he win?"

Brennan picked up the deck of cards in his right hand and made several one-handed cuts. Then he showed Keaton the bottom card. It was the ace of spades. "Long run, nobody wins. Otherwise we couldn't stay in business. But Morton had his moments. He was a loose bettor. Loved long shots. Every now and then he'd hit one and live it up like a big spender."

"But most of the time he lost?"

"Most of the time. Sometimes he even left owing us money. But we carried him. He always settled up before his next visit. Well, almost always."

"Almost always?" Keaton asked, emphasizing the word "almost."

"This Memorial Day he showed up with his account still in arrears. Bill staked him and carried his debt."

"Is that usual?"

Brennan shrugged. "Depends on the customer. Morton had been coming for a long time."

"How long?"

"At least twenty years. That's how long I've been here."

"How'd he do playing with house money?"

Brennan performed another series of cuts with his right hand and the ace of hearts replaced the ace of spades on the bottom of the deck. "He never did get back to even. Left owing a little more than he did when he showed up."

"How much was that?"

"Nearly a hundred grand."

"Bill let him gamble a hundred grand on the cuff?"

"He'd been good for it in the past."

"No wonder you showed up at his funeral."

"Wasn't like that. I sorta liked the guy." Brennan smiled. "I did ask a couple of questions about his estate, though."

"What did you find out?"

"Widow was about to divorce him, but she gets everything, which doesn't appear to be much. Not nearly enough to cover his losses, anyhow."

"So Little Bill will write it off?"

Brennan shrugged. "Nature of the business. Happens sometimes. Even if Morton had the money in his estate, it would be tough for us to collect."

"He came here pretty often. Did he have any friends in town?"

"Besides me, you mean?"

"Besides you."

Brennan shook his head. "None I know of. When he was on a winning streak, he'd find a few temporary friends of the female persuasion. But those faces changed regularly. And he hadn't had a winning streak recently."

"What about Blaze Stender? Did Morton ever mention him?"

"He talked like they were good buddies. But I noticed when Blaze was pitching, Lanny would bet against him every chance he got. That strategy never worked very well until Blaze was just about washed up. Then Lanny would load up the line against him and laugh about it."

"Anything else you can think of about Morton?"

"Nothing out of the ordinary."

Keaton turned off his recorder. "Well, then, I better be going. Thanks for your time."

Brennan did another one-handed shuffle and brought the ace of diamonds to the bottom of the deck. "Sure you wouldn't like to play a little poker?"

The laughter from the adjoining room called to Keaton, but

he shook his head. "No. I've been watching you handle that deck. I think poker would be a losing proposition."

"How about a meal, then? Little Bill said I should get you whatever you want."

"No, thanks. I've got a column to write."

Another one-handed shuffle brought the ace of clubs to the bottom of the deck. "Everybody's got to eat. And there's a game just getting started in the Robert Byrd room."

A whoop of joy came from one of the card rooms. Keaton's stomach growled. He knew he shouldn't stay, but he felt rooted to his chair. His palms began to sweat and his chest vibrated. It took a few seconds to realize the vibration was caused by the cell phone in his vest pocket.

He stood, excused himself, turned his back on Brennan, and answered the phone.

"Lloyd, it's Meri Atkins. I thought you should know this right away. AP just released a story claiming Blaze Stender was one of that group of players that tested positive for steroids in two thousand three."

"Are you sure?" Keaton said. "Those results were supposed to be anonymous and confidential."

"That's what A-Rod thought too."

"Oh, shit. I'll follow up on it." Keaton snapped his phone shut and shoved his chair back under the poker table. "Thanks for your time, Ben." In spite of the bad news about Stender, he felt a clear sense of relief. "I'm afraid I have to run."

CHAPTER TEN:
THE PASTEBOARD MEMORIAL

KEATON'S KORNER

An anonymous source has leaked the news that Blaze Stender tested positive for steroids in 2003. Not illegal steroids, mind you. Until 2004, baseball hadn't banned the steroids he is accused of using, and the drugs themselves were legally available through prescriptions.

The news surfaces at a time when Blaze cannot answer his faceless accuser. There's a familiar pattern here. Whenever a star player, like A-Rod or Blaze, makes big news, some anonymous source conveniently leaks the results of the blanket tests made in 2003, which were themselves supposed to remain anonymous. These tests of 1,198 ballplayers were made to determine the extent of baseball's drug usage, with the explicit agreement that the names of players who tested positive were not to be revealed to the teams or the athletes themselves, let alone to the media.

So let's review. Blaze Stender allegedly tested positive for drugs that were not banned either by society or by baseball at the time he was tested. His career did not last long after the tests, and he recorded a lackluster six wins and seventeen losses over that injury-plagued period, so it's hard to argue that the steroids helped his performance in any way.

What's the problem here? Let me suggest that the real problem is one that's not being discussed: the violation of Blaze Stender's civil rights. Although the results were supposed to remain anonymous, it's reported that major-league baseball and the

132

*players union have a list of one hundred four names of players
who tested positive in those blanket tests of 2003. Given the
way the names of A-Rod and Blaze have been leaked, the other
one hundred two players can hardly be resting easily. Where's
the ACLU when you really need it?*

As Barb Stender bent over the dining-room table to light two
candles, her black scoop-necked sweater dipped to reveal a tiny
mole between her collarbone and her left breast. She straightened, pursed her lips to blow out the lit taper, and motioned for
Keaton to sit across the table from her.

"That's quite a spread," Keaton said. "The salmon looks
delicious."

"I'm glad you could come. I finally got my house back, so I
decided to do something with it."

Keaton took a sip of the chardonnay he'd brought from the
living room and sat down. "Yes. I saw that the TV vans have left
your front yard."

"They got tired of waiting. Then some basketball player I
never heard of promised to apologize to his wife for numerous
infidelities. The vans are in the wife's front yard now."

"Think they'll be back?"

"Not unless they find Blaze's body. There's no end of scandal
to keep the press occupied elsewhere."

"How are you doing?"

"Got my house back." She took a sip of wine. "Now I need
to get my life back."

"Anything I can do to help?"

"Just keep on working on Blaze's story." Her blue eyes
sparkled in the candlelight as she peered over the rim of her
wineglass at Keaton. "Thank you for defending him in your
column today. That whole business of anonymous leaks is really
disturbing."

"Those samples were never retested to make sure the findings were accurate. Do you think Blaze actually used steroids?"

"I'm sure he didn't in his peak seasons." Barb shrugged. "Toward the end of his career, I just don't know. He was injured so often. And he was trying everything to keep his arm going."

"But you don't know for sure one way or the other?"

"You live with a man for over twenty years. You think you know him. Still, he spent half the season on the road. And those last years before he retired, he was moody and withdrawn." She shook her head. "I just don't know. About the steroids, I mean. But his trainer, Andy Younker, would know. Have you met him?"

"Yes, right here at Blaze's card table. He was part of the poker group." Keaton tried to make his voice sound casual. "In fact, this Friday would be the next regularly scheduled card game, wouldn't it?"

Barb shrugged. "I guess. That was Blaze's party."

"What would you think about my contacting the players and inviting them to a game here anyhow? Kind of a memorial game. In Blaze's honor."

"Why would you do that?"

"To listen to his friends reminisce about Blaze in a familiar setting. It would give me a chance to talk to Andy Younker. And I'd like to have an informal chat with Dennis Youngman as well." Keaton hesitated. "And there's something else."

"What else?"

"Someone in the game's been cheating. Blaze and I were planning to find out who."

Barb swallowed quickly and put down her fork. "Cheating? In Blaze's game? How do you know?"

Keaton explained how he'd noticed the nicked cards and the way new nicks turned up after he'd introduced a fresh deck.

"But that's so hard to believe," Barb said. "Blaze has known most of those men nearly as long as he's known me. They're his best friends."

"He was as surprised as you when I showed him the cards. We thought with both of us looking for the cheat he wouldn't be hard to spot."

"Do you think you could spot him by yourself?"

"I think so. I'd like to try. I feel I owe it to Blaze."

Barb stroked the neckline of her sweater. "I hate to bring this up. But should you even be playing poker?"

"I sat in the last game for half of the evening with no apparent side effects. I even won a little." But he remembered the lure of the games at Little Bill Ellison's casino. And he had to admit he'd hatched the idea for a Stender memorial game on the drive back from East Wheeling.

"All right, then. I'll call the group. Their names are all on one card in the family Rolodex."

"Advertise it as the Blaze Stender Pasteboard Memorial."

"Pasteboard?"

"Gamblers' slang for cards."

Barb held out her wineglass, and Keaton refilled it and topped off his own. She ran a crimson fingernail around the rim of her refilled glass and asked, "You said you wanted to talk to Dennis Youngman as well?"

"I felt I needed a better feel for Blaze's finances."

"Blaze's finances predeceased him. I thought Dennis made that clear."

"I know. I just wanted to get a feeling for his spending patterns when he was still flush."

"But why?"

"I've been looking into Lanny Morton's finances. He was getting large cash windfalls from somewhere around four times every year."

"What does that have to do with Blaze?"

"I can't help feeling that Blaze and Lanny were connected in some way we don't understand. They were best friends in college, they came up to the majors together, and they died together."

"But they broke up before we were married. Over that bitch Lanny took as his practice bride. No mystery there."

"Then why were they together on Blaze's boat when it hit the breakwater?"

"I can't even tell you what Blaze was doing out in that storm." Barb patted her lips with her napkin. "Surely you don't think Blaze was the source of Lanny's windfalls?"

"I don't know what to think. I talked to Lanny just before the accident though. He was effectively unemployed, and I don't think he could have known many people with access to the kind of money he was getting on a regular basis."

"What kind of money are we talking about?"

"Enough so that East Wheeling casinos let him gamble on the cuff for a hundred grand."

"My God. But that kind of money couldn't have come from Blaze. Not without my knowing about it."

"You're certain of that?"

"Dennis gave me copies of Blaze's financial records the day after the accident. You were there, remember? I went through the last ten years. There weren't any checks of that size that couldn't be accounted for." She stood and handed Keaton her wineglass. "Take our drinks to the living room. I'll go get the records and we can have a look."

Keaton set both wineglasses on the living room coffee table and settled into a corner of the overstuffed couch while Barb disappeared upstairs. She returned with two large loose-leaf binders, a black one labeled TAXES and a red one labeled BANK STATEMENTS.

Instead of sitting on the couch, she perched on the stuffed arm next to Keaton and leaned across him to open the red folder. Her blonde hair brushed his cheek and he was aware of the citrus aroma of her perfume as she pointed to the first page of the bank statements.

"There are ten years' worth of statements here." She thumbed a tab and flipped to a page about a third of the way through the folder. "Let's look at one of the last years Blaze pitched. His earnings varied from year to year. But our expenses stayed pretty constant."

Barb ran her fingernail down copies of checks cashed in the month of January. "Every month, Dennis typed up checks for our regular expenses and Blaze signed them."

"There's a check for two hundred thousand to the Tommy Fund," Keaton said. "Surely that's not a monthly expense."

"No, that was quarterly. Blaze made sure he gave at least a million a year to the fund. Even after the first bubble broke and we had to eat into our capital to do it. Then, of course, the second bubble broke and we didn't have any capital left."

"Four quarterly payments of two hundred grand don't add up to a million dollars."

"No. Blaze made up the balance with personal checks." She flipped over a page and found a handwritten check for sixty thousand dollars made out to the Tommy Fund.

"Why not just do it all with one check?"

Barb shrugged. "What with endorsements and performance bonuses our income was never regular. Especially after Blaze retired. He wanted to be able to vary the amount he gave from quarter to quarter to reflect our income."

"Couldn't Dennis do that?"

"Blaze liked to be in charge."

Keaton leafed through two years' worth of checks. "The only large amounts he paid out personally were for the Tommy Fund and his credit cards. The extra checks to the fund varied between forty thousand and seventy-five thousand dollars per quarter. Everything else is just small change. Certainly not enough to fuel Lanny Morton's gambling habit."

"Why on earth would you even think Blaze might be paying off Lanny?"

"Somebody was. He had no visible means of support. And he wasn't in the majors long enough to earn a pension of any size."

"So you thought Lanny was doing what? Blackmailing Blaze?" Barb flipped the notebook shut. "What on earth for?"

Keaton shrugged. "I have no idea. It was just a shot in the dark. I must say I'm glad it didn't hit anything."

Barb took the loose-leaf binder from Keaton's lap, stood, and pressed it hard against her chest. "You'll forgive my saying so, Lloyd, but I'm sure Blaze would have preferred that you concentrate on his baseball records rather than his financial records."

"I'm just trying to get a complete picture of his life."

"Who have you talked to so far?"

"Besides Lanny, I talked to Webb Bruna, Anne Morton, and Rosemary Spinetti."

Keaton was trying to decide whether to mention Gentle Ben Brennan when Barb interrupted, saying, "That's a three-to-one ratio of gossip to substance."

"Actually, I didn't get any gossip out of Rosemary. And I'm counting on you to fill in whatever substance I may have missed."

"I'm happy to help out. But let's get something straight. I don't expect to join the ranks of the wives of Kobe, Tiger, and all those god-awful cheating politicians who stand quietly while their husbands apologize to the world for screwing around. For one thing, Blaze is not around to apologize. For another, I wouldn't keep quiet."

"Did Blaze have something to apologize for?"

"Lots. But not for screwing around. They say that the wife is always the last to know. But let me tell you this. As a Southern gal, I come from the Lorena Bobbitt school for counteracting marital infidelity." Barb chopped her free hand like a cleaver in front of Keaton's crotch. "Blaze knew how I felt about infidelity before he married me. And I knew Blaze had a roving eye before I married him. Those two ladies you talked to weren't his only targets. But I never heard a word of gossip about his eye or his penis wandering after we were married. Have I made myself clear?"

Barb's outburst unnerved Keaton. "I'm sorry I upset you." He finished his wine, set his glass down on the coffee table and stood up. "Maybe I'd better be going."

Barb stood and took a step backward. "No. I'm the one who's sorry. You don't have to go. Stay and have some coffee." She laid the binders down on the coffee table. "You've had quite a bit to drink. Are you sure you're okay to drive back to Menckenburg?"

Keaton blinked. He felt all right, but he knew his blood-alcohol content must be flirting with the legal limit. "I'll be okay. I know the roads by heart."

Barb put her hand on his arm. "You're welcome to spend the night here. The guest room is all made up."

Keaton flexed his fingers to relieve their sudden tenseness. "No. I've got to pick up my dad. Liz has been watching him all day."

"Call her. I'm sure she'd understand."

Keaton shook his head. "No. It wouldn't be fair to her." The last thing he wanted was to tell Liz he'd be spending the night in Barb Stender's guest room. He could imagine his ex-wife's voice freezing the phone line.

"Well, then. Be careful on the road. I'll set up your poker game for Friday night. Those boys are big drinkers. Better plan to stay over after the game."

"I'll do that." Keaton backed halfway down the front walk, watching Barb silhouetted in the doorway. Then he turned and hurried to his car, feeling the same relief he'd felt leaving Little Bill Ellison's casino without sitting at a poker table.

Keaton counted out a hundred dollars' worth of red, white, and blue chips at each of the eight places around Blaze Stender's octagonal poker table and took several decks of cards from the cabinet under the trophy shelves. He considered putting one of the two nicked decks from the last game back into play, but that would have put two cheaters at the table, and he knew he could hold his own against the evening's competition without the help of marked cards. So he laid two fresh, unopened decks on the green felt table covering and returned the remaining decks to the cabinet.

Barb came in carrying a large silver tray loaded with lunch-meats, cheese, lettuce, and sliced bread for sandwiches. She set the tray on the sideboard next to a large bowl filled with pretzels and two smaller bowls holding mixed nuts and M&M's. "Drinks are in the fridge," she said, nodding toward the low refrigerator next to the sideboard.

"I know the drill." Keaton waved his hand at the sandwich spread. "Thanks for taking care of all this."

"Not a problem." Barb seemed poised to say something more when the doorbell rang.

"That'll be the first of your guests. I'll get the door." She backed out of the room, stopping in the doorway to blow him a kiss and say, "Good luck."

Barb returned with Stender's trainer Andy Younker in tow. His muscular frame filled the doorway, and he was wearing the same black leather jacket and what looked like the same black T-shirt he'd worn to the previous game.

"I'm glad you came early," Keaton said. "I wanted to talk to you about my column in the *Herald* this morning."

"The steroid business," Younker said. "I thought you nailed

it. They weren't illegal at the time, so what's all the fuss about?"

"You were his trainer. Was he on steroids?"

"What's the use of denying it? Somebody leaked the test results."

"How long had he been juicing?"

"Depends on what you mean by juicing. He'd been using cortisone for a long time. It's a steroid, but it's still legal. After his last injury, he tried damn near everything to get his arm back. Primobolan, testosterone. Anything he could get his hands on."

"But he wasn't taking anything illegal before he was injured?"

"No. And like you said in your column, what he finally took wasn't illegal when he took it. Baseball didn't outlaw it until after those tests in two thousand three, when they found they had enough juicers to stock four full teams. And whatever Blaze took sure didn't help his performance any. So what's the big deal?"

"The Hall of Fame voters make it a big deal. They've been reluctant to vote for any player who has the slightest hint of steroids on his record."

"Shit," Younker said. "I didn't think of that."

"Any idea where Blaze got the steroids?"

"I got him the cortisone. As for the rest, I got no comment."

"You're talking steroids, aren't you?" Red Gilles, Stender's catcher when he started out with Cleveland, entered the room. "Those tests were a travesty." He sat down at the poker table. "I can tell you Blaze never used steroids when I was catching him. Never needed 'em."

The room began to fill up. Webb Bruna arrived, waved at Keaton, and took a seat at the table. He was followed by two men Keaton hadn't met. An intense, rail-thin balding man wearing a cardigan, and a stocky middle-aged man whose craggy face looked vaguely familiar.

"We had a no-show, so we scoured our list of substitutes," Bruna explained, and introduced the newcomers. The balding man was Bob Kessler, the doctor in charge of the Tommy Fund, and the man with the familiar face was Terry Zaccone, a onetime utility infielder with several major league teams.

Keaton shook hands with the two newcomers and asked Bruna, "Who couldn't make it?"

"Denny Youngman," Bruna said. "I think he's still brooding over the way you exposed his dealer-friendly game."

"Too bad," Keaton said.

"I don't have Denny's green eyeshade, but I'll be the bank in his place." Bruna collected a hundred-dollar buy-in from each player.

The last two players to arrive were Dale Lewis, Stender's neighbor, and Steve Parnell, Stender's agent. When everyone had grabbed drinks and settled around the table, Keaton stood and said, "Welcome to the first annual Blaze Stender Pasteboard Memorial." He took out his pocket recorder and set it on the table next to his stack of chips. "You all know I'm working on Blaze's biography. I was hoping you might share your thoughts about him during the game and won't mind if I record them."

He didn't tell them he was also recording the game with a small video camera that poked out through the webbing of a baseball glove on the trophy shelf across the room. The extra observation post doubled his chances of catching whoever was marking cards and, in case it became an issue, could provide recorded evidence of the cheat's activity.

"I'll tell you one thing about Blaze," Terry Zaccone said. "He was the most superstitious man I ever met. And I've met plenty playing baseball. If he were here, he'd be plenty pissed that you're sitting in his chair."

"God, yes." Steve Parnell laughed. "Remember that night

you took his place and refused to leave it. He swore at you the whole evening."

"I don't want to hear anything bad about the Blazer," Red Gilles said. "He was the most generous man I ever met. Never left the field until every last clamoring kid had gotten his autograph."

"He was generous with his money too," Bob Kessler said. "His checks to the Tommy Fund came in regular as clockwork, even when he had financial trouble."

"So his financial trouble was common knowledge?" Keaton said.

"Everyone in this room knew he was having troubles," Dale Lewis said. "He bitched nonstop about his losses. I don't think any of us really knew how bad they were."

"You've got to realize a lot of us invested in the same Ponzi scheme," Webb Bruna said. "Denny Youngman was really high on it. None of us got hit nearly as hard as Blaze, though."

"Well, if Blaze were here, I know what he'd say right now," Steve Parnell said.

"What's that?" Keaton asked.

"How's about shutting the fuck up and dealing those cards. We came here to play poker, not gossip."

The group laughed, and Keaton slid the cellophane off a fresh deck of red bicycle cards.

Steve Parnell won the right to deal first, anted ten dollars, and announced a round of Texas Hold 'Em, dealing Keaton a six of clubs and seven of hearts. Keaton didn't mind that his hand was poor, he was happy just to be back in the game. He fingered his cards, squaring them up against the green felt and waiting for his turn to fold.

The game settled into an easy rhythm. Keaton wasn't getting many cards worth playing, but he didn't care. He bided his time, folding early, enjoying the banter and watching the other players.

Andy Younker stayed in every pot far too long, hoping for a miracle that never came. He had to buy a fresh stack of chips after the first six hands had been dealt. Steve Parnell kept up a steady line of patter, becoming quiet only when he had a good hand.

Of the two new players, Bob Kessler provided a running commentary laced with jokes that seemed to have no connection with the cards he held. The other substitute, Terry Zaccone, frowned and deliberated over each decision, fingering his chips and moving them grudgingly into the pot on the rare occasions when he called a bet. After watching Zaccone groan and grimace his way to winning a hand of seven-card stud with a well-hidden full house, Bob Kessler, who had contributed a good share of the large pot by pushing a losing flush, said, "Should have known better than to bet against you, Zack. You're tighter than a nun's cunt with your chips. Used to drive Blaze crazy."

After the first round of eight deals, a fair number of chips had migrated to the stacks in front of Terry Zaccone and Webb Bruna. Everyone had had a chance to handle the cards, but Keaton couldn't see any signs of nicks around the edges.

Keaton finally won a pot halfway through the second round of deals, raking in enough chips to put him a little ahead of the game. That's what he loved about poker. You didn't have to win all of the hands, or even most of the hands. You just had to manage your money well enough to come out with more than you went in with.

The second and third rounds of deals came and went, and the cards still looked as fresh as when Keaton had slit the cellophane and opened the decks, with no nicks on the edges or any other visible marks.

Maybe the cheat knows I'm on to him, Keaton thought. Or maybe tonight's no-show, Dennis Youngman, had been marking the cards. Youngman had insisted on calling a game that gave him a healthy advantage whenever he dealt. It wasn't hard to imagine he might have been skewing the odds a little more by marking a few cards.

The fourth time it was Keaton's turn to deal, he anted ten dollars and announced a game of seven-card high-low. Sitting immediately to Keaton's left, Terry Zaccone stayed in the pot through the first five cards, agonizing over every betting decision. When the sixth card was due, he lapsed into his quandary mode, frowning, fidgeting and fingering his chips over the decision to call a twenty-dollar bet.

As the dealer, Keaton slid the top card of the deck forward slightly, indicating he was set to deal and Zaccone was holding up the play. The move was too subtle to pressure Zaccone into a decision, but it was a revelation to Keaton. Glancing down at the deck, he could see the protruding face of the top card reflected in the beveled edge of the table. It was the six of clubs.

He looked around the table. Where the green felt cover ended, the blond maple edges in front of all the other players had been rounded so that they wouldn't reflect a recognizable image. But the blond edge in front of him had been sanded flat and polished into a mirror-like surface canted at just the right angle to provide a glimpse of the card faces as they were dealt.

Keaton didn't need a hidden camera to locate the cheat at the table. The cheat was the man who usually sat in the chair he now occupied. Blaze Stender himself.

CHAPTER ELEVEN:
AMNESIA ACRES

KEATON'S KORNER

My recent column on the eligibility requirements for the Hall of Fame generated a firestorm of responses that focused, not on a player's records and ability, but on the three extra criteria of integrity, sportsmanship, and character. Some respondents argued that these three criteria had been ignored so much that they were essentially meaningless and should be stricken from the entrance requirements, while others argued that the criteria should be strictly observed and even used to expel existing members.

Now it's no secret that the Hall of Fame includes some unsavory characters. Among living members there are former drug users, admitted cheats (a spitballer, and at least two pitchers who doctored baseballs to improve their breaking stuff), and a repeat DUI offender. And the roster of deceased immortals includes Ty Cobb, a rabid racist and sociopath, at least two former Ku Klux Klan members, and numerous alcoholics and gamblers. The greatest player of all time, Babe Ruth, imbibed libations illegal in his day and was said to be something of a philanderer.

The Hall of Fame is inconsistent (some might say hypocritical) on this point, since their integrity clause is currently invoked as an excuse for barring players accused of using steroids. Mark McGwire, who broke the single-season home-run record and has more home runs per at bat than any player in the history of the game, was recently rejected by eighty percent of the eligible Hall of Fame voters, presumably because he admitted he'd used steroids before baseball outlawed them.

Baseball is balancing itself on an unstable double standard. Eventually, the pendulum will swing back so that a player's on-field performance will once again become the predominant consideration for Hall of Fame membership. The final word on this argument comes from Buck O'Neill, the Negro League player, manager, and spokesman. Responding to fans outraged that he could have voted for the notorious racist Enos Slaughter's entry into the Hall, he told Sports Illustrated, *"You can't know what's in a man's heart . . . Could he play or couldn't he play? That's what matters."*

Keaton poked the scrambled eggs around the plate with his fork. He'd never been much of a breakfast eater, and his stomach didn't feel ready for any food at all. Barb Stender sat across the table from him on her screened-in patio, looking far too cheerful for any hour of the morning.

"I waited up for the game to finish," she said, "but you were still going well after midnight."

"The game ran till three in the morning. Nobody wanted to stop." *Myself included,* Keaton thought.

"Did you find the cheat?"

Keaton shook his head. "Not really. We played all night with two fresh decks, and I never saw a single nicked card."

"Somebody could have tipped the cheater off. I hope you don't think the absence of marked cards last night means that Blaze was the cheat."

Keaton repositioned his eggs. "Blaze wasn't the only regular who was absent last night. Dennis Youngman didn't show either."

"There's just no way Blaze would cheat his friends. He wasn't that kind of man."

"You'd get no argument from the gang last night. They had nothing but praise for him." Keaton set his fork down and rubbed his queasy stomach. He wanted to change the subject. "Bob Kessler was particularly high on your husband. He did say one thing I want to check out, though."

"What's that?"

"He said Blaze gave the same amount to the Tommy Fund year after year. In good years and bad."

Barb's voice tightened. "Are we back to that again?"

"It's important, Barb. I'd like to get to the bottom of it."

Barb waved her hand at the sunlit garden beyond the patio screen. "This is the kind of day to go walking in the park. Or boating on the lake. Dale Lewis has been letting me borrow his cutter. Wouldn't you rather be on the lake than rooting around canceled checks and stale tax returns?"

"Of course. But I've got deadlines to meet."

"I'll offer you a trade. I'll swap you two hours with Blaze's tax records for two hours with me on Lake Erie."

"Sounds like a deal." When Barb left to get Blaze's financial records, Keaton cleared the breakfast table of dishes and dumped his eggs down the garbage disposal. He was sitting at the table sipping tea when Barb returned with the two binders labeled TAXES and BANK STATEMENTS.

She set the binders down in front of Keaton and said, "Two hours. No more."

After his previous stint with Stender's records, Keaton knew just what he was looking for. He took his pen and a sheet of scratch paper and copied several rows of figures from the bank statements. Then he checked five years' worth of tax returns and examined several batches of canceled checks. After forty-five minutes he closed the binders, called Barb back in, and said, "All right. I think I know what's going on."

"From the look on your face, I'm not going to like it."

"Probably not. Let's review what we already know. At the beginning of every quarter, Dennis Youngman typed out checks for two hundred thousand to the Tommy Fund. Then Blaze would augment those donations with handwritten checks that ranged between forty thousand and seventy-five thousand each quarter."

Keaton turned his scratch pad so that Barb could read the rows of figures. "But those random checks always added up to two hundred thousand each year. At least for the five years I checked."

"But that squares with what Bob Kessler told you. Blaze gave the same amount every year."

"That's what Blaze claimed on his tax returns. But I don't think that two hundred thousand in handwritten checks ever made it to the Tommy Fund."

"Why not?"

"Let's take a look at these two canceled checks from the days when banks still returned them with their statements." Keaton turned over two canceled checks and shoved them to the middle of the table. "Dennis Youngman prepared one of these checks and Blaze prepared the other, handwritten one. They're both stamped with the name of the Tommy Fund and the bank ID. But the handwritten check is countersigned with the written name 'Tommy Fund.' "

"What's wrong with that?"

"Don't you think it's a little strange? If there's a signature, why wouldn't it be someone's name? Like Bob Kessler. Or Bob Kessler for the Tommy Fund. But not just Tommy Fund. And the rubber stamp covers most of the signature."

"I still don't see what you're driving at."

"I think someone went to the bank and opened an account with a name like Tommy Fund."

"But how could anyone get away with that?"

"Look at the signature. Look at Blaze's handwriting on the other side. They're both pretty sloppy. The second letter of the last name could be an *a* just as easily as a *u*. And the signature tails off at the end. What we took for a *d* could be an *a*, followed by an *l*."

"Well, Blaze's penmanship was never exceptional. But there's no question it's his handwriting on the front of the check. So what are you getting at?"

"I think someone with a name like Thomas Fanal or Thomas Funel has an account at your bank and Blaze has been paying that person two hundred thousand dollars a year."

"And claiming it as a donation to the Tommy Fund on our income tax?"

"Well, a two-hundred-grand donation could save you as much as a hundred thousand dollars a year in taxes."

"But both checks have the Tommy Fund stamp on the reverse side."

"It would be easy for Blaze to get a stamp from the fund and use it on the canceled checks to throw off an auditor."

"So you think Blaze might have opened that account himself?"

"He could have. But that's taking a pretty big risk just to dodge your tax bill. There'd be jail time if he was caught. I still think it's more likely someone was blackmailing him."

Barb shoved the scratch paper and canceled checks back across the table. "Look. I want you to stop this right now."

Keaton gathered up the checks and folded them inside the scratch paper. "Don't you want to find out who might have been blackmailing Blaze?"

"You haven't convinced me he was being blackmailed. Maybe this was just some elaborate tax dodge. Maybe the money really went to the Tommy Fund. It doesn't really matter to me." She gathered up the two binders and clutched them against her chest. "Lloyd, I'm broke. It's bad enough to find out Blaze might have been giving away two hundred thousand a year. But my signature is on those tax returns along with his. That makes me liable for any penalties, as well as any jail time."

"I wasn't intending to go to the IRS."

"I know you weren't. But once you start digging, there's no telling what your shovel might hit or who might notice the stacks of dirt."

Keaton was formulating an argument when his cell phone played the opening bars of "The Gambler."

"That's your ringtone?" Barb said. "Cute."

Keaton checked the phone. It was Liz calling. He stood, excused himself, and turned his back on Barb. Liz's voice came through tight with stress. "Lloyd, where are you?"

"Still in Cleveland. I'm going over some things with Barb Stender."

"Well, tear yourself away from her. Your father needs you."

"Is he missing again?"

"No. He's right here. But he's on a rampage. His apartment is a god-awful mess. And he keeps ranting and calling me Martha."

"Oh, God." He could hear his father's voice in the background, saying, "Can't find those goddamn notes."

"You've got to come right away," Liz said. "It's time to put him in one of those homes you've been looking at."

"I still have a few to check out."

"There's no time. He needs help now."

John Keaton's voice came through clearly. "Don't need a home. Already got a home."

"I'll leave right now." Keaton ended the call.

Barb raised an eyebrow. "Trouble?"

"My dad," Keaton said. "He's losing it."

"I'm sorry. Is there anything I can do?"

Keaton pocketed his cell phone. "I'm afraid I'll have to take a rain check on that boat trip."

Barb set the two loose-leaf binders down on the breakfast table. "The glaze had pretty much gone from the day anyhow."

Keaton headed for the door. "I'll be back in touch as soon as I get Dad sorted out."

Barb just stared down at the binders. "You do that."

Keaton swung his Escort out of the Stenders' driveway and headed for Interstate 71. The subject of his biography was turning from Dr. Jekyll into Mr. Hyde before his eyes. In the space of a week, Blaze Stender had been revealed as a steroid user, card cheat, and tax dodger. And something even darker may have fueled what looked to be over twenty years' worth of blackmail payments.

Keaton patted his pocket, where he'd put the scratch paper with two canceled checks folded inside. At least he knew how to start tracking down the recipient of those payments.

Keaton wasn't prepared for the scene that confronted him when he opened the door to his father's apartment. Open books, newspaper sections, and magazine pages were strewn on every flat surface. A waist-high mound of clothing, shirts, jeans, underwear, and socks occupied one corner of the living room. In the kitchen, what looked like every plate, pot, pan, bowl, cup, saucer, and glass in the house had been washed recently and set draining on the sideboard.

His father sat at the small kitchen table, staring morosely at a can of Stroh's. Half of a broken dinner plate lay under the table near his stocking feet. "I want those notes," John Keaton said without looking up from his beer.

Liz shook her head. "I'm sorry, Lloyd. I just can't keep on doing this. He was fine last night, but he's been yelling for some set of notes all morning. I think they belonged to his father, but I don't have the slightest idea what they look like. When I couldn't find them, he became abusive. Kept calling me Martha. And worse."

"I need those notes," John Keaton said. "And the columns."

"I'm sorry you had to go through this, Liz," Keaton said. "It's my problem. I've called the Stauder Center. They can take him today."

"Don't want to go to any center," John Keaton said.

"It's just for a little while, Dad. It'll be like a vacation." Keaton ignored Liz's look of disbelief. "We'll need some time to clean this place up and find your notes."

"Need those notes. Gonna make me a book."

Liz pointed to a suitcase near the door. "I packed what I thought he'd need right away."

"That's good. The rest can come later." Keaton took a pair of loafers from the top of the mound of clothes in the corner. "Put your shoes on, Dad."

John Keaton shoved his feet into the loafers. "Not leaving without those notes."

Keaton grabbed the suitcase by the door. "We'll find them and bring them out later."

"I'll stay here and look for them," Liz said. "Clean the place up a little. Pack a few more of your things."

John Keaton rose heavily from the kitchen table. "Don't bother packing any more stuff. I'll be back."

Keaton's dad maintained a sullen silence for the first ten minutes of the trip. Then he said, "This place we're going. Is it the one that 'makes a difference one resident at a time'? Or the one where you 'forget home maintenance and embrace health-care security'?"

John Keaton's sardonic quotes were the first sign that he had read any of the brochures on managed-care facilities that Keaton had given him. After a while all the pamphlets had started to look alike to Keaton. Lots of pictures of elderly faces that obviously belonged to actors looking far too healthy and happy. "I don't remember the advertising, Dad. I picked the place that looked best to me. The one I'd like for myself."

"Why don't you move in there, then? I'll go back to the apartment."

"I've got to make a living, remember? So we can afford your new digs." He hadn't yet figured out how they could afford the move. That's why he had put off making the arrangements. And why he'd needed the advance on the Stender biography.

"I don't know why I just can't move in with you. Your mom and I took care of your granddad until he passed."

"Granddad didn't have Alzheimer's." It was the first time Keaton could remember using the A word in his father's presence.

"The hell he didn't. They just didn't have a word for it then."

The starched woman who showed Keaton and his father to his father's new living quarters wore a nametag that read "Hi! I'm Tiffany" and was the same person who had escorted Keaton on his exploratory visit. Keaton recognized many of the same canned phrases—"round-the-clock care," "registered nurses always on duty," and "five-star rating"—interspersed with lots of references to "loved ones." She opened the door to a two-room apartment that would have been spacious for a hotel room but was a little cramped for living quarters. "A lot smaller than the place I was just run out of" was how Keaton's father put it.

Tiffany answered his objections by sliding back a glass door leading to a flagstone walkway that wound its way through a small garden and a stand of beech trees before coming to a concrete wall. "Our garden area gives you more space by providing access to private pathways that are secured to prevent wandering."

John Keaton stuck his head through the open door, brought it back in quickly, and made a face like a man with his foot in a bear trap.

Undeterred, Tiffany continued her sales pitch. "Our aim here is to maximize the ability and comfort of loved ones experiencing memory loss."

"Honey," John Keaton said, "I've plum run out of loved ones. Otherwise I wouldn't be here."

"That's where we come in, sir," Tiffany said. "We've found that family members can't do it all by themselves."

"Why not? I did."

Tiffany seemed to have run out of sales pitch. She handed the apartment keys to Keaton and said, "I'll leave you to make yourselves at home. You can find me at the front desk if you have any questions."

As soon as Tiffany left, John Keaton plopped down into an overstuffed easy chair, raising a puff of dust. "Well, here we are. Amnesia Acres."

"I'm sorry, Dad."

"I'm sorry too. Apologize to Liz for me, will you." Keaton's dad slouched deep into the chair's cushions. "I just don't remember any of it."

"It's all right. She understands."

"I do want to find those notes, though. They're records your grandfather kept. Along with his newspaper columns." John Keaton sat up straight. "I had this idea. I'd like to edit a book of columns. His, mine, and yours. The best stuff we ever wrote. Three generations of Keatons. What do you think?"

Keaton was moved by the suggestion. Both by the idea and the realization that its completion was beyond his father's capability. He blinked to clear a sudden dampness in his eyes. "I think it's a great idea, Dad. I'd like to help. In any way I can."

"Well, then, find me those notes so I'll have something to do. Otherwise I'll go crazy cooped up here."

Back in his father's apartment, Keaton found that Liz had organized the once-scattered books and magazines into neat stacks and packed another suitcase with clothes to be transported to the Stauder Center. Next to the suitcase were four large loose-leaf binders filled with plastic sleeves holding his father's *News* columns. A note from Liz was taped to the top binder. "These are your dad's. Couldn't find your granddad's."

Keaton gathered the binders under his arms and took them back down the hall to his own apartment. Coupling his dad's columns with his own would give them two-thirds of the source material they needed for the book his dad wanted.

When Keaton was starting out as a reporter, he'd preserved his columns the same way his father had, by protecting batches of clippings in plastic sleeves and filing the sleeves in loose-leaf binders. He'd even kept it up long after computers revolutionized the newspaper business. When Meri Atkins saw him clipping his columns and shoving them into plastic sleeves, she laughed out loud. Now he kept his columns on neatly labeled CDs, one disc for each year. But the early columns were still in binders on the floor of his bedroom closet, in file boxes buried beneath other file boxes.

In order to reach his early columns, Keaton had to clear out the file box he'd put in last, which held the scrapbooks Barb Stender had given him. Sitting on top of the box was the scrapbook Stender had cobbled together himself. Whereas the scrapbooks Barb had prepared held clippings neatly scissored and pasted in chronological order, Stender's own scrapbook bulged at the seams with a hodgepodge of sports pages, game programs, and issues of old magazines.

Keaton had already examined and cataloged the contents of

Barb's scrapbooks, making detailed notes he would use in describing Stender's team-by-team journey through the major leagues. But the disorganized mess of Stender's own scrapbook had looked too forbidding. Having pulled the box out of his closet, though, Keaton decided to look through its contents.

As Barb had told him, most of the sports pages and game programs in Stender's scrapbook were from cities he had visited on the road. From time to time he would sort through these and pass some along to Barb for inclusion in her own orderly records. But Stender's scrapbook pages held more than yellowing sports sections and dog-eared magazines. Jammed between the pages were old letters, wedding invitations, snapshots, birth announcements, and pictures of Blaze's high school teams in Colony, Oklahoma. The old letters and high school pictures, in particular, were great fodder for the biography, and Keaton was sorry he hadn't opened the scrapbook sooner. He had taken Barb at her word that all it contained were clippings waiting to be processed.

A small brown envelope had been taped to the inside back cover of Stender's scrapbook. It contained tiny one- and two-paragraph snippets from obituary notices. There were obituaries for Stender's mother and father, as well as his son Tommy and an uncle, Bus Stender. In addition to family members, there were obituary notices for Rosemary Spinetti's husband John and Ken Caminetti, the former MVP who had died of drug abuse, as well as two other adults whose names Keaton didn't recognize: David Oke and Dr. Thomas Fulton.

The envelope also held short obituaries of three Oklahoma teenagers. A boy named Gene Varney who had died after being beaned in a high school baseball game, and two young women. One, Charlene Kilgren, had died in childbirth. Another, Edie Weber, had succumbed after three years in a coma. Keaton checked the dates of the teenagers' obituaries. Both Gene Varney and Charlene Kilgren were of the right age to have been in high school with Blaze Stender, but the Weber girl was six years younger than the pitcher and had grown up in a different part of the state.

CHAPTER TWELVE:
CALLED TO ACCOUNT

KEATON'S KORNER

I was reading some of my father's old Cleveland News columns and came across one that speaks directly to the issues raised in my recent scribblings regarding the requirement that members of Baseball's Hall of Fame be of good character. During my father's tenure at the News, a passel of do-gooders invoked this requirement as an argument for evicting Tris Speaker, the greatest center fielder of his day, from the Hall of Fame because the Texas native had been a member of the Ku Klux Klan in his youth.

My father responded that those people calling for Speaker's eviction on the basis of his youthful associations should have paid more attention to his later life. Speaker was a goodwill ambassador for the Cleveland Indians in 1947 when they made Larry Doby the first African-American player in the American League. Doby came to the Indians straight from the Negro Leagues, where he had been a middle infielder. At the time, the Indians had two future Hall of Famers, Lou Boudreau and Joe Gordon, playing short and second, so there was little chance that Doby would see much playing time in the infield.

To solve the problem, Tris Speaker, the former Klan member, was hired to coach Doby in the center fielder's art. He did his job so well that the Indians won the World Series in 1948, Doby's first year in center field. In 1998, when Doby was inducted into the Hall of Fame himself, he acknowledged Speaker's contribution to his career in his induction speech.

Speaker's role in coaching the first black player in the American League affords another example of the folly of creating blacklists based on one-time affiliations and trying to read a man's heart instead of his deeds when casting votes for baseball's Hall of Fame.

Keaton had erased the number from his cell phone's directory, but he wasn't surprised to find that he knew it by heart. He punched it into his phone and after three rings the raspy voice of Little Bill Ellison came on the line with the ka-ching of slot machines in the background.

"Been hoping to hear from you after your visit, scribe," Little Bill rasped. "Got some bets you want to place?"

"No. Got a favor I'd like to ask."

"We usually quote pretty long odds on favors. But there's no harm in asking."

"Remember about a year ago when I placed a bet for a friend on the National League Championship Series and pretended it was my own money?"

"How could I forget? Your bet and others like it that night damn near broke us."

"Well, you took pains to let me know I wasn't fooling anybody when I said I was betting my own money. You quoted my bank balance and not only told me exactly where the money had come from, but also how much the donor had left in her account and where she'd gotten the cashier's check that went into my account. It was all pretty impressive."

"We were showing off a little. But we do need to be able to check a player's credit in a hurry, so we maintain a few eyes inside the banking system."

"I'd like you to use those eyes to check out a bank account for me."

Little Bill cleared his throat loudly and said, "And just who does this account belong to?"

"I don't know that. It's under a phony name in First Cleveland. I'm hoping the deposit and withdrawal patterns will help me put a real name on the account."

"And why would you want to do that?"

"Call it a reporter's curiosity."

"Wouldn't have anything to do with your interest in Lanny Morton, would it?"

"I can't tell you that. Can you do it?"

"Oh sure we can do it. But why should we?"

"Call it a favor for a friend."

"Last time I did business with you, friend, you damn near broke my entire operation."

"The time before that, you did break mine. I'd say we're even."

"That's not much of an argument in favor of your favor."

"Never hurts to have a friend in the Fourth Estate. Lots better than having an enemy with daily access to newsprint."

"My daddy always said, 'Never argue with anybody who buys ink by the barrel.' "

"Your daddy must have been channeling Ben Franklin."

"What's the name on the account?"

"I can't quite read the signature. But I've got the number of the account."

"That'll do."

Keaton read the number from the reverse side of Blaze Stender's handwritten check.

"I'll be in touch," Little Bill said. "I'm curious to see what this turns up."

"So am I, Bill. So am I."

Before leaving for his office, Keaton stopped by his father's apartment. Liz had packed a suitcase full of clothes to be taken to the Stauder Center and located notebooks with his father's columns, but had been unable to find any of his grandfather's writings. His father had insisted they were somewhere in the apartment, but his father's memory could hardly be trusted.

Even so, Keaton wanted to search for his grandfather's work, both out of curiosity and loyalty to his father. His own apartment was a mirror image of his father's, and Keaton knew from his own experience that the kitchen cabinets afforded far more storage space than he needed as a bachelor.

Liz would never have looked in the kitchen for writing files, so that was where Keaton started and finished his search. Two file boxes had been crammed into a cabinet beside the sink that also held a popcorn popper and an aluminum roaster full of pots and pans. The two boxes contained loose-leaf binders holding his grandfather's newspaper columns. Each neatly labeled binder held two or three years' worth of columns starting in 1916 and running until 1950.

Keaton riffled the pages of the earliest binder and stopped at a column singing the praises of Tris Speaker. He'd just written a column of his own mentioning Speaker, and was curious to see what his grandfather had to say about the man who was generally recognized as the best fielding center fielder of his day. His grandfather had written:

An old-timer spent a couple of afternoons watching the Gray Eagle, Tris Speaker, patrol center and a large portion of right and left fields, and he remarked: "If I had a ball club consisting of just Speaker, Walter Johnson, and any old catcher, I could win the pennant in either league. The opposition couldn't ever hit Walter, and even if they did, they couldn't hit past Tris."

Keaton put a paper clip on the binder page to mark the column and pulled the rest of the binders out of the box. Packed under the binders were stacks of oblong notebooks with blocks of advertising on their hard brown covers that made them look like old *Farmers' Almanac*s. Keaton opened the top notebook and could barely keep his hands from trembling. The pages were covered with tiny precise handwriting that he recognized from the birthday cards his grandfather had sent him every year until he died.

Amazing. His grandfather had hung onto his notes as a working reporter. After living through the Depression, he probably couldn't bear to throw anything out. He might even have cultivated his neat, precise handwriting to make the most of the thin, bound notebook pages.

The notebooks would be a treasure trove for the compilation his father was contemplating. Keaton stifled the urge to stay home from work and lose himself in the clipped, terse sentences. Instead, he repacked the binders full of columns in a single box to be delivered to his father and organized the handwritten notebooks in another box he could examine at his leisure. Then he left for his office.

Keaton had barely settled into his cubicle when his phone rang and Little Bill Ellison's voice rasped, "Got that information you wanted."

"That was quick."

"In my business, you've got to be able to check credit before the customer leaves the casino."

"Makes sense. What did you find out?"

"Lots of interesting stuff. The account belongs to a man named Thomas Fanal. Like you said, the name was phony. So was his street address. He got his mail at a PO box in University Heights."

Keaton felt a rush. Lanny Morton lived in University Heights. "That's interesting. What else did you find out?"

"We could only go back three years, but it looks like Blaze

Stender was the only person to deposit money in the account. He put checks in the first week of every quarter. Forty to sixty grand a pop. But he missed the last two quarters."

"What about withdrawals?"

"Guy mostly used ATM machines. Probably didn't want any tellers to recognize him. Maxed out the daily limit as soon as the deposit hit. Usually found machines around University Heights. But here's a surprise. Or maybe not. Several times he used the ATMs right here in our casino."

"And I'll bet Lanny Morton was visiting you every one of those times."

"Guess that wasn't much of a surprise after all."

"No. I suspected the money was going to Lanny."

"Think he had something on Stender?"

"I had a strong hunch."

"But you came to me rather than the local cops."

"Hard to get a warrant on the basis of a reporter's hunch." And he didn't want to risk sending Barb to jail for tax fraud.

"So you weren't surprised about Lanny. Here's something that might surprise you, though. First thing Mr. Fanal did soon as Stender's quarterly donation hit was to split it into equal halves. Half of each deposit went into a First Cleveland account in the name of a Mr. Stephen Brown."

"Let me guess. Another phony."

"Phony as a stripper's stage name."

Keaton flipped to a fresh page in his notebook. "What can you tell me about Mr. Brown?"

"Same as Mr. Fanal, he got most of his money from ATMs. But his were in Oklahoma."

"Where in Oklahoma?"

"Mostly in a place called Ponca City. Ever hear of it?"

"No." Keaton called up a map of Oklahoma on his computer. Ponca City was just north of Red Rock, the location where

Blaze Stender and Lanny Morton had been pulled off the road on their first trip to spring training.

Keaton thanked Ellison, hung up, and called Barb Stender. "Barb, I'd like you to check Blaze's phone bills for the year."

"What am I looking for?"

Keaton checked his notes and gave her Lanny Morton's number in University Heights.

"Anything else?"

"I want to know about any calls to Oklahoma."

"His sister still lives there, you know."

"That's okay. Get all the numbers. We can separate his sister's later."

"What's it all about?"

"The University Heights number is Lanny Morton's. It looks as if he was on the receiving end of all those checks Blaze wrote to Thomas Fanal disguised as Tommy Fund donations."

"So he was blackmailing Blaze?"

"Looks like it."

"But how? What could Morton possibly know that would be worth so much money?"

"That's what I want to find out."

"Why do you want Oklahoma numbers?"

"Some of Blaze's money wound up in Oklahoma. Could be somebody there was in cahoots with Morton. Or maybe he just had a needy relative back in his home state."

"Anything else I can do?"

Keaton paged through his notes. "Blaze had an envelope full of obituary snippets in his scrapbook. Most of them are names I recognize: his mom and dad, your son Tommy, an uncle named Bus Stender. But there were five names I couldn't place."

"What are they?"

"Tom Fulton, Gene Varney, David Oke, Charlene Kilgren, and Edie Weber."

"Tom Fulton was the Stenders' family doctor when Tommy died. I always thought a better doctor in a bigger hospital might have saved him, but there we were in East Nowhere, Oklahoma."

"I'm sorry." He couldn't think of anything else to say.

After a pause, Barb said, "David Oke was Blaze's uncle on his mother's side. His favorite uncle. A civilizing influence compared with his rough-edged father. The other three names I don't know."

"All three died in their teens. One in a baseball accident. One in childbirth, and one in a coma."

"What a shame. Sorry I can't help you with their names. When do you need those other phone numbers?"

"As soon as possible."

"I'll get right on it."

Keaton pulled the obituary notices for Gene Varney, Charlene Kilgren, and Edie Weber out of Stender's envelope and Googled their names without getting any useful results. Then he went next door to Meri Atkins's cubicle. "I need to consult the generation that has mastered the Internet."

Meri looked up from her computer. "At least you're starting to recognize your limitations. What can I do for you?"

Keaton laid the three clippings on her desk. "I've got three obituary notices here. They're probably at least twenty years old, and I'm guessing they're from an Oklahoma newspaper. How do I find out more about the subjects?"

Meri scooped up the clippings. "You give them to your trusted Girl Friday."

"If I do that, how will I ever learn to accomplish anything on my own?"

"You won't, and your trusted Girl Friday will take over your job when your shortcomings become apparent to management and they put you out to pasture."

"Pasture sounds pretty good right now."

Meri looked at both sides of the clippings. "No dates. No newspaper snipes. How do you know they're from Oklahoma?"

"They were with a batch of other Oklahoma obituaries in Blaze Stender's effects. All three died as teenagers, and that's where Blaze was as a teenager."

"So this task relates to Blaze's biography rather than our newspaper business?"

"It could turn out to be newsworthy. If not, I'll mention you in the book's acknowledgments. That's Girl Friday, right?"

"For now. By the time the book comes out, I'll have taken your job."

"Well, don't dawdle. I'm sniffing pastureland even as we speak."

The phone rang in Keaton's cubicle.

Meri shrugged. "Landline. That's about your speed. Better answer it."

Barb's voice came over the receiver. "I've looked up those numbers you wanted."

Keaton juggled the phone, his notebook and a pen from his shirt pocket. "Let's have them."

"Blaze called Lanny once in the last six months. Two days before the accident."

"He was probably setting up the boat trip. What about Oklahoma calls?"

"He called his sister twice. Once in March and once in May. There was another call I didn't recognize. To a number in Ponca City."

"That's the one I want. What's the number?" After Barb gave him the number, he asked, "When did Blaze make the call?"

"One week before the accident."

"All right. Thanks. You did good."

"What are you going to do?"

"Rattle a cage or two."

After he hung up, Keaton checked his notes from his conversations with Webb Bruna. He was pretty sure he knew who belonged to the Ponca City number. He might as well call and find out for sure. If he was wrong, he could just apologize, hang up, and do a little more homework.

He punched the number into his office phone.

A deep-fried male voice answered, "Yeah?"

"I'm trying to reach Cletis Raptor."

"Well, you've reached him. Now what do you want?"

"Mr. Raptor, my name is Lloyd Keaton. I'm a reporter with the Menckenburg, Ohio, *Herald*. I've been hired to write a biography of Blaze Stender."

"What's that to me?"

"When Blaze was a rookie going to his first spring-training camp, you arrested him and Lanny Morton for being left of the center line."

"If you say so."

"I'd like to talk to you about it."

"That was a long time ago."

"But you still remember them."

"They was famous baseball players."

"Not when you knew them."

"No. But later on they was."

"So you kept up with them?"

"Just through the sports pages."

"And you haven't spoken to either of them since that night you pulled them over?"

"No. Why should I?"

In his notebook, Keaton wrote, "Lies about recent contact." Then he said, "Tell me about their accident."

"Not much to tell. It was raining pretty good and they hit a phone pole."

"And you pulled them over later on."

"Their door was a-flappin', and the Injun was speeding."

"Had they been drinking?"

"Not to excess. If they had been, I'd of jailed them."

"But you did keep them overnight."

"I don't recall."

"Do you recall meeting with the Mammoths' management?"

"Now you mention it, they did lawyer up."

Keaton wrote, "Mammoths' management = lawyering up" and then said, "And then you let them go?"

"We reached an understanding. And they agreed to pay for the telephone pole."

"Did they pay for anything else?"

"Likely there was a fine. I don't recall. Like I said, it was a long time ago."

"Did the boys appear to be on friendly terms with each other?"

"They spent the night in a cell together. I didn't watch over them. Wasn't no fistfights nor ass groping reported. They left together the next day."

"So it was just an ordinary traffic stop. How big was the fine?"

"I told you, I don't recall the details. Where's all this going?"

"I think something happened on that trip to change the course of their lives. I'm trying to write the story of those lives, fill in a little color and background. And it's not every day a man gets arrested for being left of the center line. Anything you could tell me would help."

"I've told you all I can recollect."

"Well, if you think of anything else, I'd appreciate it if you'd call me." Keaton gave Raptor the address and phone number of the newspaper and hung up. He looked down at his note pad. Raptor had lied at least three times. About the boys not being drunk, about the bribe the Mammoths paid for their release, and about not having any recent contact with Blaze Stender.

Maybe he should have waited before calling, developed more of a plan of attack. He could have called Raptor on any of his lies, but that would only have put him on his guard and probably ended the conversation. But at least he'd established that there was no innocent explanation for Blaze's call.

Keaton set his notes aside and went to work on his next day's column. He had finished it and was about to quit for the day when he looked up to see Meri Atkins standing in the entrance to his cubicle.

She waved a sheet of paper and said, "Girl Friday reporting."

"That's pretty quick service."

"Well, I wanted to finish so I could get back to undermining your position of power."

"I'm still impressed. You tracked down all three names?"

"Wasn't too hard. The families were all still in Oklahoma. Couple of false starts, couple of dead ends, but eventually I got through."

"What did you find out?"

Meri glanced at the paper in her hand. "The Varney boy was killed in a high school baseball game. He was in the on-deck circle when the batter hit a foul line drive that caught him behind the ear. One of those things where he felt all right and the hospital let him go, but the pressure built and he died the next day."

"What was the connection with Blaze?"

"Blaze hit the line drive. But nobody blamed him. I talked to the boy's father. He had nothing but praise for Blaze. And nothing but bitterness for the medical profession."

"Amazing. I thought I knew Blaze petty well, but I'd never heard that story."

"Not the kind of thing high schools or hospitals want to spread around."

"What about the two girls?"

"Charlene Kilgren was a sophomore at Oklahoma State University. What the press listed as birth complications was actually a botched abortion. Family had no idea she was pregnant, let alone who the father was."

"So there's no connection with Blaze?"

"He was a senior at OSU the year she died. The fact that he kept her obituary says something. But when I asked about boyfriends, I hit a dead end."

"How'd you get these people to talk?"

"Promised anonymity. Told them I was a reporter doing a story on something related to the obituaries. Deaths in high school sports, childbirth, long-term comas."

"What about the girl in a coma?"

"Edie Weber. That was a tough one. She'd been in a coma for three years after being struck by a car. Hit-and-run. I talked to her father. He made the decision to pull the plug. Could barely talk about it twenty-plus years later."

"Over twenty years. When exactly was the accident?"

Meri laid the sheet of paper on Keaton's desk and pointed to the date. Keaton's eyes followed Meri's finger. Edie Weber had been hit by a car on the same date Blaze Stender and Lanny Morton had started their ill-fated drive to spring training.

CHAPTER THIRTEEN:
A MATTER OF TIMING

KEATON'S KORNER

For the coming week, Keaton's Korner will be taken over by my colleague Meredith Atkins while I take some time off to attend to personal business. You'll find Meri to be knowledgeable not only about the baseball pennant races, but also the football debuts of the Buckeyes, Bengals, and Browns, as well as local school athletics. I'm leaving you in good hands and I know you'll enjoy her unique perspective on the Menckenburg sports scene.

Keaton took two days to get his father settled in at the Stauder Center and then flew to Tulsa, where he rented a car and started out on the same route Blaze Stender and Lanny Morton had followed on their drive to spring training in Tucson.

The first stop he made was to visit Vernon Weber, the father of the hit-and-run victim whose obituary had turned up in Blaze Stender's scrapbook. Weber greeted Keaton sitting on the porch of his home wearing a leather jacket against the prairie winds that were announcing the start of the football season. The man didn't seem to fit well in his own clothes or his own skin. The jacket was at least one size too large for his frail shoulders, and his face was fixed in the blank stare of a music major in a calculus class. It was a lost look Keaton had seen quite often recently on the faces of other tenants in his father's nursing home.

"I appreciate your willingness to talk with me on such short notice," Keaton said. "And I'm sorry to have to bring up the past."

Weber sat motionless in a wooden rocking chair and stared out at his parched brown lawn. "The past is all I've got left."

"Tell me about your daughter and her accident."

"About her coma, you mean?"

"About her coma and everything that led up to it."

Weber had been holding a framed picture and a scrapbook on his lap, and the rocking chair squeaked as he leaned forward to hand the picture to Keaton. "Edie was our only child. We scrounged to send her to a private high school in Tulsa. I wanted her closer to home, but she got along real well there. Was head cheerleader her senior year. Won a couple of statewide beauty contests."

Keaton stared at the picture of a pretty cheerleader with blonde bangs and a confident smile while her father related the story of his daughter's accident.

"February of her senior year, Edie started coming home for weekends. She was dating a local boy, Ernie Jenkins. He was at OSU, but his family was in real estate and had a big home about ten miles from here."

Weber's voice was flat, resigned. "Anyhow, Ernie took Edie to a Saturday-night movie. On the way home, he ran out of gas. Well, they took an empty gas can from his trunk and started out walking. It was a dark night on a desolate road, and they'd walked about a mile when she was hit. Car knocked her forty feet, but the driver just kept right on going. Didn't even slow down. Happened so fast, Ernie didn't see the car coming or going."

Weber shook his head. "Why couldn't the driver have stopped? I've asked myself that over and over. It took Ernie quite a while to get help. The road was deserted and it started in to raining pretty hard. If the driver had stopped or Ernie had got help quicker, things might have been different."

Weber shrugged. "As it turned out, Edie was in a coma over three years. Her mom and I kept hoping she'd snap out of it, but she never showed any signs she might do that. And the bills were eating us alive."

Weber raised a trembling hand. "Not that I wouldn't have kept paying if I thought there was a chance she'd wake up. But the doctors just kept shaking their heads.

"Finally, we couldn't take it anymore. We were a religious family, but we decided to cut off life support. Doctors took care of it. I sure couldn't manage it. Damn near killed my wife Virg. Hell, it did kill her. She just faded away after Edie died. We tried all kinds of pills for depression, but none of them worked. She hung on for two years, but in the end she wouldn't even get out of bed. Curled up in a fetal position, just like Edie at the end. Just didn't want to live."

Weber clutched the scrapbook in his lap. "After Virg died, I tried to track down the driver that had hit Edie. I mean, he'd robbed me of everything I held dear. And the police had never found a thing."

"After five years, how did you start?" Keaton asked.

"I figured, see, that if the guy was drunk and driving crazy he might have hit something else. Or run into trouble down the road."

Weber opened the scrapbook and took out a dog-eared highway map. He unfolded three sections of the map and smoothed them on top of his scrapbook. A thick red pie-shaped wedge had been outlined on the map with its point at the location of his daughter's accident.

Weber waved his hand over the wedge, which extended due west of the accident site. "The car that hit Edie was headed west. If the driver was drunk or stoned, he might have had more trouble that evening. I figured out how far he might have gone before sobering up or stopping. Gave him three hours. Then I talked to every sheriff, police station, and state patrol office within that range.

"The trail was five years cold, but most of the lawmen had records going back ten years. I looked up every traffic stop made the night Edie was hit. It was a Saturday night, so there were a lot of them. But the police were helpful, and I had plenty of time to sift through the list. I came up with three pretty good suspects. One had been stopped in Enid, one in Stillwell, and one in Red Rock."

Keaton felt a surge of excitement. He repeated, "Red Rock."

The edges of Weber's mouth inched up in a faint imitation of a smile. "I thought that might interest you. The lady from your office said you were doing a piece on long-term comas, but I looked you up on Google. You've done all your reporting on sports in Cleveland and Menckenburg, so I figured you were more interested in Morton and Stender than in Edie."

"I'm sorry," Keaton said. "I'm afraid that's the case."

Weber waved a frail hand over the map. "No need to apologize. I want to help anybody who wants to find out what happened that night."

"So tell me what you found out in Red Rock."

"Well, those boys hit a telephone pole a little to the east of Red Rock. I understand Morton, the driver, was pretty drunk."

"But he wasn't charged with drunk driving."

"No. But the deputy at the station house remembered him. He thought somebody put the fix in to keep his breath from being tested."

Keaton nodded. "The Mammoths sent a lawyer. But I thought the fix just covered drunk-driving charges. Are you saying they made a hit-and-run felony go away too?"

"No. That lead never panned out. I thought I'd hit pay dirt in

Red Rock, but the timing was off. Morton and Stender were being booked in Noble County about the same time Edie was hit back here in Osage County."

"There's no chance somebody made a mistake? Recorded the wrong arrest time?"

Weber sighed and shook his head. "No chance. I talked to two local deputies and they both vouched for the record."

"Was one of them named Raptor?"

"I talked to Raptor. He's the officer that pulled them over. He wasn't very cooperative. But he seemed sure of the time. The deputy who was most helpful was the officer on duty at the station house when they were brought in and booked. He was absolutely certain of the time. His name's Hightower. I see he's worked his way up to sheriff since I talked to him."

"What happened to the other two leads you turned up?"

"One fellow hit a truck head-on and was killed instantly. Timing wasn't quite right for him either. The one from Enid had an alibi. He'd been at work when Edie was hit."

Keaton returned the picture of Weber's daughter. He wanted to leave the man with some words of hope but couldn't think of any. The best he could manage was "I'm on my way to Noble County. I'll look up Hightower and Raptor and let you know if I uncover anything new."

" 'Preciate it."

"I'm afraid that's not much help."

Weber tucked the photo and scrapbook under his arm and stood up. "Don't apologize. It's more help than I've gotten in twenty years."

Keaton's first stop on the road to Red Rock was the site of the accident that had been the focal point of the wedge on Vernon Weber's map. At the edge of a sweeping curve, a shiny new road sign read LAKESIDE LANE, and a large billboard announced the development of Lakeside Acres, with model homes available for viewing through Jenkins Realty.

Low-hanging branches and overgrown weeds had taken over the edge of the roadway, so that Keaton had to drive beyond the accident site to find a safe place to park. Walking back, he saw two places where skid marks and crushed weeds marked the paths of recent failures to hold the road. After twenty-five years, drivers still had trouble negotiating the blind curves.

To get a sense of timing, Keaton got back in his car and tried to find the spot farther down the road where Morton and Stender had clipped a telephone pole. It took him just under an hour to get from the site of Edie Weber's accident to the rural Red Rock fields where the two pitchers had run off the road, but all the poles along that stretch of highway stood straight and looked evenly weathered. Whatever damage had been done to the countryside had long since been healed by nature and road crews.

Another half hour of driving took Keaton to the Noble County seat of Perry, where the two had been jailed overnight. There was no question about it. If they had been picked up anywhere close to the time of Edie Weber's accident, there was no way they could have been responsible for it. But why else would Stender have kept a copy of Edie's obituary? And why else would hush money have found its way regularly to Radar Raptor?

There was only one way Keaton could make sense of it. Once Raptor had learned of Edie's accident through her father's visit, he might have linked her death to Stender and Morton, doctored their booking time to throw Weber off the scent, and then blackmailed the two baseball players. Maybe there'd been something suspicious about Stender's auto, something that didn't quite match their story about hitting a telephone pole, something that didn't make sense until Vernon Weber wandered into the Noble County sheriff's office five years later and spoke with Raptor.

While Noble County Sheriff Wes Hightower was only one or two pounds lighter than Central Casting's image of a rotund Okie sheriff, he appeared to be several IQ points brighter. When Keaton asked what he remembered about the night Morton and Stender had spent in his jail, he got right to the point. "First thing I remember is the time they came in, if that's what you're getting at," he said. "My shift was scheduled to end at midnight and they came in around ten till. I booked them and stuck around past quitting time."

"Why'd you do that?" Keaton asked.

"Hell, I'm a baseball fan. Those boys had taken Oklahoma State to the College World Series, and Stender was the Indians' number-one draft pick. We hadn't had anybody that famous in our jail before or since. At least, not till we nabbed Timothy McVeigh."

"So you're sure of the time."

"Sure as sunrise. You must have been talking to old man Weber. My heart goes out to that man, but there's no way those two boys could have hit his little girl. I was booking them just about the time that hit-and-run driver left her in the weeds."

"Did you see their car?"

"Just to glance at when I finally went home. Driver's door was stove in pretty bad where they wrapped it around that pole. Radar Raptor was the arresting officer. He got a better look at it."

"What time did you finally leave?"

"I stuck around until the boys were bedded down. Left about two, I guess."

"How'd they seem to you?"

"Were they drunk, you mean? They were both so high they would have needed a stepladder to tie their shoes. Either one of them could have probably pissed a hundred proof. But we never tested them."

"Why not?"

Hightower shrugged. "It was Raptor's call. Can't say I blame him. I'd probably have done the same thing. We'd taken them off the road so they weren't a danger to anyone. A DUI arrest that night might have ruined their lives."

"They seem to get along with one another?"

The question was the first one Hightower hadn't seemed to anticipate. "With each other? Hell, they were two scared college kids. More worried their lives might be screwed up than who to blame for getting them drunk."

"Or whose fault it was they hit the pole?"

Hightower shrugged again. "That road. That rainstorm. Blood-alcohol levels had to be twice the legal limit. They're lucky they didn't have a worse accident. Morton was driving when Raptor stopped them. He'd have been charged. But I didn't hear either one of them bad-mouthing the other."

"But they never were charged."

"Not with anything serious. Being left of the center line, as I recall. I came back early the next morning to check up on them. Like I said, they were local celebrities. By that time the Mammoths had a couple of men on the scene."

"You think money might have changed hands?"

Hightower stared out his window, then cleared his throat and said, "Off the record, you never could be sure with Raptor."

"The Mammoths GM at the time claims it cost them ten grand."

Hightower whistled softly. "That must have been a department record. I know I've never heard about a bigger boost. For the record, though, we don't operate that way anymore. Not on my watch."

"Whatever became of Raptor?"

"Took early retirement. Just after I took over the department and made it plain there'd be no more pay for play. He's got a nice place on Lake Kaw. Living pretty high on the hog, I hear. You planning to drop in on him?"

"That seems like my next move."

"Better let me give you directions. His place isn't so easy to find. It's off the beaten path near the Indian reservation in Osage County."

"Back the way I came," Keaton said.

Hightower spread a county map out on his desk and pointed to a blue area shaped like a straight razor. "He's on the north shore of Lake Kaw."

"Right across the lake from the site of Edie Weber's accident."

"Crash," Hightower said.

"Excuse me?"

"Crash. The federal government doesn't want us calling them accidents anymore. They're all crashes. The word 'accident' implies nobody's to blame." Hightower shrugged. "Course, in this case, we really don't know who's to blame."

"I can't imagine Vernon Weber cares whether you call it an accident or a crash. Either way, it cost him his daughter and wife and ruined his life."

"That's for sure. I'll call Raptor and let him know you're on your way to visit him. He's not the friendliest fellow, but he may warm up a little if he thinks you're there on official business. He still depends on our retirement checks."

Keaton stood. "That would be a big help."

"Give the bastard my regards."

Before leaving to visit Radar Raptor, Keaton left a message for Little Bill Ellison asking if his sources could determine when the payments to Thomas Fanal and the Ponca City bank had begun.

Radar Raptor's retirement home was a stone hunting lodge

on the north bank of Lake Kaw. Too big to be called a cabin, and too small for a hotel, it was down a private road that cut through a pine forest. The road ended at the lake, where a fifteen-foot pleasure boat was docked at the end of a wood pier.

Raptor came down the stone steps from a porch that was not quite as long as a runway. A short, skinny man with a wispy gray goatee that needed either cultivating or cutting, he greeted Keaton by saying, "Like I told the sheriff, there's nothing I know I didn't already tell you on the phone."

"That's okay," Keaton said. "I've looked over both crash sites and have a better idea of what's going on since the last time we talked."

"There's only one crash site, far as I know."

"There's the one around Red Rock where Morton and Stender hit a telephone pole, and one right across this lake where Edie Weber was killed."

"That's a whole different jurisdiction. And it didn't have nothing to do with them two ballplayers. I was booking them in Perry when she was hit."

"Can we go inside? I'd like to talk a little about that."

Raptor shrugged and led the way up the stone steps. His front door opened onto a massive room lined with racks of hunting rifles and the mounted heads of deer, moose, and other game.

Keaton looked up at three chandeliers made from interlocking deer antlers and stared at the profusion of mounted heads on the walls. "You've got more horns here than a convention of cuckolds. Did you shoot all these animals yourself?"

"Well, they didn't get here by running headlong into the other side of them walls."

"You must be a pretty good shot." Keaton walked around a pool table and sat on a stool in front of a shiny oak bar backed by a rack of hunting rifles neatly placed in alternate slots of a showcase and a display of dueling pistols framed against red velvet. "Sheriff Hightower confirmed what you said about the time you booked Morton and Stender at the station house. It was a little before midnight."

"He should know. He was on duty at the time." Raptor shook his head. "I can't see why you're so all-fired sure we made a mistake in the booking time. If any mistakes were made, they could just as easy have come at the other end of the line."

"With the accident report, you mean. Seems like people would be more careful about getting the time of a fatal accident right than making sure of the time a couple of college kids were booked for charges that were never filed."

Raptor stroked his wispy beard. "You would think so, wouldn't you?"

"Are you saying a mistake was made at the other end? That the Weber accident happened earlier than it was recorded?"

"I'm saying there's no reason to believe a mistake was made on either end. What makes you think them ballplayers had anything at all to do with Edie Weber's death?"

"Just this. For a number of years, Lanny Morton has been sending sizable amounts of money to a bank account in Ponca City." Keaton watched Raptor to see how he'd take this revelation. "Seems strange that he'd be doing that just to cover up an accident involving a telephone pole he busted twenty-five years ago."

If Raptor was surprised that someone had traced the flow of money from Stender to Morton to Ponca City, he didn't show it. He sighed, shook his head, and moved behind the bar. "Who knows why injuns do anything. Maybe he was planning to retire around here."

"I doubt it. But if that was his plan, it didn't work out."

Raptor squinted at Keaton. "What did you say your name was again? Hightower told me, but my memory's not what it used to be."

Keaton handed him a business card. "Lloyd Keaton."

Raptor took a pair of glasses from his shirt pocket. "Eyesight's even worse than my memory. Only need these for seeing, though." He scanned the card, then pocketed it. "Menckenburg, huh? That near Cleveland?"

"Couple of hours' drive."

Raptor opened the pistol showcase behind the bar and took out a revolver. "So somebody's been tracing funds from Cleveland to Ponca City."

Keaton stared at the revolver. "That's right."

Raptor spun the revolver's cylinder, then took a box of cartridges and made a point of inserting one in the cylinder. "Following somebody else's money around don't sound like much fun. Could even be unhealthy."

"Well, the newspaper business hasn't been healthy in years."

Raptor inserted another bullet and spun the cylinder again. "What's the newspaper business got to do with this?"

"Several of my coworkers at the paper have been tracking those funds. Just in case you thought I've been working alone." Keaton wished he'd told someone besides Little Bill Ellison about the trail of hush money. And hoped that wish didn't show in his face.

Raptor put another bullet in the cylinder and spun it again. "But you're here alone. If you really had any evidence of payoffs, you'd have come with cops. At least that's what I think. What do you think?"

"I make it a point never to argue with a man holding a gun."

Raptor lifted the revolver until the barrel pointed at Keaton and spun the cylinder again. "This? This is just a nervous habit."

"Well, it's making me nervous, all right. I didn't bring any cops. But Sheriff Hightower knows I was coming here. And my newspaper colleagues know about the payoffs."

"Colleagues. That's a strange word. Do these colleagues have names?"

"Meri Oliver and Eddie Atkins." Keaton switched surnames to add a level of protection, quickly realized it wasn't much protection, but still hoped he sounded convincing. "By now, though, they've probably leaked what they know to most of the office."

"You keep on hinting you know more than you really do." Raptor lowered the revolver. "Believe me, you don't want to do that. This doesn't concern you." He spun the cylinder again. "No, I have to think you don't have the full picture. You may have traced money to Ponca City, but you don't know where it went after that. And it's not so easy to get information out of bankers here in Oklahoma."

Raptor laid the revolver on the bar in front of him. "So right now you've got no cops and no warrants. And, for all you know, any money that came to Ponca City has already been spent. Trail could be colder than the shady side of a witch's tit."

Keaton thought a fair share of the money had gone into his immediate surroundings, but he didn't say so. He kept his eyes on the revolver and tried not to look around the room.

"Hell," Raptor said. "For all you know, Morton could have been sending money to his folks. His ma still lives here in Osage County."

"The kind of money he was sending would have bought a palace here. Does his mother have a palace?"

"Money to his ma makes more sense than money to a blackmailer. You haven't got a clue as to who he'd be paying off or why."

"Edie Weber's death seems like reason enough."

"To make that stick, you're going to have to figure out how them boys could have been in two places at once. I told you, I was booking them in Perry about the same time the Weber girl was run over."

"Could be somebody made a mistake reporting the time."

"Well, it sure as shit wasn't me. You think there was a mistake, you'd best be talking to the folks in Osage County."

"That sounds like an exit line." Keaton wanted to get out before Raptor picked up the gun again. He edged off his barstool and backed away. "Maybe I'll do just that."

Keaton drove as fast as he could back out the gravel road from Raptor's lodge, turned onto the main highway, and checked his rearview mirror until he was sure Raptor wasn't following him. He kept his hands from trembling by clutching the steering wheel and pulled into a parking lot behind a Burger King that hid his car from the road.

His pulse had almost returned to normal when his cell phone rang. Little Bill Ellison was calling with the results of the search Keaton had requested. Ellison's contacts had been unable to access any deposit or withdrawal records more than ten years old. But he was able to find out when Thomas Fanal had opened his account.

Keaton wrote down the date and did the math in his head. The account had been opened about twenty years ago, roughly five years after Stender and Morton had driven to spring training and Edie Weber had been struck by a hit-and-run driver. Just about the time Vernon Weber would have visited Radar Raptor's station house in Perry trying to track down his daughter's killer.

CHAPTER FOURTEEN:
ANOTHER SET OF EYES

Sheriff Todd Black Elk of Osage County was twice as wide as a cigar-store Indian and almost as expressive. He scratched his back on the edge of a metal file cabinet, stared hard at Keaton, and then answered his question in slow, measured tones. "For the record, I knew Lanny Morton. Went to high school with him. A year behind him, actually. Played first base when he was a senior. We only lost one regular-season game and got to the state finals. Lanny went on to OSU and signed with Cleveland. Me, though, I couldn't hit the outside curve."

The sheriff mimicked swinging at a low outside pitch and missing, causing his solitary black pigtail to bounce over his shoulder. He flicked it back behind him and said, "Football was my game. Wasn't fast enough to make it big, though. Played a little JC, then hooked up with the sheriff's department."

"And you said you remember the Weber accident," Keaton said.

"Hell, yes, I remember it. First big unsolved case we had after I joined up. And everybody in the county knew Edie Weber. Knew who she was, I mean. Pecan Queen. Miss this. Miss that. Hard to explain now, but back then, fresh off the reservation, you just knew she was way out of your league. Made her seem even more special."

Black Elk paused and shook his head. "Not so much like that anymore. Not when you're sheriff, anyhow. But back then, there wasn't many of us in law enforcement. Edie was the belle of the county, and I was convinced I could crack the case. Combed the accident scene, took photos, looked for skid marks."

"Were there any?"

Black Elk shook his head. "None. Like the driver never even seen her. Knocked her forty feet into the weeds. Still got the evidence box, if you'd like to see it." Black Elk leaned over his desk and spoke into the intercom. "Martha, bring me the box on the Weber accident. It's in deep storage with the other cold cases."

"That usual?" Keaton asked. "To keep evidence that long?"

Black Elk shrugged. "Most of our fatals clean up pretty easy. Passengers in a car. Friday-night drunks. Motorcyclists who lose it on the curves. Every year or so, though, we get a hit-and-run case we can't close. Probably thirty to forty evidence boxes back where I sent Martha. Drivers who got away from us."

The deputy returned with a brown file box and set it on Black Elk's desk.

The sheriff ran his uniform sleeve over the layer of dust on the box lid, lifted it, and took out a large manila envelope. He opened the envelope and fanned out about a dozen eight-by-ten color photographs on his desktop. "Took most of these myself."

Black Elk pointed to a close-up of the road surface. "That's about where he hit her. No skid marks you can see." He held up a longer view of the empty roadway. "No skid marks before or after the impact. Just kept right on going. Left her in those high weeds you see there. Couldn't even spot her from the roadway."

Keaton felt out of his element. He had no idea what to look for in the photos. He pointed to two pictures of a blue Corvette parked alongside the highway. "Who belongs to the Corvette?"

"That's Ernie Jenkins's 'Vette. He'd run out of gas. I took those pictures before it was towed away."

"Why'd it have to be towed? Why not just fill the tank?"

"Turns out a stone or something had left a hole in the underside of the gas tank. He didn't know it at the time, though. They were walking to find a gas station when she was hit."

Keaton returned the photos to the envelope and put the envelope back in the evidence box, laying it on a plastic container that held the smudged print dress he'd seen in the photos of the victim. "You've kept the girl's clothes?"

"Her mother couldn't stand to look at them. And her dad wanted us to have anything that would help us find the driver."

"So you investigated on your own."

"Oh, yeah. First thing I did was to look for other accidents that night. I made the connection with Blaze Stender and Lanny right away. But I checked with Wes Hightower over in Noble County and found out the timing was off. Edie was hit just about the same time Wes was booking the two boys."

"You talked to Hightower, not Radar Raptor?"

"Well, I was pretty green, but I knew if you wanted the straight scoop from Noble County, you didn't go to Raptor. And Wes and I had done some training together."

"But later on you sent Vernon Weber to Raptor."

"I didn't exactly send him to Raptor. I felt sorry for the man. He'd lost his child and his wife and wanted to do something about it. I helped him mark up his map and put him in touch with all the law-enforcement agencies that might have come in contact with the hit-and-run driver. He plowed a lot of the same ground I'd already been over."

"But that was five, maybe six years later."

"He was desperate to do something. And I figured it couldn't hurt. One more pair of eyes. That's why I don't mind spending time with you. You might see something I missed."

"Everything I see points to Stender and Morton. Any chance the timing of the accident might be off?"

Black Elk shrugged. "Don't see how. I logged in Ernie

Jenkins's call myself. Got him to tell me exactly what he did after Edie was hit. It was a pretty desolate road back then. Took him half an hour to get to a phone. I tried it myself. Followed his path. Took me half an hour too."

"Whatever became of Jenkins?"

"He's still around. Solid citizen. Big family. Rich real-estate developer."

"What was he like back then?"

"Rich young prick floating on his daddy's money. But that accident scared the piss out of him. Made him grow up a little. Just a little, not a lot. Now he's a rich older prick trying to grow what's left of his daddy's money."

"Think he might be willing to talk to me? About the accident?"

"I'm guessing he wants to keep that part of his life dead and buried. But he'd likely do it if I asked him to. He owes me a few favors."

"Favors? For something you did that night?"

Black Elk smiled. "Only thing I did that night was get some dry clothes and try to calm him down. There were other nights, though, when he came out cleaner than he might have after run-ins with our officers." Black Elk nodded toward the corridor leading to his jail cells. "He slept off more than one drunk right here without being charged for DUI."

"Funny, you don't strike me as a compassionate lawman."

Black Elk shrugged. "Local cops did it for me back when I was young and had a wild hair up my butt."

"So you're just giving a little back."

"Our jails are already chock-full. Be a sorry world if everybody got what was coming to them."

Before Keaton drove off for the meeting Black Elk had set up with Ernie Jenkins, he called Meri Atkins at the *Herald*.

"Nice to hear from you," she said. "You ready to retire out there on the open range?"

"When I do retire, the only open range I want to see will be in my kitchen. Right now, though, I need a favor."

"Name it."

"That seems too easy. Does that mean you'll do it?"

"Not necessarily. I'm just saying 'Name it.' "

"All right. I want you to find me somebody who investigates accidents. Somebody good who can interpret evidence that's over twenty years old. I need him fast. And since I'll probably be paying for it myself, I need him to be cheap."

"Hmm. Good, fast and cheap. That's a tall order. Might be able to find two out of three. But good and fast don't come cheap. And fast and cheap might not be very good."

"See what you can do. How's the column going?"

"I generated a firestorm with my first effort. Set a record for reader responses. You'll probably still be digging out from under them when you get back."

"What was the topic?"

"The sport that regularly reports the most serious injuries in the US. Know which one that is?"

"I'd guess football."

"You'd be wrong. It's cheerleading."

"Cheerleading's not a sport."

"That's part of the problem. If it were a recognized sport, schools and the feds might pay more attention to safety."

"So why isn't it a sport?"

"Lots of folks are dead set against making it a sport. Feminists think it fosters the wrong image of womanhood. Title Nine backers worry cheerleading would take slots for women away from more traditional sports. And there are businesses raking in around three hundred mil a year controlling competitions and uniform sales."

"So these folks are flooding you with letters and e-mails because you'd like to make cheerleading a sport?"

"You bet. But I'm getting just as many responses from people who agree with me."

"Record numbers, you say?"

"Oh, yeah. Our boss is really impressed. I'll send you a copy. So you can deal with the issue when you get your column back. If you get it back, that is. Remember what happened to Wally Pipp."

"One day off and he lost his job to Lou Gehrig."

"And you're going to be gone a whole week."

Ernie Jenkins was showing model homes in his real-estate development on Lake Kaw, just down a newly paved access road from the site where he and Edie Weber had been walking when she was struck by a hit-and-run driver.

Keaton parked his rental car beside a BMW convertible and found Jenkins in the living room of the newest model home, looking out through a picture window. Enough underbrush and trees had been cleared to give him a clear view of the deep blue lake water and vacation homes under construction on adjacent lots.

The realtor had jet-black hair and wore a yellow sport shirt whose open collar lapped over the lapels of a white linen sport coat. He turned his head when Keaton entered, but made no effort to move away from his view. "I want you to know I'm only talking to you as a favor to Sheriff Black Elk. I don't see any point in dredging up Edie's death after all these years. It's bad enough we ended up building out here without having to talk about it as well."

"I'm hoping if we get a few details straight, we might still find the driver," Keaton said. "Some things just don't make sense right now."

Jenkins slid open a glass door and stepped out onto a deck, where he lit a cigarette from a silver case. "None of it ever made sense. Edie was a beautiful young woman with her whole life ahead of her."

Keaton followed Jenkins out into the chilly air. "It would help if I heard your side of the story."

"Nothing to tell. It's all part of the official record. We ran out of gas a mile or so back down the main road. Started walking west. I thought we'd catch a ride for sure, but that didn't happen. Back then nothing much was developed out here. Wasn't near as much traffic on the road."

"So you were low on gas?"

Jenkins took an angry drag of cigarette smoke. "No, I wasn't low on gas. My tank was punctured somehow. Must have caught a flying rock."

"What made you decide to walk west?"

"What?"

"I was wondering why you walked west. The nearest gas station in that direction is a Shell station that's still two miles from here, or about three miles from where you stopped. But there's a Seventy-Six station just two miles back in the other direction."

"What the hell, I don't even know if that Seventy-Six station was around back then. I knew about the Shell station. Knew it was open twenty-four hours. And I thought there was a good chance of getting a ride in that direction."

"But you didn't see any cars."

"Not until that one hit Edie. We'd just rounded that curve before that access road you just come down, and it snuck up behind us. I never saw it coming."

"What color was the car?"

"Hell, I'm not even sure it was a car. Could have been a pickup. It knocked Edie into the weeds and I ran right to her. I guess I wasn't thinking very straight."

"Hard to know what to do when something happens that fast. What did you do next?"

"Tried to find a phone. First house I tried, nobody was home. So I went on down the road. Finally found a house with lights on. They called nine-one-one."

"How long did all that take?"

"About half an hour, I'd guess." Jenkins shook his head. "If we'd had cell phones back then, the way we do now, or if I'd busted into that first home I come to, Edie might be alive today."

Jenkins stubbed out his cigarette on the back of the deck railing and dropped it over the side. "Took me quite a spell to get over Edie. I sure don't appreciate having you bring it all back up. What do you hope to get by all this grave robbing?"

"It'll give Vernon Weber some peace if he knows what happened. And you ought to want to see the driver brought to justice."

"Hell, that driver's long gone. And nothing you do will bring Edie back." Jenkins stalked back into the house. "I've said as much as I care to on this here subject."

Keaton thanked Jenkins for his time and returned to his rental car. Before switching on the ignition, he checked his cell phone and saw that Meri had called back.

"You're in luck," Meri told him. "I've found an accident investigator who seems to be good, fast, and cheap."

"How'd you do that?"

"For cripe's sake. I'm a reporter. You must remember what that was like. I asked around. This guy's supposed to be the best within five hundred miles."

"When could he get here?"

"Soon as you need him. You said you wanted fast. And he lives in West Virginia, so his prices aren't inflated."

"Who is this paragon?"

"Calls himself a failure analyst. Name's Owen Allison."

CHAPTER FIFTEEN:
I KNOW WHAT HAPPENED

Keaton stood just beyond the security exit at the foot of Concourse A of the Tulsa airport the next morning wondering how he would recognize Owen Allison. Meri had told him, "Don't worry, he'll recognize you," but he couldn't help feeling apprehensive. His frame of reference for Southern investigators ranged from a folksy Andy Griffith to a redneck Rod Steiger and he was wondering where Allison might fit into that spectrum when a tall man with flecks of gray in his close-cropped brown beard tapped him on the shoulder.

"You must be Lloyd Keaton," the man said with an easy smile. "I'm Owen Allison."

"How'd you recognize me?" Keaton asked.

"Miss Atkins said you'd be wearing a fedora that's fifty years out of date."

Keaton shrugged. "It's my father's hat. He was a sportswriter too."

"Your father wasn't John Keaton, was he?"

"Yes. You know him?"

"I'd read your dad's columns when I was a kid visiting my grandparents during the summer. They lived in Ohio, and I grew up rooting for the Reds and Indians. He was pretty good."

"Yes, he was," Keaton said, trying not to emphasize the past tense.

Allison waved off Keaton's offer to help with his battered roll-aboard suitcase and followed him up an escalator into a parking garage.

"You're not quite what I expected," Keaton said. The man towing the suitcase didn't bear the slightest resemblance to either Griffith or Steiger. More like a bearded Harrison Ford.

Allison smiled. "If you're from West Virginia, it takes a little time to convince people that *The Beverly Hillbillies* wasn't a documentary."

Keaton laughed. "I didn't exactly expect bare feet and a straw hat. But you don't even have a recognizable accent."

"I lost my twang naturally. Left home after high school and got a bachelor's degree in engineering from Marquette and a master's in operations research from Stanford. Then I worked for quite a while in the San Francisco Bay area."

Keaton threaded his way through rows of parked cars. "What took you back to West Virginia?"

"A number of things. Mostly my mom, though. She has Alzheimer's and doesn't want to leave the family home, so she takes some looking after."

"That's tough. I just put my dad in a home before I left Menckenburg. Who's staying with your mom?"

"I've got a foster son at Arizona State University. He was at home full time this summer. Then there's a combination nurse/ housekeeper who comes three times a week, and neighbors drop in fairly regularly."

"Sounds like you've got it under control."

"You never really get it under control. But we've got the coping pretty well organized."

Keaton stopped behind his rented Taurus and popped the trunk. "Is your mom fairly lucid?"

Allison wrestled his roll-aboard into the trunk and slid into the passenger seat, pulling onto his lap the computer case that had been slung over his shoulder. "She's in and out. She says she doesn't mind losing brain cells one at a time. The thing that really scares her, though, is that the rest of them seem to be gathering for a mass escape."

Keaton laughed. "That's pretty funny. Hard to laugh about Alzheimer's, though."

"Hard not to laugh sometimes."

On the way out of the airport, Keaton asked, "What the heck is a 'failure analyst,' anyway?"

Allison smiled. "I try to figure out why dams break, bridges drop, cars wreck, mines fail, things like that. After the fact, mostly. It's a mix of accident reconstruction, engineering, anthropology, pathology, systems analysis, and plain old problem solving."

"Ever try to solve a problem that was twenty years old?"

"Helped to solve a fifty-year-old murder once. Man's body was unearthed during interstate reconstruction. Turns out he'd been planted there after uncovering a bid-rigging scheme when the interstate was first built. I've had a few cases that went back one or two years as well. Why don't you tell me more about your problem?"

Keaton filled Allison in on his meetings with the local sheriffs and outlined the problem as he saw it, emphasizing the discrepancies in timing that made it seem that Blaze Stender and Lanny Morton couldn't have hit Edie Weber. When he finished, he asked Allison, "Where'd you like to start?"

"With Sheriff Black Elk and his crash records. You said they seemed to be fairly complete."

Sheriff Todd Black Elk personally brought the evidence box into the interrogation room next to his office and hovered over Owen Allison as he sifted through the contents of the box. Allison set aside the cellophane wrapped clothing on top of the crash reports and spread out the eight-by-ten photos that Black Elk had taken of the accident scene and Ernie Jenkins's disabled Corvette.

"No skid marks at all," Allison commented.

"Son of a bitch didn't even try to stop," Black Elk said.

"Was it raining when she was hit?"

"Don't know," Black Elk said. "I remember it was raining when we got the call."

Allison pointed to the photos of Jenkins's Corvette. "Looks like it wasn't raining when they abandoned the Corvette. It's dry underneath except for what looks to be a pool of gasoline in the dirt under the gas tank."

"I was there when they towed it away the next morning," Black Elk said. "Even after the storm had blown over, you could still smell the gasoline."

Allison turned his attention to the photos of the accident scene. "When did you take these?"

"Next day," Black Elk said. "We were way too busy with paramedics that night to worry about photos."

"So you were there that night," Allison said.

"First on the scene," Black Elk said. "Just a little ahead of the ambulance."

Allison pointed to a photo of the roadside. "So her body must have been in the weeds there, beyond the curve."

"That's right. You couldn't see it from the road."

Allison nodded, gathered up the photos, and returned them to the evidence box. Then he opened the binder holding the coroner's report and began jotting notes on a quad-ruled tablet. After a short time, he looked up at Black Elk. "Was it clear she was hit by a car? These head injuries are consistent with trauma from a blunt instrument."

"Car knocked her thirty or forty feet," Black Elk said. "She hit her head on a rock when she landed."

"How did her body look?"

Black Elk extended his arms straight over his head. "Like she was sliding headfirst for home."

Keaton remembered Vern Weber sitting motionless on his porch. "Sliding for a home she'd never reach."

"Was the ground wet underneath her?" Allison asked.

Black Elk's brow furrowed. "It was wet all around her. Underneath? I just don't know."

Allison riffled the pages of the coroner's report. "Dr. Eugene Bak signed the autopsy papers. Is he still around?"

Black Elk shook his head. "Doc Bak died eight, maybe nine years ago."

Allison said, "Too bad," and went back to his note taking. The only sound in the room was the whir of the rotating fan that ruffled the pages of his notebook.

When he finished with the coroner's report, Allison turned his attention to the cellophane-wrapped clothing that had been on top of the photos and written reports. He set aside the scuffed flat-heeled shoes and focused on the yellow print dress, still flecked with burrs from the roadside weeds. "You kept all her clothing?"

"Parents didn't want it back," Black Elk said. "I thought it might be useful someday."

"It is." Allison took a small camera from his briefcase, smoothed out the print dress, and snapped off two photographs.

"See something?" Keaton asked.

Allison pointed to a thin red crescent just below the waistline of the dress. "Could be the paint around a headlight."

"That's what I thought, too," Black Elk said. "But we didn't have any cars to match with it."

"And Blaze Stender's red Mustang was long gone by the time anyone made the connection," Keaton said.

"Even when we made the connection, we couldn't make the timing fit," Black Elk said.

"It's past two o'clock," Keaton said. "How about a lunch break? You can fill me in on what you're thinking."

"Want me to send out for some sandwiches?" Black Elk asked.

Allison returned his camera to his briefcase. "I could stand to stretch my legs." He stood up. "Tell me, Sheriff. Where would this man Jenkins have gone to get his Corvette repaired?"

"He had it towed to Tom Ramies's garage. Right here in town. Best mechanic in the county. Pretty good with body work, too."

"Is he still around?"

"Tom Junior runs it now. Would have been Tom Senior back in the day."

"Think we could stop by there on the way to lunch?"

Black Elk shrugged. "Don't see why not. Don't know what Ramies could tell you, though."

"Maybe nothing. I'd just like to know what became of Mr. Jenkins's Corvette."

The three men left the sheriff's office, walked two blocks in the cool autumn afternoon, and turned down a narrow alley that led to a garage where a potbellied man in a grimy undershirt sweated under a racked pickup.

Sheriff Black Elk introduced the man as Tom Ramies Junior, and explained that his two guests were interested in the Corvette that Ernie Jenkins had been driving on the night Edie Weber was killed.

Ramies took a rag from the hip pocket of his jeans, wiped the grease off his hands, and said, "I was two years behind Edie in high school. Sure do remember her, though. Remember the Corvette, too. We had it in here plenty. Old Ernie ran the wheels off damn near every car his daddy bought him."

"What about the time you had it after the Weber accident?" Allison asked.

Ramies frowned. "That was a little before my time. I helped out some back then, but I sure don't recall . . . You know what, though? I bet Dad would remember."

"Could I talk to him?" Allison asked.

Ramies led the men into the tiny office built into the back corner of the garage. They bunched around the lone desk as Ramies put on the speakerphone and dialed his father's number. "Dad," he said, "I've got Sheriff Black Elk here with a couple of fellows who want to talk about the time Edie Weber was killed. I told them you'd remember it just fine."

"Oh my, yes. 'Bout the worst accident I can remember."

Owen Allison leaned over the speakerphone and introduced himself. "What can you tell us about the Corvette Ernie Jenkins was driving?"

"Not much to tell. Barely anything wrong with the car. Had a little gouge half the size of your pinkie right smack in the middle of the gas tank. Damnedest thing I ever saw."

"Big enough for all the gas to leak out, though," Allison said.

"Oh, yeah. But small enough so's I could have patched it easy with a weld. But Ernie wouldn't have none of that. Insisted on getting a brand new tank."

"So that's what happened?" Allison asked.

"Customer knows best. Cost about a grand more than a weld would have. But Ernie was always free with his daddy's money."

"Anything else you can tell us about the car?" Allison asked.

"No. We just had to wait for the new tank to be delivered. Pretty easy job. Had lots tougher ones with Ernie's cars. He's been a real good customer over the years."

They thanked Ramies Senior and Ramies Junior hung up the phone. Turning away from the desk, he said, "That was just like Ernie Jenkins. Surprised he didn't get a new ashtray every time one filled up."

"Rich or poor, it's nice to have money," Allison said.

"Well, hell, Ernie inherited it all anyhow, don't you know," Ramies said. "Now he's fixin' to spoil Ernie Junior the same way. He was in the other day asking what I thought about the new model 'Vette for when Junior turns sixteen."

"What'd you tell him?" Keaton asked.

"Told him I couldn't think of a better birthday present." Ramies grinned. "More business for us, don't you know. Like father, like son."

Keaton, Allison, and the sheriff ate lunch at a Mexican restaurant a block away from Ramies's garage. Over tacos and beer, Keaton asked Allison what he thought about the evidence he'd been studying.

Allison stared into his beer mug. "This whole business of reconstruction is a little like sausage making. It's best not to let the client see the work in process. Much better to wait for the finished product."

"But you think you know what happened that night."

Allison dipped a tortilla chip into a mound of guacamole. "I've got a pretty good idea. But there are still a couple of loose ends dangling."

They arrived back at the sheriff's office to find Ernie Jenkins fuming in the waiting area near the front desk. He didn't wait to tear into Todd Black Elk. "What the hell are you up to? Old man Ramies tells me you've been asking questions about my old Corvette. I told you yesterday there's no point in picking at those old scabs. Nothing you do will bring Edie back. All you're doing is opening old sores. You keep at it, and I'll by God have your badge."

The sheriff raised one hand as if he were trying to stop traffic. "Calm down, Ernie. We're trying to solve a vehicular homicide. There's no statute of limitations I know of. And you've got no call to be upset. You're about the only man in the county with a perfect alibi. You were walking with Edie when she was hit."

"And I don't like having those memories dredged up. It's not easy thinking I might have gotten help quicker. And now you'll have people thinking there was something wrong with my Corvette."

Owen Allison spoke up. "There was something wrong with it. There was a hole in the bottom of the gas tank."

Jenkins wheeled around. "I don't know who you are, mister, but that sure as shit wasn't my fault."

The sheriff stepped between the men and introduced Allison, who said, "So long as you're here, you can help us with a question. Was it raining when the car hit Edie?"

"What the hell has that got to do with anything?"

"It would help us make sense out of some of the crash-scene photos," Allison said.

"I sure don't see how."

"You don't have to see how it helps, Ernie," the sheriff said. "Just answer the man's question. Was it raining or not?"

"It was raining, okay? Now will you let it alone?"

"The county doesn't pay me to let it alone, Ernie," the sheriff said. "And these two gentlemen are trying to help out."

"You keep on the way you're going, and the county won't be paying you much longer. I'll by God see to that."

"That's your privilege as a voting resident, Ernie," the sheriff said. "But right now you're interfering with county business. Unless you've got something constructive to add, I'd appreciate it if you'd get out of this building."

"Why you shit-kicking half-breed." Jenkins raised a fist, and Black Elk caught it just under the wrist and forced it down.

"You don't want to be doing that, Ernie," the sheriff said. "It's not going to sit well with your clients if you get thrown in jail for assaulting a peace officer. You'd best leave, and you probably want to do that under your own power."

Jenkins jerked his hand back and stood sputtering as Black Elk turned and asked Allison, "What else's on your agenda?"

"I think I'd like to see the accident site."

"It's changed a lot, you know," Black Elk said. "Ernie here is putting in a big development out there."

"I understand that," Allison said. "I'd like to see it anyhow. Maybe you could get me an old map showing what it was like at the time of the accident."

"That won't be too hard," Black Elk said. "All the big changes are pretty recent."

Black Elk disappeared into his office, ignoring Jenkins, who stormed out of the building, trying unsuccessfully to slam the heavy oak door.

"Man could use a character transplant," Allison said after the door closed.

Black Elk returned with a road map. "Don't worry about Ernie. His bark's worse than his bite."

"I don't think I'd like to be within range of either," Keaton said.

"He's not a bad guy," Black Elk said. "All his money sort of went to his head."

"Not much there to impede its progress." Allison took the map from Black Elk. "This looks just like what I need."

"I've been out there," Keaton said. "I can drive you."

"Well, you know where to find me if you have any more questions," Black Elk said.

Keaton and Allison thanked Sheriff Black Elk and drove to the curve in the road where Edie Weber had been struck down. Allison paced off the distance from the newly paved side road to the spot where he calculated Edie's body had landed in the weeds. Then he knelt, poked at the ground, wrote in his pocket notebook, and finally rose and pointed at the sign advertising Lakeview Estates. "Let's drive down that new road and take a look."

Keaton made a U-turn and headed down the road to Ernie Jenkins's development while Allison unfolded Black Elk's map. "This would have been a gravel road when the accident happened," he said.

Keaton pulled into the parking area reserved for Ernie Jenkins's model home. There were no other cars in sight.

Allison walked away from the model home down to the rim of the lake. Then he turned and headed for the pine forest on the other side of the access road. At the edge of the forest, he knelt and picked a burr off his pants cuff. "All right, I think I know what happened."

Before he could straighten up, a shot rang out, and the pine branch over his head burst into pieces.

CHAPTER SIXTEEN: UNUSUAL SUSPECTS

A second shot thudded into the pine tree next to Keaton. He scrambled behind the wounded pine as Allison dove to the ground.

Two more shots whistled through the leaves.

Keaton peeked out from behind his tree. "Flashes came from that stand of pines beyond the model homes. At the edge of the lake."

Allison crawled for the cover of the pines. "Let's head inland. The more trees we can get between us and those bullets, the better I'll feel."

The two men turned their backs on the lake and ran, hunched over, about a hundred yards deeper into the woods.

They pulled up at the edge of a small clearing. "Shooting's stopped," Allison panted.

Keaton yanked out his cell phone. "I'm calling Sheriff Black Elk before the shooter decides to come through the woods hunting us."

"Don't do that," Allison said. "He could be the one shooting at us."

"You think he's the blackmailer?"

Allison shrugged. "How the hell would I know?"

"You said you knew what happened."

"I know about the accident, not about the blackmail."

"Then what makes you think it could be Black Elk shooting at us?"

"I know you've pegged Raptor as the blackmailer. But Black Elk had access to the same information, and he knew we were headed here."

"So did Ernie Jenkins. Maybe he really did see the hit-and-run car. I wouldn't put blackmail past him."

"He was just a college kid at the time."

"Maybe he was behind in his tuition payments." Keaton stared at his cell phone. "We need to get help. I'll call Sheriff Hightower from Noble County."

"Same problem as Black Elk," Allison said. "He had enough information to try blackmail if he put it all together."

"We can't just sit here."

"Call both your sheriffs," Allison said. "Even if one of them is the blackmailer, it's not likely they're in cahoots. Tell them to tear down the access road with their sirens blaring. If we wait until they're both here before we show ourselves, we should be pretty safe."

"Good idea. I'll call Hightower first. He's got more distance to travel." Keaton called the Noble County sheriff's office and explained their situation. As he shoved his phone back into his pocket, he said, "Hightower's on his way."

"Let's start circling toward the access road," Allison said. "Find a spot where we can't be seen but can hear the patrol cars coming."

They left the clearing and circled toward the access road. After five minutes, Keaton stopped and called Sheriff Black Elk. When the call ended, Keaton pocketed his phone, frowned, and shook his head.

"Something the matter?" Allison asked.

Keaton shrugged. "He didn't sound surprised to hear we were under fire. Said he'd get here right away. Said he was close by."

"Not too close by, I hope."

The two men picked their way through the forest, trying to make as little noise as possible. They stopped every few minutes, straining to hear any sounds of pursuit.

A siren screamed as they neared the access road. "That must be Black Elk." Keaton checked his watch. "Ten minutes since I called him. He really didn't have far to come."

"We'll stay out of sight until he has company," Allison said after the siren had stopped.

Keaton's cell phone shattered the silence. He ducked behind a log as if the phone's ring were the signal for an artillery barrage and mouthed the word "Black Elk" to Allison.

Black Elk's voice was loud enough for Allison to hear over Keaton's cell. "Where the hell are you guys?"

"We're still in the woods," Keaton whispered into his phone. "We headed inland to get away from the bullets and just kept running. If you stay where you are, we'll meet you at the model home parking lot."

Keaton ended the call, and the two men made their way to the edge of the access road. A few minutes later, a second siren blared as Sheriff Hightower barreled down the road toward the lake. Keaton and Allison followed, keeping within the shelter of the trees that paralleled the road.

When Keaton and Allison reached the lake, they found the two patrol cars nose-to-nose in the model home parking lot, their motors idling and their bar lights flashing. The two sheriffs were leaning against their vehicles.

Sheriff Black Elk stepped away from his vehicle as soon as the two men appeared. "Where you guys been?"

"Somebody was shooting at us," Keaton said. "We weren't anxious to come back until you guys were in sight."

"Show me where you were ambushed," Black Elk said.

Allison led the way. Instead of going straight to the edge of the water and following the beach to the point where they heard the first shot, he took a circuitous route through the woods.

"Went all the way around your rump to get to your elbow," Black Elk said when Allison stopped at a tree near the water's edge. "Why not take a direct route?"

"In case the sniper's still out there, I didn't want to be a target any longer than necessary," Allison said. He knelt beside the tree. "I was here when the first shot was fired. It clipped that branch overhead."

"Then what?" Black Elk asked.

Allison pointed to a long gouge in the matting of pine needles at his feet. "I dove into the woods."

"There were three more shots." Keaton pointed to the tree he'd used for shelter. "It sounded like one of them hit that tree."

Black Elk examined the tree Keaton identified. He stood on his toes and probed a point about seven feet above the ground. "Looks like a bullet hole right here."

Black Elk dug out the bullet with a pocketknife, being careful to bring out plenty of tree so the bullet wouldn't be scarred. He examined it and showed it to Wes Hightower. "Looks like thirty caliber."

"Sniper rifle," Hightower said.

Black Elk backed up against the tree and scanned the lakefront. "Probably came from that stand of trees beyond the housing development."

"That's what we thought," Allison said. "We took off in the opposite direction and called you guys."

"It's my jurisdiction," Black Elk said. "Why'd you call both of us?"

"When the shooting started, I'd just figured out what happened to Edie Weber," Allison said. "I thought you'd both want to know."

"No shit?" Black Elk scanned the opposite shore. "Think that had anything to do with your drawing fire?"

"Could be," Allison said.

"Maybe you'd best tell us, then," Black Elk said.

"Easier to do back in your office with the evidence box," Allison said.

Black Elk swept his eyes over the housing development and the neighboring woods. "What do you think, Wes? Should we wait till tomorrow to beat those bushes across the way?"

"Shooter must be long gone by now," Hightower said. "But it's your jurisdiction, so it's your decision."

"I'll stake out a couple of men, see nothing's disturbed." Black Elk pocketed his knife. "Let's reconvene at my office."

Back in Sheriff Black Elk's interrogation room, Owen Allison laid Edie Weber's cellophane-wrapped dress on the desk alongside the photos Black Elk had taken of the accident scene and Ernie Jenkins's Corvette. "You need to understand," Allison said, "that I'm ninety-five percent sure of what I'm going to tell you, and I can show you circumstantial evidence to support my story, but I doubt if that evidence would stand up in court after all these years."

"Fair enough," Black Elk said.

"Let's start with the accident itself," Allison sad. "I don't believe Ernie Jenkins has been telling anything like the whole story. Take this dress. It's covered with burrs front and back, all around the hemline and higher."

"She landed in the weeds," Black Elk said.

"Face down," Allison said. "That would account for a few burrs on the front of her dress. In order to cover her hemline like that, she must have been running through the weeds." Allison propped his foot on the desk to show the burrs surrounding his pants cuff. "Her dress looks like our pants after today's run."

"There was no sidewalk along the road," Black Elk said. "And they walked nearly a mile before she was hit."

"No sidewalk. But according to your photos, the weeds had been cleared along the berm. And there was so little traffic, why not walk in the road? That's where she was hit." Allison tilted the folded dress to show them the waistband. "And she wasn't hit from behind, which is how Jenkins described the accident."

"I wondered about that," Black Elk said.

"How do you know?" Hightower asked.

"The red crescent imprint left by the headlight fixture is on the left side of her dress. The car caught her on the left hip."

"Maybe she turned when she heard it coming," Black Elk said.

"I think it all started at the lake, just about where we were today," Allison said.

Black Elk frowned. "Shit. Of course."

"You'll have to spell it out for me," Hightower said.

"Look at the two people involved," Allison said. "We've got a beautiful, popular high school senior who has a good reputation, and, by all accounts, is fairly religious. And we've got a randy college boy with relatively few scruples."

Allison laid the skirt aside. "And there's one piece of clothing absent from this collection."

Black Elk nodded. "No panties."

"That site by the lake is under development now," Allison said. "But at the time of the accident there was just a gravel road leading to the lake. Teenagers used it to park and pet, I'm guessing."

"I'm getting the picture," Hightower said.

"About time," Black Elk said.

"Get off it," Hightower said. "You're twenty-five years late yourself."

"So we've got an innocent young woman with a blood-alcohol

content beyond the legal limit, and a randy college boy," Allison said.

"Didn't anybody check Jenkins's blood-alcohol content?" Keaton asked.

"Hell, he was walking, not driving," Black Elk said. "At least that's what he told us. We didn't really set out to test Edie's alcohol level. It just came out in the blood workup."

"But what puts them at the lake?" Hightower asked.

Allison pointed to the dress. "Those burrs, for one thing. And the fact that Edie was hit from the left side. Here's the way I see it. Jenkins drove down to the lake and parked. Edie was a little drunk. He tried to take advantage. By the time he got her panties off, she panicked, left the car, and ran."

"Picking up those burrs," Keaton said.

"Exactly. Jenkins followed her. Maybe in his car on the road. Maybe on foot through the woods. She managed to stay ahead of him."

"Wise chief say squaw can run faster with pants off than brave with pants down," Black Elk intoned, mimicking the Indians in old black-and-white Westerns. "Make-um rape difficult."

Nobody laughed.

"She was still ahead of him and still running when she hit the main road," Allison said, "and ran right in front of Blaze Stender's Mustang."

"Hit from the left side. It fits," Hightower said. "But how did Blaze Stender get into this? The timing still doesn't fit."

"I'm coming to that," Allison said. "Jenkins knew he'd look pretty bad if he told what really happened."

"You're telling us he left Edie by the side of the road and went back to arrange an alibi?" Hightower said.

"It's the only thing that makes sense," Allison said. "The weeds hid her body from any traffic. He could be pretty sure she wouldn't be found until he had his story ready."

"That explains something I didn't understand when I talked to Jenkins yesterday," Keaton said. "He said the place where we were standing brought back memories of the accident. But he was at the lake, not on the road where she was hit."

"But he must have known a quick response might have saved her." Black Elk shook his head. "And all you've got is speculation based on a few burrs and an offhand remark about the lake bringing back memories. Hardly enough to ruin a man's reputation."

"Actually, we've got a lot more than that." Allison held up the photo of Jenkins's disabled Corvette. "Here's the one piece of evidence that might actually stand up in court."

"What's that?" Hightower asked.

"It's the photo I took of Jenkins's Corvette before they towed it away," Black Elk said.

"See how the rain has drenched the grass all around the car. But it's dry underneath. Except for that big splotch under the gas tank. You said you could still smell the gasoline the next day," Allison said to Black Elk.

"That's right, you could," said Black Elk.

"So?" Hightower said.

"Think about it," Allison said. "Young stud driving with a beauty queen. Last thing he's watching is the gas gauge. But let's say he's got a hole in the bottom of his tank. By the time he realizes he's in trouble and has to stop, there shouldn't be any gas left in the tank to leak out." Allison tapped the photo. "But there must have been half a tankful on the ground under the car."

"More than enough to get him to a gas station," Keaton said.

"Jesus Christ," Hightower said. "So he left Edie there in the weeds, drove back up the road, and punctured his own gas tank."

Allison nodded. "Old man Ramies said he'd never seen a puncture quite like it. A tiny gouge right smack in the middle of the tank's bottom. Couldn't figure out how a stone flung by a front tire could have done that kind of damage."

"So you think Jenkins caused his own leak, and then went off on foot to find help?" Hightower said. "My God, that could have cost the paramedics at least an hour."

"And delayed the accident report by an hour," Keaton said. "So that the hit-and-run car would have been at least an hour farther down the road than we ever thought possible."

"So it could have been Blaze Stender's Mustang," Hightower said.

"Almost certainly," Allison said.

"Just because of the red color?" Black Elk said. "That's pretty thin."

"There's one piece of evidence we haven't shared with you yet," Keaton said. "For at least twenty years, Blaze Stender and Lanny Morton have been sending a hundred grand a year to a bank here in Ponca City."

"Blood money?" Hightower said. "Who's been collecting it?"

"We were hoping you'd help us find that out," Keaton said.

"That's my jurisdiction," Hightower said. "I think I can handle it."

"Anybody else know about this?" Black Elk asked.

"Just the people in my office who've been tracking the funds," Keaton said. "And Stender's wife. And their accountant," he added, thinking that the more people he cited, the safer he and Allison were likely to be.

"Any other evidence we should know about?" Black Elk asked.

"Well, we're back in the realm of speculation," Allison said. "But you were here yesterday when I asked Jenkins whether it was raining when Edie was hit."

"And he said it was," Black Elk said.

"But not right away," Allison said. "He stalled. He had to think about it. That doesn't make sense for an image that should be branded in his brain."

"Are you saying it wasn't raining?" Black Elk said.

"If it happened the way I just laid out, it wasn't raining when she was hit or when Jenkins abandoned his car. But it was raining when he reported the accident. So he had to stop and figure out what the weather was like when his version of the accident happened."

"And that's why he stalled," Keaton said.

"That's pure speculation," Black Elk said. "I've seen innocent men stop and think twice before answering when you ask them their name."

Allison held up the photo of Jenkins's Corvette. "I'd say this is more than speculation. Jenkins had to be lying about the way the accident happened."

"All right, I'm sold," Hightower said. "So you think he was shooting at you today? When he saw you poking around the place where it all started?"

"Could have been Jenkins," Allison said. "Could have been the blackmailer."

"Could be Jenkins is your blackmailer," Black Elk said. "Maybe he saw more of the hit-and-run car than he let on. Hell, if he was in his own car, maybe he followed it."

"Could be," Keaton said. "Or it could be the blackmailer is ex-deputy Raptor. He kept Stender and Morton overnight and had a good look at their car."

"Or anybody who had access to the information I just laid out," Allison said.

"That could be almost anybody in my office," Black Elk said. "That's a pretty long list. And it's not one I'll be happy checking out."

"But I'd say those two names you mentioned, Jenkins and Raptor, head the list of prime suspects," Hightower said. "They both seem to be living a little higher on the hog than you'd expect from their circumstances."

Black Elk stood and fanned out the photos on the desk. "Let's say all this is true. Who do we have we can prosecute? The hit-and-run car is long gone and both the ballplayers are dead."

"Ernie Jenkins lied to us twenty-five years ago," Hightower said. "He sure as hell impeded the progress of our investigation."

"I'm pretty sure the statute of limitations on lying doesn't stretch that far." Black Elk squared up the photographs into a single pile. "Besides, a good lawyer could trample all over our evidence and leave us on the hook for false-arrest charges, or slander, or worse."

"But Vern Weber has a right to know what really happened," Keaton said.

"His daughter's dead," Black Elk said. "Let her rest."

"One thing we do have is a sniper on the loose," Hightower said.

"And a blackmailer," Keaton said. "Who could be the same person."

"Dark out now," Black Elk said. "We'll comb the shooting site by the lake first thing tomorrow. See what we can come up with."

"And I'll see what I can find out about those Ponca City deposits," Hightower said. "Do you have an account number?"

Keaton copied a number on an empty page of his notebook, tore the page out, and handed it to Hightower.

"Should I ask you how you got this?" Hightower asked.

"You don't want to know," Keaton said. "Some of our workers prefer to labor in obscurity. But the source is impeccable."

Black Elk returned the photos to the evidence box. "I can't

216

believe we didn't put this together ourselves."

"You had no reason to suspect Jenkins was lying," Allison said.

"Why not? His mouth was open. That's usually a dead giveaway." Black Elk smiled. "Injun know white man speak with forked tongue."

"What's next on your agenda?" Hightower asked.

Keaton shrugged. "Dinner. I'll stick around a day or so. See what you guys turn up."

"Unless you think you need me, I'll head home tomorrow," Allison said. "I've done all I can with the evidence, and being a target makes me nervous."

"Where you fellows staying?" Black Elk asked.

"Starlite Motel. Off Route Sixty in Pawhuska," Keaton said.

"I'll have my guys keep an eye on it. You should be okay, though. Whoever was shooting at you must know you've gotten the law involved, so it's too late to try to silence you or scare you off."

"That's all very logical," Allison said. "And I'd take some comfort from it if it weren't for the fact that we'd just come from your office when he shot at us."

Keaton and Allison picked up a pizza and a cold six-pack of Budweiser to take back to their motel. After they'd double-locked the door and closed the curtains, they sat on separate beds while Keaton popped open two beers. He handed one to Allison. "That was a pretty impressive display you just put on."

"The key was the pool of gasoline under the Corvette. Once you know for sure Jenkins has been lying, it all falls into place."

"The local law had that same information for twenty-five years, and it still hadn't fallen into place."

Allison sipped his beer, lifted a slice of pepperoni pizza from its greasy box, and handed it to Keaton. "That's not quite true.

Somebody figured out enough to blackmail Stender and Morton."

"And you don't think it was Raptor?"

"I'm just saying I don't know. Could have been Raptor. Could have been Jenkins. Could have been either of those two lawmen we just left."

Keaton laid the pizza slice on a napkin on the bedside stand. "But who shot at us today? And why?"

"Pretty much the same list of suspects. Jenkins might have wanted to keep us from uncovering his lies. The blackmailer might have just wanted to scare us off."

"Or wanted us dead."

"Not a happy thought." Allison washed down his pizza with a swig of beer. "At least now the local law knows as much as we do."

"So nobody has anything to gain by killing us."

"That's what Black Elk said, but it doesn't make me feel any safer. If the shooter was Raptor or Jenkins, they may not know we've been to the cops."

"And in any case, they couldn't know what we told the cops."

"Unless the shooter was one of the cops," Allison said. "Black Elk turned sour when I suggested anyone in his office could have put together the information the blackmailer needed."

"But he'd have no reason to come after us," Keaton said. "Hightower knows as much as we know."

"You're talking as if there were some logic to all this. Strictly speaking, the sniper never had much to gain by shooting us. But that didn't stop him."

Keaton paused with his pizza slice halfway to his mouth. "You're saying we could still be in somebody's sights."

"I'd like to believe we're safe. But there's certainly no guarantee. The blackmailer may think we're close to identifying him."

Something metallic clattered to the floor in the room next to theirs.

The pizza turned to cardboard in Keaton's mouth. He swallowed hard. "What was that?"

Allison went to the window and pulled the curtain back just enough to permit a peek out. "Family with a baby moving in next door."

"Is the baby armed?"

"Carrying a rattle and a pacifier. Neither looks lethal. A black coupe was circling the parking lot, but it's gone now."

"All of a sudden I don't feel too safe here. We're sitting ducks if anyone wants us dead."

Allison came away from the window. "Let's stop sitting. Let's pack up and get out. Find an anonymous motel near the Tulsa airport where nobody knows our names."

Keaton closed the pizza box and stood up. "Makes sense to me."

"We won't bother to check out. Or tell anyone we're going. Put some space between us and the shooter. Take a little time to think. We can call anybody we need to tomorrow from Tulsa." Allison cocked his ear toward the window. "What's that?" He peeked through the curtain again. "That black coupe is still circling."

"Black Elk said he'd have men keeping an eye on the motel."

"Somehow that doesn't make me feel any safer." Allison released the curtain. "They've cleared out. Let's load the car fast. Then maybe we can time their next round and leave before they come back."

They packed their suitcases into the trunk of their rental car, then went back inside and kept watch behind the curtain.

"Here it comes," said Allison.

The black coupe circled the parking lot twice and disappeared.

"Let's go," Keaton said.

The two men clambered into the rental car, and Keaton drove out of the parking lot onto the main street of Pawhuska. He traveled four blocks with one eye on his rearview mirror, then merged onto a four-lane highway leading to Route 60 and hit the accelerator.

"Tulsa, here we come," Keaton said.

A siren sounded behind them, and the flashing red light of a police car pulsed in their rearview mirror.

Chapter Seventeen:
A Fine Fix

Keaton slowed and the flashing lights drew closer. He swore and pulled over to the side of the road, then propped his wrists on the steering wheel so they would be in full view of the approaching officer.

Instead of placing his hands where they could be seen, Owen Allison reached for his cell phone. He couldn't decide whether to dial nine-one-one or activate the recorder, but quickly figured that if the occupants of the patrol car meant to harm them, nine-one-one wouldn't be much help. So he activated the recorder.

Keaton watched in his rearview mirror as a hulking figure emerged from the patrol car and patted his holster. The flasher on top of the car turned the face of Todd Black Elk alternating colors of red and blue.

Black Elk strolled toward the rental car, blocking out the setting sun with his bulk. He waited for Keaton to roll down the driver's window, then rested his forearm on the sill and said, "You boys going somewhere?"

"Tulsa," Keaton said. "Owen has an early flight and we both thought we'd rather be somewhere where nobody was shooting at us."

"Like you to turn around and come with me, if you don't mind," Black Elk said.

Keaton's hands tightened on the steering wheel. "Why?"

"After hearing your story about Radar Raptor, Wes Hightower drove out to visit him. Found him dead."

"What happened?"

"Looks like his gun went off while he was cleaning it." Black
Elk tilted his Mounties-style hat back on his forehead. "At least,
that's what somebody wants us to think."

"What do you want with us?" Keaton asked.

"You talked to him a couple of days ago. Might have been
the last to see him alive. Like you to take a look at his place and
fill us in on the details of your visit." Black Elk straightened and
tapped his fist on top of the rental car. "Turn this around and
follow me."

Keaton watched Black Elk return to his patrol car in the
gathering dusk. "What about it? Think it's a trap?"

"He had us just now if he wanted us." Allison turned off his
recorder and punched a number into his cell phone. "I think I'll
let a few friends know where we're going, though. And who
we're going with. Just in case."

The three chandeliers made from interlocking deer antlers cast
eerie shadows in the main room of Radar Raptor's hunting
lodge. Raptor himself was slumped over a bloodstained table,
his one remaining eye staring unblinkingly at the flashes from
the police photographer's camera.

A greasy rag and a cleaning rod lay on the fringe of the pool
of blood that had leaked from Raptor's damaged head, while a
revolver lay on the wood floor just beneath his dangling right
hand.

Sheriff Hightower whispered instructions to two deputies and
a photographer, then turned and nodded to Keaton. "Thanks
for coming. Near as we can tell, you were one of the last people
to see Raptor alive. And this afternoon you told us you thought
he might be involved in a blackmail scheme." Hightower pointed
toward Raptor's slumped body. "Hoped you might be able to

shed some light on this."

Keaton shrugged. "Looks like he was cleaning his gun and either discharged it accidentally or decided to commit suicide. The gun on the floor looks like the one he used to threaten me two days ago."

"You didn't tell us anything about a threat," Hightower said.

"Wasn't a direct threat exactly. He took the revolver out and toyed with it while I was asking him about Edie Weber and the money Lanny Morton had been sending to Ponca City."

"You asked him about blackmail payments?" Black Elk said. "While he held a gun on you? I'd say your balls outweighed your brains."

"I made it plain I wasn't the only one who knew about the payments," Keaton said. "And he didn't exactly hold the gun on me. Just spun the cylinder, sighted down the barrel, and then tried to look like he was measuring me for a coffin."

"Was he sitting where he is now?" Hightower asked.

"No. He was standing at the bar."

"Anything changed since you were here?"

Keaton swept his eyes over the room. "Antlers all seem to be in place. When I talked to him, though, it was a little brighter in here. But he still had to put on glasses to read my business card. Joked about only needing them for seeing. I can't imagine he'd try to clean his gun without wearing his glasses, but I don't see them anywhere."

Hightower gestured toward the gun racks and pistol displays on the lodge walls. "Hell, Raptor could probably clean every weapon here blindfolded."

"Maybe, but would he?" Keaton pointed at a gun rack behind the bar. "And that gun rack. When I was here, rifles were stacked in alternate slots. Now there's an extra rifle between the first and third slots on the left-hand side."

Hightower tapped the extra rifle with his pen. "This the one?"

"Yeah," Keaton said. "That slot wasn't filled when I was here two days ago."

"What do you make of that?" Hightower asked.

"Could be that's the gun that fired on us today."

"It's the right caliber," Black Elk said.

"So are most of the rifles on the rack," Hightower said. "We can check them all against the slug we dug out of the tree. If they match, either Raptor was your sniper or somebody went to a good deal of trouble to make us think he was."

"If Raptor was on the other end of that rifle this morning," Black Elk said, "you two would be dead now."

"How long's he been dead?" Keaton asked.

"Coroner says at least three hours. I found him a couple of hours ago," Hightower said.

"So it happened after we left your office," Keaton said to Black Elk.

"Well, don't worry," Black Elk said. "We've got no reason to suspect the two of you."

Wish I could say the same about the two of you, Keaton thought. But he said, "That's a load off my mind. Of course, you had us under surveillance."

"Lucky we did," Black Elk said. "You might have left town without tipping us off about Raptor's glasses and the extra rifle."

"I'm pretty sure you'd have figured it out." Keaton's cell phone vibrated. He checked the screen, saw that the caller was his ex-wife, and excused himself to take the call.

He turned his back on the corpse, walked away from the bloody table, and whispered into the phone, "Liz. What's going on?"

"It's your dad. I think you better come right home."

"He hasn't wandered away from Stauder's, has he?"

"No. He hasn't wandered away. Davy and I have visited him

the last two days. They seem to be taking good care of him."

"What is it, then?"

"It's his mind. He's finally acknowledged what's happening, and he's panicking. He's asking for you. Says you two have a project planned. Says he wants to finish it before his mind is a blank slate. It's heartbreaking, he's so desperate."

Keaton sighed. "I'll get there as soon as I can."

He pocketed his phone with such force that Hightower asked, "Trouble?"

"Problems at home," Keaton said.

"Have to get back?"

Keaton looked at Raptor's lifeless body. "Yes. Are you about finished with me here?"

"You've been most helpful," Hightower said. "But I don't have any more questions. If some come up, I could ask them just as easily by phone. What about you, Todd?"

Black Elk shrugged. "You guys have solved one mystery and looks like you've left us with another. I'd say we're even. I know how to reach you if I need to."

Keaton turned to Owen Allison. "What time's your flight out tomorrow?"

"Ten in the morning."

"Maybe I'll join you."

"Happy for the company."

As soon as they got back on the road to Tulsa, Owen Allison said, "Look, if you think it's important to have someone on site here, I can stick around."

Keaton checked his rearview mirror. No one seemed to be following them. "I appreciate the offer, but I don't think there's anything to be gained by sticking around. And there's a lot that could be lost if we're still a target in someone's mind." *And,* Keaton thought, *as a practical matter I can't afford to pay for much more of your time.*

As if he'd read Keaton's mind, Allison said, "You wouldn't have to pay my salary. Just cover my expenses."

"It's not a question of pay," Keaton said. "It's more a question of capabilities. I brought you here to look into the mystery of Edie Weber's death. That was your area of expertise, and you solved the case. Beautifully, I might add. What's left now is the mystery of who shot Radar Raptor. That's the kind of mystery the cops are trained to solve."

"But it's almost certain that Raptor's shooting is linked to what we uncovered about Edie Weber's death."

"I'll grant you that, but poking into Raptor's death is the cops' job. It would be too dangerous for an outsider. Somebody has already shot at us. I can't ask you to stay around. We got what we came for. Whatever else you might uncover isn't worth the risk."

"But you were going to stick around yourself, until that call came about your dad. Raptor's killing may be the cops' job, but you've already reasoned out more about his death than the two of them put together." Allison braced his right hand against the dashboard and turned toward Keaton. "There's a good chance it was Raptor who was shooting at us. If that's the case, there's no more threat."

"According to Black Elk, if it was Raptor shooting at us, we'd both be dead."

"Unless he just wanted to scare us."

"Well, if that's what he wanted, he succeeded. But it might not have been Raptor. Might have been somebody we haven't met. Or Ernie Jenkins. Or one of those lawmen we just left."

"I think we can rule out Sheriff Black Elk," Allison said.

"You're the one who put him on the list. This morning when we were running for our lives."

"If Black Elk wanted to kill us, he just had us dead to rights back at that traffic stop and on the back roads leading to Raptor's. And he's the one who preserved the evidence of the Weber crash all these years. Without his photos and Edie Weber's dress, I never could have figured out what really happened."

"That dress could just as easily have supported blackmail as accident reconstruction." Keaton shook his head. "No, with or without Black Elk, there are just too many potential snipers out there. I can't in good conscience ask you to stay to do a job that's really mine. To tell the truth, I'm a little relieved to be traveling out of sniper range myself. Let's give the professional lawmen time to do their stuff. We can always go back later."

"You're the boss," Allison said. "Incidentally, our plane leaves at seven-thirty tomorrow morning. We're connecting through Chicago."

"I thought you said ten o'clock."

"If one of those lawmen is after us, I thought I'd give him a chance to sleep in."

Keaton and Allison checked into a motel near the Tulsa airport just before midnight. Even though he had an early flight, Keaton was too wired to sleep. He thought about Raptor's death, weighing the possibilities. Since suicide seemed unlikely, what sort of motive might move someone to murder Raptor? According to Hightower, Deputy Sheriff Raptor could count at least one enemy on every page of the local phone book. But he'd been retired for nearly four years. Given the timing, it stood to reason that his death was somehow linked to Edie Weber's death and the blackmailing of Blaze Stender. Maybe Raptor had an accomplice who wanted to be sure to remain anonymous. If that were the case, it made sense that the accomplice might be found in the Noble County sheriff's office.

He took out his computer and e-mailed Liz his flight details and arrival time, asking her to pass the information along to his father. He wished he'd taken the time to start working with his dad on three generations of Keaton columns before leaving for Tulsa. If only they'd conceived the project earlier, before his dad's brain started to shut down.

Thinking of his father's project reminded Keaton that he'd packed one of his grandfather's handwritten notebooks to read on his trip. Until now, he hadn't had a chance to look at it. He dug into the bottom of his suitcase and retrieved the long, thin bound notebook whose hard brown cover was imprinted with ads for patent medicines, soaps, and cigarettes.

Keaton thumbed through the notebook pages. Dates were written in the upper right-hand corner of each page in his grandfather's precise, economical handwriting. Two of the last pages in the book caught his eye. The first, dated January 4, 1927, began

Spoke says:
Leonard's story is pure BS.
Dutch is a gutless whiner who had it in for Cobb.
Claims Cobb shortened career by overworking sore arm.

Keaton took a deep breath and tried to steady his hands. "Spoke" would be Tris Speaker, his grandfather's favorite Cleveland player. Leonard would be "Dutch" Leonard, a journeyman pitcher who made headlines around the 1926 Christmas holidays by accusing Speaker and Ty Cobb, two of baseball's reigning superstars, of conspiring to fix an unimportant game between the teams they managed, Cleveland and Detroit, late in the 1919 season.

His grandfather's notes evidently came from interviews made when the story broke seven years after the suspect game had been played. Keaton knew the broad outlines of the story and how it eventually played out.

On the basis of Leonard's testimony and incriminating letters from Cobb and Cleveland outfielder Smokey Joe Wood,

American League President Ban Johnson initially forced Speaker and Cobb to resign quietly and paid Leonard twenty thousand dollars to suppress the letters, which Johnson felt would damage baseball's image. Upon review, Baseball Commissioner Kenesaw Mountain Landis overturned Johnson's ruling, exposed the attempted cover-up, exonerated Speaker and Cobb, and allowed them to return to the game with different teams. The two superstars finished their careers and were among the first players elected to Baseball's Hall of Fame.

The guilt of Cobb and Speaker had been debated endlessly by contemporary sportswriters and, in later years, by baseball historians. Keaton examined his grandfather's notes for some indication of what he'd found and what he felt. The initial page continued,

Q: What about the letters?
Spoke: They don't mention me.
Sounds like Wood bet against us. Unforgivable.
I bet, sure. You know that.
But you've never seen me bet against my own team.
Q: Was the game on the up and up?
Spoke: Absolutely. I went 3 for 5.
Does that look like I was dogging it?

The next page was dated January 5, 1927, and headed with a list of names and phone numbers, along with the same question he'd asked Speaker, "Was the game on the up and up?"

Graney: Sure it was.
We sloughed off some late season games.
But only games that didn't affect the standings.
Everybody did it.
But we never threw none.

Myers: It was a play-for-fun game.
But it wasn't rigged.

An entry at the bottom of the page read

Barnard has conclusive proof something was wrong.

And was followed by the notation

Appt. 1 pm Jan 8

The names of the interviewees on the second page meant nothing to Keaton. He Googled them and, after a bit of searching, found that Jack Graney was Cleveland's leadoff hitter in the suspect game, while Elmer Myers was the Cleveland pitcher accused of serving up batting-practice pitches in the Tribe's nine-to-five loss.

The last entry was intriguing. The Barnard of the notes, who claimed to have conclusive proof of wrongdoing, was Ernest S. Barnard, president of the Cleveland ball club. Unfortunately, the claim came on the last page of the notebook. Or what turned out to be the last page. The last two pages had been torn out, so that only their stub ends peeked out from the notebook binding.

Had his grandfather uncovered something in his meeting with the Cleveland president that he couldn't face or didn't want to write about a friend? Evidence he didn't want to share? It must have been tough seeing his good friend and favorite player accused of profiting from bets made on a rigged game. Still, it was hard to imagine that a dedicated reporter would destroy his notes on such an important subject. Maybe there was some simpler explanation. Maybe Granddad just needed a couple of blank sheets of paper for some other purpose, like a grocery list. He'd have to wait until he got home to see if the next notebook in the series contained a record of his grandfather's meeting with the Cleveland president.

Most of the notebook pages had tiny, nearly invisible numbers penciled in the lower right-hand corners. At first, Keaton assumed they were page numbers, but then he noticed they seemed to range randomly from –100 to 125. He couldn't make out any pattern in the seemingly random entries until he found a penciled notation to the left of one of the numbers. The notation read: *Reds 110, Phils –130; Sox 115, Tribe –135,* the betting lines on two of the day's games. Keaton smiled. The entries represented the outcome of the day's wagers. Granddad had been a betting man.

CHAPTER EIGHTEEN:
GETTING AND FORGETTING
THE GOODS

KEATON'S KORNER

It's apparent from your letters and e-mails that you enjoyed Meri Atkins's columns during my vacation as much as I did. Her columns debating whether cheerleading should be a sport generated almost as many responses as my columns debating whether Pete Rose's banishment is justified.

This being Ohio, letters regarding Pete Rose continued to arrive during my absence. Most wanted to know how I could uphold Rose's banishment while insisting that Hall of Famers should be judged by what they did on the field, not what happened off it.

Let's be clear about this. I strongly believe that entrance into the Hall of Fame should depend on a player's performance, not his personality. But Pete Rose violated two of the cardinal rules of baseball and received the prescribed penalties.

These rules and penalties have been around much longer than Rose. Commissioner Kenesaw Mountain Landis installed them in 1927 after ruling that superstars Ty Cobb and Tris Speaker were innocent of charges that they had conspired to fix a late-season game in 1919. Two of the rules instituted by Landis at the time are directly relevant to Rose's case. The first provides for "Ineligibility for one year for betting any sum whatsoever upon any ball game in connection with which the bettor had no duty to perform," while the second promises, "Permanent ineligibility for betting any sum whatsoever upon any ball game in connection with which the bettor has any duty to perform."

There is overwhelming evidence that Pete Rose violated both these rules, which are posted in every major-league clubhouse. Pete has earned his banishment, regardless of his records on the field of play.

Every level space in his father's assisted-living quarters, from tabletops and windowsills to chair seats and the kitchen drain board, was covered with small stacks of plastic sleeves containing newspaper columns. There were few visible traces of the pristine apartment they had visited when shopping for retirement homes. Keaton gathered up two stacks of columns and cleared a corner of the couch while his father walked over and around the stacks on the floor.

"I'm sorry, Lloyd," his father said. "I really want to help. Every day I start organizing stacks of columns. The next day I can't remember what I was thinking. Or why. So I start all over." He shook his head. "Sometimes I forget before I get back from lunch."

Keaton looked at the columns he'd cleared from the sofa before sitting down. One of his grandfather's on the 1920 World Series; three by his father on Roger Maris, foul balls, and Bob Gibson; and one of his own on steroids. The only apparent connection was the subject of baseball and the surname of the authors.

"It's okay, Dad. Let's just reorganize these and stack them all by author. One pile for granddad, one pile for you, and one pile for me. Then you go through your columns and pick out the ones you'd like to see in print again."

John Keaton shook his head. "But I need to know how they all fit together. That's what I can't seem to manage."

"Don't worry about that. I'll take care of the connections. We could do a chapter on famous teammates. Granddad wrote about Ruth and Gehrig, you covered Maris and Mantle, and I've interviewed Jeter and A-Rod."

John Keaton bent over and lifted a stack from the floor. "I wrote a lot about Feller and the fifty-four season."

"That could be another chapter. Granddad covered the nineteen-twenty Series, you and he were both around when the Indians won pennants in forty-eight and fifty-four, and I covered the Tribe in ninety-five and ninety-seven before I left Cleveland." *Left Cleveland,* he thought. A euphemism for blowing everything that mattered to him.

"I get it," John Keaton said. "I just need to remember it. What are some other topics?"

"Well, we could do a chapter on scandals. Granddad covered the Black Sox and the Cobb-Speaker affair, you interviewed Pete Rose, and strikes and steroids happened on my watch."

"That's it. That's the kind of thing I wanted to do. I just couldn't . . ." John Keaton's hands spread and trembled, then came together as he interlaced his fingers. "Couldn't make the connections."

"It'll work out. I'll make a list. We'll start some stacks and label them. Teams, teammates, World Series, scandals. We'll think of a few others. Labels will help you make the connections." He tore some pages from his pocket notebook to start making labels. The torn pages reminded him of the missing pages in his grandfather's notebook. "How well did Granddad know Tris Speaker?"

"Speaker was a good friend of Dad's. He gave me an autographed ball once." John Keaton paused and frowned. "Or maybe that was somebody else."

"Did Granddad think he was guilty back in nineteen twenty-seven?"

John Keaton shook his head. "I can't remember what I thought yesterday. Older memories come a little easier, but they're all random. You can't expect me to remember what my father thought when I was a child."

"I just thought he might have mentioned it."

John Keaton sighed. "Not to me. At least not that I remember."

Keaton stood, patted his father's shoulder, and scooped up the rest of the columns scattered on the couch. "Let's just get these columns sorted by author and start labeling some subjects. Then I'll take you out to Max and Erma's for a good restaurant dinner. Help you forget the institutional food here."

"That's one good thing about my condition. I forget about the food every night."

Back in his own apartment, Keaton organized his grandfather's columns in chronological order, then checked those that had been written at the time the Cobb-Speaker scandal broke. He couldn't find any addressing the scandal, which would have been big news in the Cleveland papers.

He did find several columns praising Speaker during the season before the scandal broke. Columns lauding his hitting prowess, defensive skills, and strategic decisions as a player/manager. But Keaton could find no mention of Speaker in his grandfather's columns after the scandal broke. Not even when Speaker retired two years later. Of course, he no longer played in Cleveland after Judge Landis reinstated him.

So it wasn't entirely surprising that Speaker would receive fewer mentions in his grandfather's columns after the scandal. Still, if Speaker and his grandfather had been good friends, it was strange that the player would suddenly receive no notice whatsoever. Had the missing pages of his grandfather's notebooks contained evidence of Speaker's guilt? The remaining collection of notebooks was randomly organized and incomplete, and he couldn't find any more handwritten entries covering the

Cobb-Speaker affair.

Keaton went online to refresh his knowledge of the scandal itself. Sportswriters of the day appeared to be evenly split on the guilt of the two superstars. After reviewing the evidence, Keaton became convinced that Cobb, at least, had bet heavily on his own team, the Tigers, an act that was legal at the time. To profit from the game, however, Speaker would have had to bet against his own team, something he told Keaton's grandfather he'd never done. Still, other Cleveland players admitted that the game in question had been played "for fun," and Speaker was known to be a gambling man.

Incontrovertible evidence never surfaced. Was there a chance that his grandfather had uncovered such evidence and sat on it, either because of his friendship with Speaker or his respect for the game? His grandfather's post-scandal silence on Speaker suggested that he must at least have had strong suspicions regarding his friend's guilt.

Keaton wondered how his grandfather might have felt, realizing that a friend, a player he respected, had been guilty of questionable conduct. The sportswriters of the day had a long history of looking the other way when public idols revealed feet of clay. Still, it couldn't have been easy for his grandfather. As a reporter, he must have been tempted to share whatever inside knowledge he had of the scandal. Had he decided that the sins of the past were best left buried there?

The possibility of shielding the public from the foibles of the famous reminded Keaton that he'd spent his first days back without contacting Barb Stender. He'd promised to share any information he uncovered regarding the reasons behind Blaze's blackmail payments and the identity of the blackmailer. He knew too much about the former and too little about the latter, and none of his knowledge was likely to be welcome.

★ ★ ★ ★ ★

Keaton split the next day between the newspaper and his
father's new quarters and then left for Cleveland in the early
evening, trying throughout the two-and-a-half-hour drive to
think of a way to soften his message to Barb Stender and put
her husband in a more positive light.

He stalled through a late dinner in the Stenders' dining room,
making small talk, and finally laid out what he'd learned in
Oklahoma while pouring the last of a second bottle of cabernet
into their wineglasses. They'd made a ritual of clinking their
glasses through the first bottle, but Barb let her refilled glass sit
untouched. "Hit-and-run? He killed a girl?" Her face was ashen
in the candlelight. "But we don't know Blaze was driving. Lanny
was behind the wheel when they were stopped for speeding."

Keaton moved his chair so he was sitting at the corner of the
table next to Barb. "That's right. But it was Blaze's car, and we
do know he was paying blackmail money to Lanny. And we
know that half of that money wound up in Ponca City."

"But you don't know who picked it up there?"

"Best guess is Radar Raptor, the deputy who stopped Blaze
and Lanny Morton that night. But somebody killed him just
before we left Oklahoma."

"To keep him from talking?"

"Most likely. Man was about as popular as an abortionist at a
right-to-life rally. A lot of people had reason to want him dead.
But that had been true for a long time, and the fact that he was
killed while we were poking into the blackmail scheme seems
like more than a coincidence."

Barb traced the base of her wineglass with a fingertip. "So
there's someone loose in Oklahoma who knows the whole story."

"The killer, you mean? It's likely. But the two lawmen who
were helping us know about the hit-and-run as well."

Barb sighed. "Will it go into your book?"

"I don't see how I can keep it out. The days when reporters covered up the foibles of superstars are long gone."

"Now they trumpet them to the world to help beef up book sales."

"That's not what I intended. And you know it."

"But it makes Blaze look . . ." Barb shook her head. "No better than a murderer."

She seemed in such distress that Keaton wanted to reassure her, to soften the blow. He reached out for her hand, and his movement startled her. Her wineglass wobbled, then splashed its contents onto her blouse and slacks.

Keaton watched the red stain blossom on her white blouse. "Shit. I'm sorry."

Barb dabbed at the stain with a napkin. "It's all right. They're both washable. I'd better attend to it right now, though." She stood and headed toward the stairs.

Keaton used his napkin to keep the wine pooling on the table from dripping to the floor. He felt awkward, uncertain. It hadn't occurred to him that Barb might want him to sit on the story. He was a reporter, after all. And it was a big story. Especially if they could nail the blackmailer and murderer.

Barb glided back to the table wearing a white silk robe that glistened in the candlelight. Her outfit made Keaton feel even more awkward. He apologized again for the wine spill.

Barb waved him off. "It's not a problem. Look. It was silly of me to think you could sweep this whole mess under a rug." The robe dipped open to show the tiny mole just above her left breast. "Can you keep it quiet for a while, though? At least until after the Hall of Fame vote?"

"Well, Blaze wanted to have the book out in time for the vote."

"That was when he thought it would help his chances. When he was still alive. Before they moved his eligibility up to next

January because of the accident. That's less than three months away."

"The publishers are going to want to see the manuscript around that time. Once they see the story, I can't control what they might say publicly."

"The publishers won't care about the timing of the Hall of Fame vote. With Blaze's boat accident, they can expect to sell a lot more books. I helped to get you on the job. I can help to get you an extension."

"So you feel that strongly about the Hall of Fame vote?"

Barb shivered and the silk of her robe rippled. "I feel I owe it to Blaze."

"The story's likely to come out anyhow. Those two lawmen in Oklahoma know all about it."

"But they've got no real proof, and nobody's left alive to charge with a hit-and-run that's twenty-five years old. Why should they care?"

"They've got a fresh murder on their hands. The motive's likely to be tied in with the blackmail. If and when they find the killer, the whole story is bound to come out."

"But until then, they're likely to keep quiet about what they know."

Keaton shrugged. "I guess that's true. They won't want to tip the killer off to everything they know." *Particularly if one of the lawmen is the blackmailer,* he thought.

"What happens in Oklahoma is out of our control. I'm just asking you to keep what you know quiet for a short time. At least until after the Hall of Fame vote." Barb touched his arm. "For the sake of Blaze's friendship."

Keaton hesitated. It had been a while since he'd thought of Blaze Stender as a friend. And now he knew him to be a card cheat, a steroid user, a probable philanderer, a tax dodger, and a hit-and-run driver.

Sensing his reluctance, Barb reached out and took both his hands in hers. "For the sake of my friendship, then." She leaned forward and the robe fell open.

CHAPTER NINETEEN:
FALLING OFF A BICYCLE

KEATON'S KORNER

Last week's column on Pete Rose elicited a firestorm of mail from outraged Ohioans proclaiming his innocence, protesting his banishment, and claiming his misdeeds were much less serious than those of known "cheaters" who were caught using illegal drugs. As I pointed out in the column, Pete was found guilty of violating the majors' long-standing rule against betting on baseball games and is serving the prescribed penalty.

The cases of accused steroid users are much different. A-Rod and Blaze Stender, for example, were revealed to have tested positive in the supposedly anonymous sampling conducted in 2003, before baseball had outlawed steroid use. Since neither man tested positive after the rule outlawing steroids was in place, it is difficult to see how they, or other players in the same boat, can be called cheaters if they violated no law. Amphetamines were banned at the same time as steroids, but I've not heard of any one-time amphetamine users being labeled as cheaters, even though amphetamines were once distributed by the bowlful in major league clubhouses.

The case of Manny Ramirez is a little different. He tested positive after baseball's ban was in place. But he served baseball's prescribed sentence, a 50-day suspension for his first offense. Both steroids and gambling had been a plague for some time before baseball finally banned them. At the current time, a first-time steroid user will receive a 50-day suspension, while a

241

first-time gambler will be banned for life. These penalties reflect baseball's judgment regarding the seriousness of the offenses. Even if you disagree with this judgment, both penalties have been well publicized and should come as no surprise to wrongdoers. In measuring the seriousness of the offense and the accompanying penalty, therefore, Pete Rose stands well apart from A-Rod, Blaze, Manny, and other accused steroid users.

Keaton woke to find Barb standing beside the bed, freshly scrubbed and dressed in tight-fitting jeans and a white blouse. "Morning, sleepyhead," she said. "I'm taking breakfast orders."

"Never touch the stuff," Keaton said. "A cup of tea is all I usually need."

Barb leaned across the bed and kissed him. "Thought you might need to replenish your strength."

He didn't know whether to smile or blush. "It wasn't exactly my finest hour."

"We got it straightened out eventually."

"That's pretty much a single entendre, isn't it?" Keaton looked around for his clothes. He could see his shirt on the floor, and his pants draped across a chair under the picture window. His underwear was nowhere in sight.

Barb smiled like a coconspirator. "I especially liked the, ah, oral favors. I knew you were good with words, but I didn't know you could do so many other things with your tongue. Blaze would never do that for me."

Keaton didn't want to think about Blaze Stender. Especially not about what Blaze Stender did in bed with his wife. "It's been a long time. My tongue was one of the few parts of my anatomy I knew I could count on."

"It came back pretty quickly. Like riding a bicycle."

Keaton sat up to get a better look around the rest of the bedroom. It had been nothing like riding a bicycle. More like catching your pants cuff in the sprocket and falling into a mud puddle with your girlfriend watching. At least the first time.

He spotted his underpants on the floor and squirmed toward them under the covers. When he got to the edge of the bed they were out of reach and it was clear he couldn't retrieve them without uncovering his nakedness. What the hell. Nothing to be embarrassed about. Barb was right. They eventually got it straightened out. He threw off the covers, left the bed, and had one leg into his underpants when his cell phone rang.

Startled, he stopped with his pants at half-mast and followed the sound, hopping on one foot toward the chair that held his slacks. He retrieved his phone from his pants pocket and pulled up his underpants before bringing the phone to his ear.

"Lloyd, are you there? Where are you?" He could hear the exasperation in his ex-wife's voice.

"Liz. What's going on?"

"I'm with your dad. He was expecting to see you this morning. In fact, he was expecting you last night."

"He knew I wasn't coming last night. I told him." Keaton shook his head. "Well, he must have forgotten."

Barb put her finger to her lips and backed out of the bedroom.

"Your dad's been rambling," Liz said. "And the place is still littered with newspaper clippings. How soon can you get here?"

Keaton sat on the edge of the bed and worked one leg into his slacks. "Not for a while. I'm in Cleveland."

"What are you doing there?"

He worked his other leg into his slacks and stood to pull them up. "Having breakfast."

"You haven't had breakfast in twenty years. What's going on?"

"I was working on the Stender book. It got to be late. I decided to stay over."

"With the Widow Stender?"

Keaton retrieved his shirt from the floor. "In her house, yes."

There was a short silence on the other end of the line. "You haven't forgotten you promised to take Davy to the Ohio State game?"

"No. I haven't forgotten. Jesus, what time is it?"

"Nine-thirty. Aren't there any clocks in the Widow Stender's kitchen?"

"I'm sorry. I wasn't paying attention."

"Evidently not."

"I'll go right to the car. I should get to Menckenburg in time to pick up Davy."

"I'll try to bring him to your dad's place. Then you'll only need to explain why you're late one time, to both of them."

Keaton buttoned his shirt and hurried downstairs to the kitchen. Liz was adjusting the flame under a yellow teakettle. "Trouble?" she asked.

"I've got to run. My dad was expecting me, and I promised to take my son to the Ohio State game."

"I was hoping we could spend some time on the lake. Dale Lewis has been lending me his cruiser."

"I'm afraid I'll have to take a rain check."

"Happy to give one. Except this time of year it's likely to be a snow check." Barb lifted one of the empty ceramic mugs next to the stove. "At least wait for your tea. It's about ready."

"I've really got to go."

Barb handed Keaton the empty mug. "I'll trust you to take this with you. You can bring it back next time you come." She ran her finger along the back of his hand. "Soon, I hope."

"Soon as I can." He turned the mug in his hands. "Listen, though. I want to clear something up."

"What's that?"

"The Hall of Fame vote. Ballots are due December thirty-first. That's just a couple of months away."

"So?"

"So, now that they've moved Blaze's eligibility up, there's no chance I could get my draft to the publisher before the new voting deadline."

"So?"

"So it was no real problem for me to promise to hold the chapter on Blaze's accident until the election's over."

The teakettle whistled shrilly.

Barb smiled. "You think I didn't know that?"

The four labeled stacks of newspaper columns Keaton had started for his father on the coffee table had grown. As if they'd cast off seedlings, they'd been joined by smaller unlabeled stacks that covered the floor and spread to the sofa, chairs, and windowsills. Keaton stepped around the stacks on the floor and found his father sitting at the kitchen table, barefoot in his red striped pajamas.

Liz stood at the sink rinsing coffee mugs. "About time," she said.

Keaton set Barb Stender's mug on the sideboard. "I got here as fast as I could. Where's Davy?"

Liz wiped her hands on her apron and unfastened it. "I didn't want to leave your dad alone. I'll go get Davy now."

Keaton waved his hands at the newspaper columns. "Looks like we're back where we started, Dad."

"I can't . . . I can't sort." John Keaton shook his head. "Need help."

Liz laid her apron on the counter. "You told me you'd cleaned up this mess."

"I did," Keaton said. "These are new stacks."

"Sorry," John Keaton said. "Need help."

Liz picked up Barb Stender's mug. "What's going on, Lloyd?"

"I told both you and Dad I wouldn't be around last night."

245

"That's not what I mean and you know it. We both expected you here this morning." Liz slammed the ceramic mug down hard on the counter and shook the broken handle at Keaton. "But you spent the night with that woman."

"I was researching the book."

"Is that what they call it now?" Liz shook her head. "I thought we were done with your evasions. Your half-truths and excuses. Your problem was always keeping your wallet shut. Not your fly."

"I'm sorry." He realized he was apologizing for past failures, not for last night. "I know I've put you through a lot."

"Don't apologize to me. Apologize to your father. He needs your attention." Liz dropped the broken cup handle in the sink and strode to the front door. "I'm going to get Davy. He could use a little attention as well."

After Liz left, Keaton checked the four stacks of columns on the coffee table, the ones he'd labeled and started building. His father seemed to have followed the labels, sorting his own writing into the stacks marked TEAMS, TEAMMATES, WORLD SERIES, and SCANDALS. When Keaton riffled through a few of the random stacks of columns on the floor, though, he could find no organizing principle.

His father shrugged. "I keep forgetting."

Keaton tapped the coffee table. "You did fine with a lot of these. I'll help with the rest. Get a few more labels. We'll pull it together."

Keaton had cleaned up most of the random stacks when his father stood up beside the kitchen table. "Liz says you're boning some ballplayer's wife."

"That's not—"

His father waved him off. "Liz knows. That's bad stuff."

John Keaton padded into the living room. As he moved, the fly on his pajamas opened and shut with each step. "Ballplayers' wives are easy marks. Husbands on the road, chased by poon tang."

"That's not the case here. The husband is dead."

"Doesn't matter. Not worth it." John Keaton raised his index finger just above his waist and shook it. "Don't ass, don't tell."

Keaton tried to avoid watching his father's open fly. "You mean, 'don't ask, don't tell'?"

"You heard me. I know what I'm saying. Damn near ruined us."

Keaton stared at his father. This was a man who'd never shared anything more private than a golf score. "Just what are you saying?"

"Your mother found out. Damn near ruined us."

"You're saying you had an affair?"

"Your mother found out. Got even, tit for fucking tat."

Keaton sat down on the couch, crushing a stack of newspaper columns. "You and mom?"

"Only thing easier than ballplayers' wives is ballplayers."

"Wait a minute." Keaton inhaled a great gulp of air. "This is a little too much."

"Way too much." John Keaton picked up a stack of random clippings. "Damn Yankees."

Keaton's cell phone rang. He picked it up, listened, said, "Okay," and pocketed it. "That was Liz. She's out front with Davy."

John Keaton shook his head. "Don't tell Liz. Anything. Already said too much."

"Of course not, Dad." Keaton rose from the couch and gathered up the newspaper columns he'd crushed. "I've got to go. We can clear all this up after the State game."

John Keaton waved his finger again. "Remember. Don't ass. Don't tell."

John Billheimer

★ ★ ★ ★ ★

When Keaton arrived at the *Herald* office on Monday morning, Meri Atkins poked her head over their shared cubicle wall and asked, "How was your weekend?"

Although he'd spent the better part of the weekend with his father, Keaton responded by listing the events he'd covered as a reporter. "Not bad. Buckeyes on Saturday, Browns on Sunday. No rest for the wicked. How about you?"

"Covered a cheerleading competition in Akron. I'm starting to wish I'd never written those columns about cheerleading being a sport."

"I thought a federal judge finally settled that argument."

"A male judge with a male agenda. He ruled cheerleading was a disorganized activity and that colleges couldn't count it as a sport in balancing their Title Nine obligations."

"If being disorganized disqualifies you as a sport, the Browns could be in big trouble. Are you going to take on the judge's ruling?"

Meri shook her head. "No. I'm burnt out on the issue. I've said everything I have to say, and no matter what side I take, half our readers get mad and write in asking for my head."

"I get the same response when I write about steroids. Maybe we both ought to back off."

"I'm letting the readers write half of today's stuff. I'm answering their e-mails. Got lots when I was filling in for you."

"What's on the mind of the public?"

"Besides weighing in on the cheerleading debate, a few folks wanted to know how to get into the newspaper business."

"In this day and age, getting into the newspaper business is a little like trying to board the *Titanic* from the iceberg."

"I can't very well write that. The economy has made lots of folks serious about finding work."

"A better question would be, 'How do you *keep* a newspaper

248

job in this market?' "

"I give up. How do you?"

"By devoting your Saturday and Sunday to cheerleading contests and Buckeye and Browns games."

Keaton's phone rang. As soon as he answered, he recognized the Okie twang.

"Mr. Keaton? It's Wes Hightower from Noble County. Thought you'd like an update on the Raptor case."

Keaton said, "Absolutely," even though he knew that if they'd found that Raptor's murder was tied to Blaze's blackmail, there was no way he could keep his vow of silence to Barb. He'd worked too hard to unearth the truth behind Edie Weber's death, and the Hall of Fame elections were still two months off. "Got the case solved?"

"It's been kinda two steps forward and one step back, but we have made a good deal of progress since you left."

"Tell me about the two steps forward."

"For one thing, it looks like Radar Raptor was your blackmailer. We can't link him directly to the phony name in the Ponca City bank account, but every time there was a withdrawal from that account, Raptor's personal savings account jumped by roughly the same amount."

"About how much did his savings jump in a year?"

Keaton heard papers being shuffled at the other end of the line. Could he trust Hightower? He certainly trusted Black Elk, who had preserved the Weber evidence and passed up at least one opportunity to put a fatal end to the questions he and Allison were asking.

Hightower came back on the line. "Looks like about a hundred grand each year."

The distance between Ohio and Oklahoma made it easy to extend Hightower the same trust he'd given Black Elk. If the sheriff's numbers were to be believed, Raptor must have been acting alone. "Sounds like Raptor's our man," Keaton said. "Any idea who killed him?"

"We've got a few leads. Ballistics tells us that extra rifle on his wall rack was the one that fired on you and your friend."

"But was it Raptor's, or was it planted?"

"Not sure. We do know this. Raptor was a real gun nut. We found detailed listings documenting over fifty weapons in his possession. He listed make, caliber, date purchased, cost, and where he got it. Every weapon on the wall was cataloged. Except for that extra rifle. It didn't make the list."

"Any prints on it?"

"Somebody had wiped it clean. But we did find two of Ernie Jenkins's prints along with yours in Raptor's hunting lodge."

"Nice work," Keaton said. "What does Jenkins have to say about that?"

"That's where we take one step backward, I'm afraid. Ernie's gone missing."

"How long ago?"

"Wife reported it a couple of days ago."

"Any leads?"

"He rented a car in Tulsa and we got hits on his credit card in Saint Louis and Fort Wayne. We've got an APB out, so he shouldn't be too hard to find."

"Saint Louis and Fort Wayne. Sounds like he's headed in this direction."

"Well, if you see him before we do, say 'howdy' and hang onto him."

"If it's all the same to you, I'd like to steer clear of him. If Ernie shot Raptor, there's a good chance he was the one firing at me as well. The shots came from his property."

"If he is guilty, he's not being very smart about disappearing. If he keeps on using his credit cards, we should be able to catch him before he does any more harm. We'll keep you informed."

After Keaton hung up, Meri poked her head over the cubicle wall. "Did I hear you say somebody had shot at you and is headed this way?"

"You make it sound more ominous than it is. Even if he is the guy who shot at me, he's got no reason to try again. I don't know anything the cops don't know."

"All the same, I think I better warn my readers off the newspaper business after all." Meri flexed the thin cubicle wall. "And then replace this wall with a brick one."

The weekend brought the first major snowstorm of the season. It bogged down Interstate 71 and clouded Keaton's field of view as he drove to Cleveland to visit Barb Stender.

Barb threw open her door and greeted him with a kiss that cleaned his tonsils and melted the snow on his lapels. "I was expecting you an hour ago," she said as she broke the clinch and led him inside.

Keaton took off his hat and overcoat. "The snowstorm followed me all the way from Menckenburg."

"Maybe we ought to stay in tonight."

"No. I promised you a dinner out. The radio says the storm should clear soon. Your driveway's a little slippery, but the main roads are okay."

Barb hung his hat and coat in the vestibule. "Well, let's have a drink here first. Give you a chance to unwind. If the radio's right, we can go out later." She poured two glasses of cabernet and joined Keaton on the couch. "Heard anything new from Oklahoma?"

Keaton reported what he'd learned about the police investigation of Raptor's death.

"So their chief suspect, this man Jenkins, has gone missing?" Barb said.

"The sheriff says he seems to be headed in our direction."

"How do they know that?"

"They're tracking his credit-card purchases."

"So the law is hot on his trail?"

"I can't vouch for the temperature of the pursuit, but they seemed confident they'll catch up with him fairly quickly, so long as he keeps using his credit card to drop bread crumbs."

"If they do catch him, that whole story of Blaze and the accident will come out."

"It will have to."

"And you'll help to see that it does."

"I'm a reporter, Barb. It's one of the biggest stories I've ever chased."

She took a sip of wine. "I suppose if you don't report it, someone else will."

"Blaze is big news, and it's a big story."

Barb patted Keaton's leg. "Then I better hope Jenkins can stay clear of the law until the Hall of Fame election is over."

"That's not impossible."

"I appreciate you keeping it quiet so far." She set her glass on the end table and walked to the picture window. "Looks like the storm has cleared. There's a beautiful moon."

"Then let's go find dinner."

"At least let me drive. You've just had a long trip."

Keaton stood up. "I'd be honored to let you drive."

Barb ran her hand around the inside of Keaton's hat as she handed it to him. "The inner band is stuffed with newspaper. Has your head been shrinking?"

"It's one of my father's old hats. Just carrying on the family tradition."

Keaton took Barb's elbow to steady her as they walked down the porch steps onto her driveway. The snow had stopped falling, but patches of ice glistened in the tracks left by Keaton's Ford Escort.

The two clung together for warmth and stability until they reached Barb's Mercedes. Keaton held the driver's door open and Barb patted his cheek as she slid behind the wheel. Then he slammed the door shut and steadied himself on the hood as he circled the car.

Keaton slipped slightly as he reached for the handle of the passenger door. He righted himself and had just swung the door open when a shot sounded and the passenger window shattered above his hand.

Before he could react, he heard another shot and felt a sharp pain in his left shoulder.

CHAPTER TWENTY:
THE FAMILY TRADITION

KEATON'S KORNER

I've been reading old columns written by my grandfather and father, and am struck by how differently three generations of writers have treated the off-field follies of baseball players. In the first half of the twentieth century, reporters traveled with the teams, sometimes roomed with the players, and served as ghostwriters for the more famous stars. Grantland Rice, the most famous sportswriter of my grandfather's day, said, "When ballplayers are no longer heroes to you, it's time to stop writing sports." This is the attitude of a public-relations flack, not a true reporter.

Because this attitude was shared by most writers, the public was spared fully developed portraits of their most popular players. Babe Ruth was a womanizing boozer; Grover Cleveland Alexander was a functioning alcoholic; Tris Speaker was an inveterate gambler. But the writers covered for them. My grandfather knew of Speaker's gambling, but praised him as a player and kept quiet about his vice.

Baseball writers were not alone in protecting admired figures. Reporters kept FDR's wheelchair out of photographs and hid JFK's womanizing from the public. This all changed for baseball in the late sixties, when Jim Bouton wrote Ball Four, which characterized some of his Yankee teammates, particularly Mickey Mantle, as carousing, womanizing drunkards. Bouton was ostracized by the baseball community, but younger reporters with no team affiliations felt free to explore the dark side of the stars.

Now, of course, anything goes. After gaining admission to the Hall of Fame, Kirby Puckett was accused of sexual assault and revealed to have cheated on both his wife and mistress. Two paternity suits helped keep onetime idol Steve Garvey out of the Hall of Fame, and Wade Boggs confessed to Barbara Walters on TV that he suffered from what he called a sexual addiction after his former mistress peddled tales of adultery to national TV and Penthouse Magazine.

It's not clear that the public is any better off knowing players' tenure at treatment centers and the names of their mistresses. With the Hall of Fame elections less than two months away, however, it's more productive if we focus on our heroes' deeds between the foul lines.

Barb grabbed Keaton's overcoat sleeve and dragged his upper torso into the passenger seat. Then she floored the accelerator, and the Mercedes fishtailed down the slippery driveway with the passenger door flapping on Keaton's dangling legs.

They thumped onto the main road, and Barb covered four blocks with the gas pedal floored before she slowed to allow Keaton to pull his legs into the car and close the passenger door. With the door closed, she picked up speed and outdistanced all following headlights, pulling up to the Cleveland Clinic's emergency entrance just fifteen minutes after the first shot had shattered the side window.

A triage nurse cut off Keaton's bloodied shirt, cleaned and examined his shoulder, declared his wound to be superficial, and applied a temporary bandage. Then she sent them back to the waiting room to fill out forms and answer questions. An intake nurse in a cubicle the size of a telephone booth examined the first set of forms and asked Keaton if he'd ever been exposed to domestic violence. In the adjoining cubicle, a middle-aged couple argued loudly with a social worker over whether their daughter, who had been admitted to the emergency room, was the victim of abuse. In the far corner of the waiting room, a stout black woman quaked with sobs.

After an hour's wait, an aide led Keaton inside to a small examination room where a young resident recleaned and redressed his wound. "You're our fourth gunshot victim this evening," the resident said. "You're a lot luckier than the others."

The resident knotted an elastic bandage tightly around Keaton's shoulder. "Already had a couple of gangbangers and a mugging victim who wanted to hold onto his wallet. He's been on the operating table for a couple of hours."

"Is that typical for a Friday night?" Keaton asked.

"Typical for a hot Friday night in the summer. Not the first big snowfall of the season. We're already swamped with traffic accidents."

The resident looped a sling around Keaton's neck. "Report back to the clinic in a week." He scribbled on a prescription pad and handed the top sheet to Keaton. "Get this filled and take a tablet if you're feeling pain. No more than four a day."

"Am I free to go?"

"Head of Emergency will have to check you out. Gunshot wound, cops will want to talk to you."

Barb took Keaton's good arm when he reappeared in the waiting area. "What's the diagnosis?"

"Just a scratch. But they want me to wait and talk to the police."

A commotion broke out near the metal detector at the entrance to the waiting area. "Policeman or no policeman," the security guard said, "you can't bring firearms in here."

Keaton recognized the plainclothes officer arguing with the security guard and led Barb to the metal detector. "It's okay,

Gerry," he said to the officer. "If you're here to see us, we'll come out."

The officer took his pistol back from the guard. "That's fine. We can talk out here in the corridor."

Gerry Waldron was no longer the youngest detective in Cleveland's police department, but his rounded features made him look at least ten years younger than his contemporaries. He tried to add a few years by cultivating a thin black mustache, but nothing he did could help him escape the nickname "Baby Face."

Keaton had worked with Waldron a year earlier, and knew that his competence and confidence belied his youthful appearance. He led Barb out the waiting-room exit and introduced her to Waldron.

"Saw your name on the incoming report and volunteered for the case," Waldron said to Keaton. "Pretty ritzy neighborhood you were in. Don't get many drive-by shootings in that neck of the woods. What went down, anyhow?"

"Don't really know," Keaton said. "It all happened so fast. I was getting into Barb's car in her driveway when we heard two shots. The first one nailed the passenger window and the second one winged me."

"I drove us out of there before there was any more shooting," Barb said.

"Where were you going in the snowstorm?" Waldron asked.

"The snow had stopped. We were headed out to dinner," Keaton said. "Barb is Blaze Stender's widow. I'm working on his biography and drove up to do some research. We had restaurant reservations."

"What restaurant?"

"Danilee's. Downtown," Barb said.

Waldron whistled softly. "Not likely to get much research done there. Lighting's so low you can barely see your hand in front of your face."

"You know the place?" Keaton asked.

"Took my wife there on our fifth anniversary. Have to wait another five years to afford it again."

A stout woman carrying a screaming baby in a blood-soaked blanket shouldered her way past them on her way to the emergency room.

"Pretty awkward talking here," Waldron said. "Maybe we ought to take a look at the scene of the crime."

By the time Waldron had radioed two patrol officers and followed Barb to her home the snow had started again, and flurries had nearly covered the tracks the Mercedes had left fishtailing out of the driveway.

Barb parked her car where it had been standing when the shooting started, and Keaton showed the policemen how far he had opened the passenger door when the window shattered.

It didn't take the officers long to find where the shooter had been standing. Snow had been shoved around beneath one of the large oaks that paralleled the stone wall surrounding the property.

"Looks like he tried to cover his tracks," Waldron said. "But you can see where he stood, and there's a break in the mound of snow on top of the wall where he cleared it."

Waldron dismissed the two patrol officers after they taped off the crime scene and a forensic team arrived to photograph Barb's Mercedes and the signs left by the shooter. Then he joined Keaton and Barb in the Stenders' kitchen.

"Shooter was either waiting for you or followed you here," Waldron sad. "Any idea who it might have been?"

Keaton shook his head. "Not sure. But it's the second time this month somebody's shot at me."

"Wasn't aware it was open season on sportswriters," Waldron said. "Why didn't we hear about the first time?"

"Happened in Oklahoma. I reported it there."

"I take it they didn't catch the culprit. If you're not sure who's been shooting at you, can you at least guess why?"

"I was in Oklahoma running down leads on an old hit-and-run case. Someone was evidently threatened by what I was finding out."

"Last time I checked," Waldron said, "hit-and-run wasn't a spectator sport. Isn't that a little off your beat?"

"I was researching a book."

Barb interrupted to say, "Anyone want a drink?"

Waldron ordered coffee, and Keaton said, "I could use several. Let's start with whatever scotch you've got handy."

"Better be careful sloshing scotch on top of the hospital's painkillers," Waldron said.

"They gave me some tablets, but I haven't taken them yet. I think I'd rather have scotch."

"So this book you were researching in Oklahoma," Waldron said. "It's the same book you're working on here?"

Keaton glanced at Barb and nodded. "A lot of the story is still confidential. Maybe you ought to talk to the Oklahoma police. I don't want to spill anything they're trying to keep secret." He gave Waldron phone numbers for Hightower and Black Elk.

Waldron pocketed the numbers. "You're the one being shot at here in my jurisdiction. Can't you give me a sanitized version?"

"At least two people had reason to be threatened by what I was investigating. An ex-deputy named Raptor and a realtor named Jenkins. Since the time someone shot at me, Raptor has been murdered and Jenkins has disappeared."

Waldron took a cup of coffee from Barb. "So do the Oklahoma police think Jenkins killed Raptor?"

"It's the most likely explanation," Keaton said. "For all they know, though, someone else could have killed them both."

"Still," Waldron said, "if no one knows where Jenkins is, could he have been tonight's shooter?"

"His credit cards suggest he's headed this way," Keaton said. "Oklahoma cops say he bought gas in Tulsa, Saint Louis and Fort Wayne."

"Sounds like we need his description."

"The Oklahoma police have his fingerprints. They know everything I know." Keaton shrugged his good shoulder. "So there's no real reason for Jenkins to come after me. Killing me doesn't buy him anything."

"Maybe he doesn't know that," Waldron said. "Or maybe he's just out for revenge."

Keaton sipped his scotch and rubbed his eyes. "Something else doesn't make sense. Fort Wayne is on the route from Tulsa to Cleveland."

"You said he was headed this way," Waldron said. "What's the problem?"

"I live in Menckenburg. You wouldn't go through Fort Wayne to get from Tulsa to Menckenburg. It's like he knew I'd be coming to Cleveland."

"Fort Wayne isn't that much of a detour. Maybe he has friends there."

"I don't want to go through life looking over my shoulder," Keaton said. "Assuming Jenkins is after me, what can I do?"

"Lie low. Vary your routine. Contact us if you see anything suspicious. How long will you be here in Cleveland?"

"I go back home tomorrow."

"We can't keep a constant watch on you, but if you let us know where you'll be, we can try to provide a police presence. I've got a few friends on the Menckenburg force. I can alert them too."

"That would be a help," Keaton said.

"Where will you be while you're here in Cleveland?"

Keaton raised his eyebrows in Barb's direction and then lifted his good arm toward the ceiling. "Right here."

Waldron smiled. "You won't be going back out to dinner, then?"

"Somehow I don't feel much like eating."

Keaton and Barb had a few more drinks and retired early. Even after several scotches, Keaton had trouble sleeping, reacting to every creak and shudder in the unfamiliar house. He got out of bed at dawn and shuffled through the pages of Blaze Stender's scrapbooks, but he had trouble concentrating on the baseball clippings Barb had collected. He had a feeling that the real story of Stender's life was off the diamond, somewhere between an Oklahoma intersection and a Lake Erie breakwater.

When Barb woke up, she tried to help with the scrapbook review, providing personal details that weren't in the clippings, but Keaton's heart wasn't in it. He apologized for being distracted and left for Menckenburg after sharing a light lunch. True to his word, Detective Waldron provided a police escort that took Keaton as far as the Cuyahoga County line.

Keaton checked his rearview mirror sporadically on Interstate 71, but began watching it regularly when he hit the Menckenburg city limits. Instead of going to his apartment, he headed for his father's nursing home, taking evasive action down several side streets to make sure he wasn't being followed.

The height of the stacks of newspaper columns in his father's living room had grown since Keaton had last visited, and the number of stacks had shrunk and no longer spread into the kitchen. Keaton had tried to help his father by starting stacks on every topic he could think of and labeling them clearly so his dad could sort his own newspaper columns with a minimum of confusion. In addition to his original piles, he'd started new stacks labeled MANAGERS, PITCHING, FIELDING, HIT-TING, HOME RUNS, ALL STARS, SALARIES, and YAN-KEES. His father had still managed to start a few random stacks with no apparent themes, but for the most part he'd added to the labeled stacks started by Keaton.

The stack labeled YANKEES held nearly twice as many columns as most of the others. It was of particular interest to Keaton, since his father's only comment after suggesting that both he and Keaton's mother had been unfaithful to each other was "Damn Yankees."

Keaton started to leaf through the YANKEES stack, arranging the columns in chronological order, while his father sat on the living room couch sipping a beer. "Last time we did this, Dad," Keaton said, "you talked about having an affair."

"I talked about you having an affair."

"That too, but you said you understood. Because of your own experience."

"Bad business. Learn from my mistakes."

"To do that, I'd need to know more about your mistakes."

Like whether you were making it all up, Keaton thought. He'd searched the Web and his own library for information on the symptoms of Alzheimer's. The ten common warning signals all involved different aspects of memory loss. Patients forgot names of intimates or what had happened to them. What Keaton wanted to know was whether patients made things up that never happened. A call to an Alzheimer's hotline gave him some insight. Sufferers sometimes became delusional, accusing family members of stealing from them. Or having affairs. So his father's accusations against his mother could have reflected paranoid delusions. Or they could have been true.

He wanted to get at the truth, but his father seemed reluctant to revisit the issue. Maybe he should start a stack of columns labeled ADULTERY and see what developed.

Keaton went on organizing the YANKEE stacks. "Dad, you always said you hated the Yankees. But you've got more columns on them than anything else except the Indians."

"Bastards were good copy."

A column on Mickey Mantle caught Keaton's eye. "Dad. You called Mickey Mantle a lush."

John Keaton set his beer bottle down and wiped his mouth with his sleeve. "He was a lush. That's what killed him."

"But you wrote this in nineteen sixty-one. Reporters were still covering up for players then. They didn't pull the covers back until much later. Not until Bouton wrote *Ball Four.*"

"Mantle was a womanizing lush. Helluva center fielder. But a womanizing lush."

"Your column compares him to Babe Ruth."

John Keaton took a long pull on his beer. "Another womanizing lush."

"But nobody wrote about it. Not in the early sixties. What did people say about this column?"

"Not a whole lot. Drinking was a laughing matter back then. Dean Martin, Jackie Gleason, they all joked about it on TV. Besides, folks didn't believe it about Mantle." John Keaton grimaced. "All-American boy. Took another ballplayer like Bouton to blow the lid off. Make them believe it."

"The Yankees ostracized Bouton. Didn't they come after you? Why'd your newspaper print this column?"

"It was a compromise. I had a bigger story they sat on. Wouldn't print the stuff I had on Dr. Feelgood."

"Who was Dr. Feelgood?"

"Some quack. Don't remember his real name. Injected Mantle with a mystery mix—amphetamines, steroids, vitamins, bone marrow . . ." John Keaton waved the hand that wasn't holding a beer. "Who knows what. Used a dirty needle. Mick got infected. Took him out of the lineup. Late in the season."

"The nineteen sixty-one season? When he and Maris were chasing Ruth's record?"

"Maris caught Ruth. Mantle didn't."

"But he might have? If it weren't for this Dr. Feelgood? Why didn't anybody know about this?"

"Big cover-up. Papers said he got an infection from playing on wet grass."

"How'd you find out?"

John Keaton picked at the label on his Budweiser. "Had my sources."

"Mom? Did Mom know Mickey Mantle?"

"Every pretty nurse in New York knew the Mick."

"But Mom was nursing in Cleveland then. The two of you were married by that time. Otherwise I'd be illegitimate."

"Somebody call you a bastard?"

"It was a joke, Dad."

"Somebody calls you a bastard, send them to me."

"If you were in Cleveland, how'd you hear about Mantle and this Dr. Feelgood?"

"Your mom. She still had nursing friends in New York."

"But you can't remember Feelgood's name?"

"Some New York Jewboy."

The answer startled Keaton. He couldn't remember ever hearing his father utter anything approaching an ethnic slur. Another of the Alzheimer's symptoms his research had uncovered.

John Keaton misread the look on his son's face. "Hell. You know I can't remember yesterday. Let alone names. Use your . . . you know . . ." He flailed about with his free hand, groping for the right word. "Your glorified typewriter."

"My computer? Was this Feelgood guy that famous?"

"Oh, yeah. It's all out there now. He did JFK. Lots of others. That Kraut actress . . ." John Keaton released his beer and waved both his hands like a frustrated conductor whose string section was out of sync. "Can't remember names."

"Don't worry, Dad. I'll look him up. But Mom knew Mickey Mantle, huh?"

John Keaton retrieved his beer. "Won't forget that name."

Keaton held up the 1961 clipping. "And you blew the whistle on him."

"For drinking. Not for screwing or doping. But nobody gave a shit." John Keaton wadded up the shreds of his Budweiser label and dropped them in the mouth of the bottle. "Talk about something else. Lots of other columns there. Forget the damn Yankees. That's one advantage of what I've got. I can forget the damn Yankees."

City editor Eddie Oliver called Keaton into his office as soon as he arrived at the newspaper Monday morning. When Keaton entered, Oliver made a show of adjusting his glasses and asking, "What's that around your neck?"

"It's a sling, Eddie."

"No. That other thing. The one dangling from a chain."

"My ID badge."

Oliver squinted through his bifocals. "Come a little closer. What's it say?"

"My name."

"What else does it say?"

"What's this all about, Eddie?"

"Just wanted to make sure it still says 'Reporter.' "

"Why wouldn't it?"

"Because if a sniper fires on one of my reporters, I'd like to know why I have to read about it in a Cleveland newspaper."

"I guess I was too busy making the news to write about it. I didn't have the whole story. Still don't. I've got the *What*, but only half of the *Who* and none of the *Why*."

"What half of the *Who* do you have?"

Keaton lifted the badge around his neck. "My name."

"So the assailant is unknown."

"He failed to leave a calling card."

"And you have no idea why someone would be shooting at you?"

"I uncovered a few unsavory facts when I was researching Blaze Stender's biography."

"When you were in Oklahoma."

"When I was in Oklahoma. On my own time."

Oliver nibbled on the earpiece of his spectacles. "Were these facts something that might interest, oh, say, the readership of a newspaper, for instance?"

"It'll make a great story when I can pull it all together. Right now it's only half a story."

"When will it be a whole story?"

"When they find whoever was shooting at me."

"So I guess I should keep my subscription to the *Cleveland Plain Dealer* paid up so I can read about it there."

"You'll read about it in the *Herald*. It'll be front-page news."

"I'll need to clear some space for that. How long will I have to wait?"

"I told you. Until the cops corral the shooter."

"And if they don't?"

"If they haven't solved the case by New Year's Day, I'll write up what I've got."

"Your New Year's resolution's going to include being a reporter next year?"

"If there are no arrests, I promised to keep it quiet until then. Either way, you'll get your scoop by New Year's."

"So for the rest of November and December you expect to

be paid for not being a reporter. Who are you to promise to suppress the news?"

"I'm the guy who's being shot at."

Meri Atkins appeared in Keaton's cubicle as soon as he returned from Oliver's office. "That sling looks awkward. Can you still type?"

"I can if I slant the keyboard sideways."

"What did the boss want?"

"Wanted to know why he didn't read about my shooting in our hometown paper."

"Can't blame him for that. How'd he feel about the shooting itself? Or should I say shootings? Did you tell him about Oklahoma?"

"No. It's a big story, and I still need to fill in some holes."

"I don't know what's going on, but it seems to me that you could use a large dose of looking after. Preferably by burly men with guns."

"The local police are watching out for me. I get an escort to and from work."

"And that's what? Thirty minutes in a twenty-four-hour day?"

"They check on me at home from time to time."

Meri arched her eyebrows. "Big whoop. So you're covered a whole hour out of the twenty-four. That's a load off my mind."

"It just doesn't make any sense."

"Random shootings never make sense. Neither do most premeditated ones."

"I just can't imagine why anyone would want to shoot me."

"Seems to me if someone wants to keep you quiet, the best way to deter them would be to go public with what you know."

"But I don't know anything the cops don't already know."

"Nobody's shooting at the cops. Maybe you know something you don't think you know. Or maybe somebody only thinks you know something you don't really know."

"I can't figure out what that might be."

"Want to know what I think? You should write your story."

"There are too many holes in it. I promised I'd keep quiet until those holes are filled."

"Just be careful one of those holes isn't your grave."

"It's my story."

"It's only your story if you're alive to write it." Meri opened Keaton's laptop. "Write down what you know. Do it right now. Put it in a safe-deposit box if you don't want to publish it yet. Encrypt it in your computer. Leave a sealed copy with me. Just get it down on paper. Maybe more of it will make sense to you then."

"Maybe you're right."

"When have I ever been wrong?" She backed out of his cubicle. "I want to hear that keyboard clacking."

Keaton stared at his computer screen. He'd promised Barb he wouldn't go public with the story until the new year. After the Hall of Fame elections. But that didn't mean he couldn't write it up now. Still, until he knew who had killed Raptor and who was shooting at him, it was only half a story.

What the hell. His father only told half of the Mantle story. And his grandfather didn't tell everything he knew about Tris Speaker. He'd just be carrying on the family tradition.

CHAPTER TWENTY-ONE:
SEVENTY-FIVE PERCENT

KEATON'S KORNER

With the Hall of Fame elections coming up soon, readers have asked me how I expect to vote. In the case of Blaze Stender, eligible for the first time following his tragic accident, the question is easy for me to answer. I believe Blaze Stender belongs in Cooperstown on the strength of his 253 wins and his year-to-year consistency as a big-game pitcher.

But, you say, what about his steroid test? It's unfortunate that steroids have played such a large part in recent elections. I think I've made my position on this issue fairly clear. Baseball was derelict in not outlawing steroids sooner, but it's difficult to demonize or penalize those players who used performance-enhancing drugs before they were outlawed. The exercise becomes arbitrary and unfair. Hank Aaron, who broke Babe Ruth's all-time home-run record, admitted he'd tried amphetamines, which were later outlawed, but no one suggests that Hammerin' Hank doesn't belong in the Hall of Fame. It's a shame that people suggest that Barry Bonds, who broke Aaron's record, should be kept out of Cooperstown because he allegedly used steroids. Bonds had established strong Hall of Fame credentials before the issue of steroids ever arose. The same is true of Blaze Stender, who reportedly tested positive in one of the last injury-plagued years of his career and retired shortly after the drugs were outlawed.

Blaze gets my vote, no question about it.

Keaton handed Meri Atkins a sealed manila envelope. "I just put a copy in my safe-deposit box. Since it was your idea, I'd like you to have one too, just in case."

Meri flipped the envelope over. Nothing was written on either side. "A plain brown wrapper. Can I read it?"

"Wouldn't that defeat the purpose?"

"I'll keep it quiet until you go public. I'd just like to know what all the fuss is about. Maybe I can help fill in the blanks."

Keaton had half anticipated Meri's request without knowing how he'd respond. Now he thought he'd like someone he trusted to know everything he knew. "All right. Just keep it a secret."

Meri slit open the envelope with her fingernail. "It'll be as secret as the real color of my hair."

Keaton was working on the next day's column when Meri appeared at the entrance to his cubicle. "The man's a shit," she said, holding up the opened envelope. "Why protect him?"

Keaton looked around his cubicle. "If you really want to discuss this, let's go somewhere a little more private."

"Conference room was empty last time I looked." Meri led the way to the glass-enclosed room, closed the door, and said, "I repeat, why protect the shit?"

"I'm waiting until the Hall of Fame vote is in. I've been arguing that the voters ought to focus on a man's baseball record and ignore any off-field antics. I'm just practicing what I preach."

" 'Off-field antics' sounds like a college prank. The man's responsible for a woman's death. Doesn't the Hall of Fame have a character clause?"

"The Hall is already filled with boozers, womanizers, gamblers, and more than a few racists. The real question should be 'could they play?' "

"I've read your columns. When most of those reprobates were

voted in, the public didn't know about their private lives."

"The baseball writers knew. And they did the voting."

Meri tapped the envelope. "This would definitely cost your man Stender a pile of votes."

"He's not my man. And there's not much doubt it would affect the Hall of Fame vote. Look at how skittish the voters have been over the issue of steroids. That's nowhere near as serious as a hit-and-run charge."

"That's right. So why cover for him?"

"There's a lot that isn't clear. We don't know if it was his car, not for sure. And we certainly don't know if he was driving. And there's an unsolved murder to be cleared up."

"Even if he wasn't driving, he was in the car. And he felt guilty enough to pay a sizable blackmail bill. That poor girl was in a coma for three years."

"What if he was asleep when it happened and didn't even know about it till much, much later?" Keaton held up his hand. "Ernie Jenkins didn't lift a finger to help. It could end up it was more his fault than Blaze Stender's."

"Jenkins does seem to be the only one left alive in this drama who might have a reason to shoot at you. You'd take that reason away if you came out with this story."

"If it is Jenkins, he must want revenge because I shined a light on something he was sure he got away with. Fingering him in public would only make him angrier."

Meri raised one eyebrow. "You keep coming up with pretty thin excuses for sitting on this story. I can't figure it out. Do you think if you sit on it until your book comes out it will pump up sales?"

"I won't deny I've thought about that. But there's not much chance the story will keep very long. The cops are likely to find Jenkins and solve Raptor's murder well before I finish the book."

"Well, then, why sit on the story at all? I don't see that you owe Stender anything. He's a real shit."

"I promised his wife I'd keep quiet until the Hall of Fame votes are in."

Meri nodded. "I can certainly see that she'd rather be the widow of a Hall-of-Fame pitcher than of a hit-and-run driver. Not to mention being a defendant in a tax-fraud case."

"Actually, she did mention that."

"Well, if her name was on a joint tax return, she's going to face fraud charges no matter when you break the story. But I don't see that you owe her any more than you owe her husband." Meri pointed at Keaton. "You have been spending a lot of time in Cleveland, even when the Browns are on the road. That's it, isn't it? You're schtupping the widow. Smile if you're schtupping her."

Keaton struggled to keep his face blank, but he couldn't help smiling.

"You smiled! I knew it!"

"I smiled because you used the word 'schtupping.' I haven't heard that since *Young Frankenstein.*"

"No need to be embarrassed. You're not the first man to neglect his duty for a piece of tail. It's a time-honored tradition. Goes all the way back to Adam. And look at the trouble that caused."

The start of the winter holiday season turned into a disaster for Keaton. He tried to satisfy his familial and romantic obligations by scheduling two Thanksgiving dinners, eating early in Menckenburg and late in Cleveland.

His ex-wife was angry that he left his father and son and the dinner she'd prepared early to slog through the snow to Cleveland, where Barb Stender, put out by his late arrival, watched unhappily as he picked at his second turkey dinner and fought to keep his eyes open after his third glass of chardonnay.

The atmosphere was as frigid as the weather in both cities, and he slept alone in Cleveland.

Determined not to make the same mistake over the December holidays, Keaton arranged to spend Christmas Day, all day, in Menckenburg with his family and his ex-wife, and New Year's Eve in Cleveland with Barb. He picked up his father early on Christmas morning and drove to the house he'd once shared with Liz and Davy in time to exchange presents. The living room in Menckenburg was much smaller than the one in Cleveland where Keaton had grown up, and there was no fireplace, but the smell of the spruce tree and the glow of familiar ornaments reminded Keaton of childhood Christmases when he was Davy's age and his grandfather had moved in with his mom and dad. As Davy thanked John Keaton for the Rawlings glove Keaton had bought, wrapped, and labeled "from Granddad," it finally dawned on him that the gifts he thought had been given him by his own absentminded grandfather had actually been picked out by his mom and dad.

His parents may or may not have had affairs, but they'd forged a full-time family, not a part-time group cobbled together on holidays and weekends. His regrets over the wreckage caused by his gambling always seemed stronger when he was with the family he'd failed to hold together.

His father's voice pulled him back from his memories. "You need oil, Lloyd."

"Excuse me?" Keaton said, before he realized that his father was talking to Davy, who was wrapping his new glove around a baseball and tying it with twine to form a permanent pocket.

"I'm Davy, not Lloyd, Granddad," Davy said. "And I don't have any oil."

"I'll get you some," Keaton said.

"All the great ones used neat's-foot oil," John Keaton said.

Davy looked up from his glove. "Tell us about some of them,

Granddad."

"What about Mickey Mantle?" Keaton said. "Tell us about him."

John Keaton frowned. "Mantle was a womanizing shit. He let his pecker run wild."

"I don't think that's the kind of information Davy was asking for," Liz said.

Davy couldn't quite collapse his grin. "That's okay, Mom."

"What about DiMaggio?" Keaton asked.

"Better center fielder than Mantle," John Keaton said. "More graceful. He screwed around too, but he was more discreet. Didn't fuck and tell. A real gentleman."

Liz stood up. "I think maybe it's time to eat."

After dinner, Davy went out to a movie with friends, and John Keaton dozed on a corner of the couch. Liz and Keaton retreated to the kitchen to keep from waking him. "You're good with him, Lloyd," Liz said, pouring the last of the merlot into his wineglass.

"Who? Dad or Davy?"

"Both. But I was thinking of your father."

"He was good with his father." Keaton sipped the merlot. "I never realized how much he had to deal with."

"What was all that about Mickey Mantle?"

"Dad thinks Mom had an affair with him."

"Before or after they were married?"

"Don't know. Dad wasn't clear about it."

"He's not clear about anything. Paranoia and persecution are par for the course with Alzheimer's patients. Why take him seriously about something so far-fetched?"

"Dad gets so worked up about it. And it's not so far-fetched. Mantle cut a wide swath through the available talent in New York when Mom was a nurse there."

"But that was when she was single."

Keaton shrugged. "Dad seems to think there might have been something later."

"What do you think? You were around then."

"Not when it would have happened. I was born just after Mantle retired."

Liz gave Keaton her "you've got to be kidding" look, a knitted brow combined with a pronounced frown. "Is that why you're so interested? You think Mantle might be your real father?"

"It sounds silly when you say it out loud. But Mom and Dad were never able to have any more children. And I know they tried."

"It's silly whether or not you say it out loud. There's no chance you're related to Mickey Mantle. Don't forget, I've seen you play softball."

"You don't think his genes might have skipped a generation? Like color blindness. After all, Davy's a pretty good ballplayer."

"I don't think there's a chance in hell there's any trace of Mickey Mantle's genes within a mile of you or your offspring. You only excel in activities that require your butt to be firmly wedged into an immobile chair. Like writing and poker."

"It's not worth talking about. I should tell you, though, that in all of last year my butt was only sitting at a poker table two times, and both those times I was in a low-stakes poker game with Blaze Stender's friends, researching his life."

"And you're keeping up with your GA meetings?"

"Absolutely."

Liz rested her hand on the back of Keaton's wrist. "That's wonderful, Lloyd. I'm only sorry it took so long."

"So am I," Keaton said.

Keaton spent New Year's Eve with Barb at a black-tie affair in the dining room of the Whiskey Island Yacht Club. Cocktails at six, dinner at seven, followed by dancing and a long, drawn-out wait for the end of the year amid dangling fish nets and helium balloons lettered with nautical phrases like "Ahoy Mate" and "Thar She Blows."

Of the eight people at his table, the only one besides Barb whom Keaton had met before was Dale Lewis, the Stenders' next-door neighbor, who had been a regular at Blaze's poker games. Lewis got progressively drunker as the evening wore on toward midnight, and kept up a steady stream of boozy laments for Blaze's absence.

"Damn shame about Blaze," Lewis said, placing his hand on Barb's bare shoulder. "If he'd taken my boat the way he'd planned, he might be with us tonight."

"He'd planned to take your boat?" Keaton said.

Lewis's hand dropped lower on Barb's back. "Loaned him the keys."

"Blaze had been having trouble with our engine," Barb said. "He wasn't sure he could get it out on the lake that day."

"How long had he been having problems?" Keaton asked.

"A month or so." Barb shifted her seat to face Keaton and detach herself from Lewis. "Blaze always managed to get it working, though."

"Good man with a boat. Good man all around." Lewis scooted his chair closer to Barb. "We sure miss him, don't we, Barb?"

Barb nodded agreement and shot an imploring glance at Keaton, who asked her to dance. On the dance floor, she said, "Dale's been a wonderful help as a neighbor, but he's never been able to hold his liquor."

"Looked to me like he was at least as interested in holding you as his liquor," Keaton said.

"He's harmless. And he has a good heart." Barb drew Keaton in closer and fingered the back of his neck as she hummed "All the Things You Are" along with the band.

Just before midnight, the partygoers crowded into the club bar to watch the broadcast from Times Square on two large TV screens and count down loudly as the ball dropped to close out the year. Barb kissed him hard on the mouth through half the strains of "Auld Lang Syne," and then whispered, "Let's get out of here."

She grabbed his hand and knifed through the singing, hugging crowd. Keaton caught a glimpse of Dale Lewis trying to catch up with them, then lost sight of him as they collected their coats and headed through the snow flurries into the parking lot. Barb slipped on a patch of ice and steadied herself against Keaton. Then she laughed and handed him the keys to the Mercedes. "You drive. I'm way too drunk."

Keaton wasn't sure that he should be driving either, but he kept a careful eye on the speed limit as Barb snuggled close to him, humming and nuzzling his neck. As soon as they got inside the door of her home, she snaked her hand into his pants and backed him up against the living room wall, saying, "Too drunk to drive, but not too drunk for other things."

They didn't make it past the living room. When the siege ended, she rolled off him and retrieved her gold strapless gown while he lay on the floor and covered himself with his limp cummerbund. She clutched her gown to her breast and knelt beside him, kissing him gently. "Happy New Year, darling."

The next morning, Barb propped herself up on an elbow in bed and blew softly in Keaton's ear. "Wake up, sleepyhead. The Hall of Fame voting deadline has passed."

Keaton rolled over to face her. "Those have to be the least likely words I ever expect to hear from a naked woman."

Barb gathered the sheet around her. "When will we know the results?"

"The official announcement is scheduled for Tuesday."

"That's two more days. Will we know ahead of time?"

"If Blaze gets in, they'll let you know in advance."

"How far in advance?"

"I don't know. It's not something I've ever worried about."

Barb ran her finger down Keaton's sternum. "I appreciate what you said in your column. About voting for Blaze."

"I meant it. I did vote for him."

"Even knowing what you know."

"I don't think a hit-and-run accident that happened before he ever pitched in the majors should affect his eligibility."

"But other voters might not feel that way." Barb leaned back and the sheet dipped, exposing her left nipple. "If Blaze doesn't make it in, do you still intend to break the story?"

Keaton looked away from her bare nipple. "It's a big story. I'll have to break it when they catch Jenkins."

"What if they don't catch him?"

"It'll be in my book. It's a big part of Blaze's life."

"And your book will be out before the next Hall of Fame vote."

"I sure hope so. That's the deal I've got with the publisher."

"I just hate to see Blaze's name dragged through the mud." The sheet slipped farther, exposing her entire breast. "It's my name too, you know."

Keaton forced himself to keep his eyes straight ahead. "There's not much point in talking about it until the votes are announced."

Barb snapped her fingers in front of Keaton's eyes. "What's the matter? Aren't you a breast man?"

Keaton smiled and shook his head. "More like a gestalt man. I'm interested in the whole picture."

Barb threw back the sheet. "Well, gestalt this."

★ ★ ★ ★ ★

Keaton was in his office working on his column when Barb called just after eleven on Monday morning. "It's nearly noon and they haven't called," she said. "They announce the results tomorrow. Wouldn't they have called by now if Blaze had made it in?"

"I don't know, Barb. I don't know their procedures."

"They must have counted the votes by now. They're not going to call. I can feel it." Her sentences were separated as if she were taking great gulps of air to accumulate enough force to expel the next clump of words.

"There's still plenty of time before the official announcement."

"Half a day is all. It's not going to happen. I can feel it."

"It's out of our hands, Barb. We just have to wait and see."

Tuesday morning's newspapers announced the results. Blaze Stender received sixty-two percent of the votes cast, short of the seventy-five percent needed for Hall of Fame membership.

Barb's call caught Keaton just before he left for the office. "What did I tell you," she said. "He didn't make it. I told you I could feel it coming."

"He did all right," Keaton said. "Polled better than Mc-Gwire. Pretty good for the first time on the ballot."

"It was the steroid thing, wasn't it? That's why he came up short."

"Could be. He only needed about seventy more votes. It's possible there are that many baseball writers who will vote against steroid users on principle."

"But he only tried them that one year. To keep his career going. And they weren't illegal when he used them."

"That doesn't matter to the zealots. But look, Barb. Sixty-two percent is awfully good for the first time out. I can't think of any player who did that well on the first ballot that didn't eventually make it in."

"But this was really his only chance. If dabbling in steroids for one season cost him seventy votes, what will your hit-and-run story cost him?"

"There's no way of knowing. The voters can be forgiving. They ignored Wade Boggs's infidelities."

"But not Steve Garvey's. I don't suppose you could sit on your story for another round of voting?"

"You know I can't. And the story may break before the book's released if the cops find whoever killed Raptor."

"What if they never find the killer? Could you delay the book?"

"I've got a contract. The publisher wants the book while Blaze is still news."

"Blaze will still be news a year from now. You got that contract because of him. And me. How can you betray us?"

"Don't even go there, Barb. A girl died. The story was bound to come out eventually."

"The story was as dead as the girl until you dug it up."

"That was my job. What happened to that girl affected the rest of Blaze's life."

"At least think about it. I can talk to the publisher."

"I have thought about it, Barb. Probably more than I should have. As far as I'm concerned, the subject is closed."

"I thought you cared about me."

"This has nothing to do with the way I feel about you."

He heard her say, "Evidently" just before the click of the receiver ended the call.

Keaton heard no more from Barb during the day, but just after he returned home the phone rang and the caller ID announced her name.

"Lloyd." Her voice was strangled, remote. As if she'd been drinking. "It's about Blaze."

"I told you, Barb. That's a closed subject."

"No. This is different. The Lorain County sheriff just called. They've found a body in the lake. They think it's his."

Chapter Twenty-Two:
Meet Me at the Morgue

KEATON'S KORNER

The Hall of Fame votes are in, and my friend Blaze Stender fell short of the seventy-five percent needed for election, even though he had a better winning percentage than over half of the pitchers already in the Hall, including Bert Blyleven, who finally made it in his next-to-last year of eligibility.

I can't argue with the collective decision of my fellow writers, who take their charge seriously and protect the exclusivity of the Hall. I can argue, though, with those sanctimonious columnists who interpreted the results as a justifiable and appropriate ban on so-called "cheaters" like Blaze and admitted steroid user Mark McGwire, as well as other sluggers who are merely suspected of using steroids before baseball banned their use. I get as tired of writing it as you must of reading it. Steroids weren't illegal when the accused players were on the field, so you can hardly call them cheaters. They are no more cheaters than the many Hall of Fame players who bolstered their performance through the use of once-legal amphetamines and still-legal cortisone (a steroid).

Even in the eyes of Hall of Fame voters, some "cheaters" appear to be more equal than others. Gaylord Perry had no trouble gaining admission to the Hall, even though he openly admitted that he regularly threw a spitball, a pitch outlawed before he was born. Other players who can legitimately be called cheaters include those who have been caught using steroids since they were banned. Manny Ramirez comes to mind here. Manny was caught and paid the prescribed penalty for his first offense—a fifty-game suspension—and I, for one, hope that when he comes up before the Hall of Fame voters they will weigh his performance on the field rather than his behavior off of it. It's what happens between the foul lines that should determine a player's fitness for Cooperstown. As for Blaze Stender, wait till next year.

Keaton drove straight to Cleveland to pick up Barb, who came out to meet him before he had a chance to get out of his car.

"Where did they find the body?" Keaton asked as Barb fastened her seat belt.

"Some teenagers ran a snowmobile out too far on Lake Erie and went through the ice near Vermillion. They got out all right, but the rescuers found a body wedged between some rocks under the ice."

"What makes them think it's Blaze?"

"He's the only male missing on the lake whose profile fits the body."

Keaton turned left out of the driveway.

"No. It's the other way. Vermillion's in Lorain County. The county coroner's office is around Oberlin College." She took a folded sheet of paper out of her coat pocket. "I've got the directions."

Keaton made a U-turn.

"It's not far," Barb said. "Could you take care of whatever identification is needed? I don't think I'm up to it."

"Of course," Keaton said. But he wasn't looking forward to it. He remembered that he could barely identify Lanny Morton after the pitcher's body had been in the water for only one day. He couldn't imagine what Blaze's remains might look like after four months.

"I'm not sure what I should be looking for, exactly," he said. "Do you know what he was wearing?"

"He liked Pendleton shirts. Wore jeans mostly." She shook her head. "So long ago. I just don't know."

In contrast to the crowd of reporters that had flocked around after the boating accident, there was only one photographer waiting in front of the Lorain County coroner's office when Keaton pulled up. He tried to stay between Barb and the photographer's popping flashes as they climbed the steps of the morgue.

The county coroner, a tall, balding man with a pronounced stoop, appeared in the doorway and blocked it long enough so that the photographer could get shots of him shaking hands with the widow. Once inside the doorway, they stood in a small vestibule while the coroner, who introduced himself as Johnnie Crain, took their coats.

"How'd that photographer know we were coming?" Keaton asked.

"This is a small town," Crain said. "Hard to keep a secret. And your husband, Mrs. Stender, well, he was a local hero."

"If it is my husband," Barb said.

Keaton noticed a large bowl filled with some kind of labels on a low table along the side of the vestibule. "Are those toe tags?"

Crain reached into the bowl and pulled out what looked like a toe tag attached to a key chain. The tag read JOHNNIE CRAIN FOR CORONER.

"They're plastic replicas," Crain said. "A little smaller than the real thing. Coroner's an elective position in this county. Always have to be hustling."

He dangled two tags on his index finger and held them out to Keaton. "Here, take a couple. They make good luggage tags."

"No thanks. I can't vote here. Why don't you save them for the newspaper photographers. If you show me the way, I'll be the one identifying the body."

The coroner nodded toward a flight of stairs to the right of the vestibule. "Morgue's just down those stairs. I'll stay up here with the lady."

Barb held out her hand, and Keaton squeezed it before starting toward the stairs. As he reached the top steps, he heard the coroner speaking into his walkie-talkie. "Mort, I'm sending Mr. Keaton down. Show him our latest arrival."

Keaton walked downstairs through double doors into a large sterile room lined with storage lockers. The smell of ammonia assaulted his nostrils as he opened the door.

A white-coated attendant waited beside the first of two steel gurneys bearing sheet-covered bodies. He introduced himself as pathologist Scott Warnasch.

"Johnnie didn't come, huh?" Warnasch said. "He's squeamish about floaters."

"So am I," Keaton said.

"Can't say I blame you." Warnasch bent and pulled the sheet back from the body on the first stretcher.

The body was better preserved than Keaton had expected, which made its appearance even more shocking. Lips and eyes were missing, and one ear and half the nose had been nibbled away. The skin was bloated and mottled, and seemed ready to slide free.

What clothing remained was tattered. Half of a blue slicker clung to the right side of the body, covering the remains of a checkered shirt and shredded blue jeans. The left arm had been stripped of both clothing and skin, and a metal wristwatch dangled above a skeletal wrist.

"Jesus," Keaton said. "I couldn't possibly make a positive identification."

"Gets to this stage, we usually need DNA or dental X-rays," Warnasch said.

Keaton pointed toward a silver belt buckle shaped like a

baseball embossed with crossed bats. "That's a pretty distinctive buckle. The wife of the missing party is upstairs. Maybe she could identify it."

Warnasch nodded. "I could take a picture if she doesn't want to come down."

"Could you do that please?" Keaton excused himself and turned his back on the body.

While the pathologist readied his camera, Keaton punched Detective Gerry Waldron's number into his cell phone. "Gerry, it's Lloyd Keaton. I'm down at the Lorain County morgue looking at a body that could be Blaze Stender's. An extra pair of eyes would be useful. Can you meet us here?"

"That's a little out of my jurisdiction."

"The accident happened in your jurisdiction. And the coroner here seems more interested in reelection than in research."

"Lot of that going around. Something fishy about the floater?"

"Just a few things I don't quite understand. It's not really my line of work."

"Be right there."

Keaton hung up and watched as the pathologist snapped close-ups of the silver belt buckle. He handed the camera to Keaton and nodded toward the shot on the screen. "That good enough?"

"Should be. Is there enough of that shirt left so you can read the label?"

When the pathologist slipped his fingers under the victim's neck, the skin shifted even more than the collar. "Label reads 'Pendleton,' " he said. "Couple of laundry marks here might help with the ID."

Keaton thanked the pathologist and took the camera upstairs to the coroner's office. Barb stood when he entered. "Is it . . . ?"

"Can't be sure." Keaton showed Barb the photo. "Recognize this belt buckle?"

Barb slumped back into her chair. "It's Blaze's. Or at least he had one like it."

The coroner put his arm around Barb's shoulder. "Should we notify the press that we've made a positive identification?"

"Your man downstairs said you'd be tracing dental records and working with the DNA," Keaton said. "Why not wait until you're absolutely sure?"

"Warnasch is a licensed forensic pathologist. I'd be inclined to follow his lead." Crain patted Barb's shoulder. "Subject to the wishes of the family, of course."

"Is there some doubt in your mind?" Barb asked Keaton.

"I'd like to be sure," Keaton said. "Let's wait and see what science has to tell us."

Barb stood. "Can we go, then?"

"Not just yet," Keaton said. "I've asked Gerry Waldron of the Cleveland PD to come and take a look."

"Why on earth would you do that?" Barb asked.

"Yes, why?" the coroner said.

"The Cleveland PD handled the original accident investigation," Keaton said. "I just wanted to close the loop."

"We have a perfectly adequate police department here in Lorain County," the coroner said.

"But you don't seem to have notified them. Or the Cleveland authorities. Maybe you thought they'd read it in your newspaper," Keaton said.

"Well, I guess we'll just have to wait, then." The coroner turned to Barb. "Can I get you something to drink?"

"No, thanks." Barb returned to her chair. "I'm not sure I could keep anything down."

It was nearly half an hour before Gerry Waldron rapped on the door of the coroner's office. Keaton made hasty introductions and led him downstairs.

"Isn't it unusual to find a floater this time of year?" Waldron asked the pathologist as he drew back the sheet to expose the remains.

"You're right. The winter water keeps the bacteria quiet and the bodies cold, like meat in your refrigerator. Come spring, the water warms up and the bacteria start working and producing gas. Then the bodies bloat and float."

"So what happened here?" Waldron asked.

"Snowmobile broke through the ice. Fun seekers got a lot more than they bargained for," the pathologist said.

Waldron pulled out a pair of latex gloves and slipped them on. He examined the corpse, touching the mottled skin and checking the reverse side of the dangling wristwatch. "You said you thought something was odd?" he asked Keaton.

"Folks on the dock who saw the boat go out said Blaze's face was covered by a hood. That slicker doesn't have a hood."

"Could be it was Morton they saw," Waldron said.

Keaton shook his head. "I saw Morton's body. He wasn't wearing a hood either."

"Anything else?" Waldron asked.

"When Blaze took me out on the water, he was wearing white slacks, a white polo shirt, and a captain's hat. Not jeans and a sport shirt."

"Could be he just wanted to impress you," Waldron said.

Keaton shrugged. "Seems like he'd feel the same way about Lanny Morton. And there's that cheap watch. Morton was wearing an expensive Rolex that belonged to Blaze. Hardly seems like a fair trade."

"When you're through with the body, I'd like to have you pack up the clothes and watch for the Cleveland Police Department," Waldron told the pathologist. Then he pointed to the side of the victim's head. "And take a look at that skull. The way the skin has discolored and shifted, something may have hit him pretty hard. Can you do that?"

"Of course I can," the pathologist said. "It's part of the standard autopsy exam. We're not all running for reelection."

As soon as they reached Barb's home, she said, "I don't understand why you thought it necessary to call in that local policeman."

"First, they should have already been notified by the coroner's office. But more important, there were a few things that didn't seem right to me. And I thought Blaze would be better served by someone who was more interested in the body than in the body politic."

Barb fished in the pocket of the coat she'd just removed and took out one of Johnnie Crain's toe tags. "I know what you mean. I didn't have the heart to refuse one the way you did." She tossed the tag into the vestibule wastebasket. "But doesn't the belt buckle remove any doubt that it's Blaze's body?"

"I couldn't make a positive ID on the basis of what I was looking at."

"I guess after all that time in the water, it was . . ."

"Actually, there was much less damage than I expected." Keaton formed a mental image of the disfiguring effects of predatory fish and skin slippage. He waved his hand. "Never mind. It doesn't bear talking about."

Barb met his hand in mid-wave, squeezed it, and led him into the living room. "I don't know about you, but I could sure use a drink."

"Are you sure?" Keaton said. "You told the coroner you couldn't hold anything down."

"His presence and that place were too upsetting." Barb went to the kitchen and returned with a bottle of merlot, two glasses, napkins, and a corkscrew. "You'll have to work for your share," she said, handing Keaton the corkscrew and the bottle of wine.

As Keaton twisted the corkscrew into the neck of the bottle,

Barb said, "Tell me about the things that didn't look right to you."

Keaton told her about the lack of hooded raingear and the inexpensive watch.

"Maybe he switched watches with Lanny Morton for some reason," Barb said.

"Pretty uneven trade, Rolex for Swatch. Take more than a player to be named later to balance it out."

Keaton was having trouble leveraging the cork out of the bottle. He sat down on the couch, clamped the bottle between his legs, and yanked. The cork popped free, followed by a splash of red wine.

"Damn!" Keaton watched as a spreading red stain covered his shirt front.

Barb started toward him with a handful of cocktail napkins, but Keaton waved her off. "It'll be all right," he said. "It'll wash out."

"Better let me soak it right now. Otherwise it'll never come clean." She hovered over him. "Come on. Take it off. If you don't, I'll do it for you."

"All right, all right, Mom. I can do it myself." Keaton unbuttoned his shirt and pulled it free of his waistband. The stain had soaked through to his undershirt.

Barb snapped her fingers. "Come on. Come on. The undershirt too. Take it all off. I'll get you one of Blaze's shirts to wear."

Keaton pulled off his shirt and undershirt. Barb gathered them up and disappeared upstairs, returning after a short time with a fresh white T-shirt and a neatly folded plaid sport shirt.

Keaton slipped into the undershirt and checked the label on the sport shirt. "Pendleton, his favorite."

"There are two drawers full upstairs. I don't know why I keep them. You're welcome to them if they fit."

Keaton buttoned the shirt, starting at the collar and finishing with the cuffs, which hung so far down they nearly covered his thumbs. Yet the body was a snug fit. "Sleeves are a little long." He unbuttoned the cuffs and rolled the sleeves up just below his elbows. "It'll do for tonight, though."

"Blaze had exceptionally long arms. It's one of the things that made him a great pitcher." Barb straightened the fabric across Keaton's shoulders. "If you don't want the shirt, just bring it back next time you come. I'll wash yours with my laundry and we can trade."

"That's pretty good service," Keaton said. "Did you always wash Blaze's shirts yourself?"

"When we first started out I did. If he was on a long road trip, there were times when he'd have them done at the team hotel, but that was so expensive. Right after he retired, I'd send them out as often as not. Their ironing is a whole lot better than mine. Recently, though, sending laundry out got to be too expensive again." She dismissed the topic with a wave of her hand. "I'd like to get back to what we were talking about. Those things that didn't look right. What do you think they might mean?"

"I've been thinking about how things might have gone bad on the boat." Keaton poured them each a glass of wine. "Blaze had called Oklahoma a week earlier. Suppose he thought all the blackmail money was going to Oklahoma and then found out Lanny was skimming some of it. They might have argued on the boat. There was probably some drinking. Maybe Lanny killed Blaze, switched their watches, maybe their jackets, and threw him overboard. But as a drunk, inexperienced sailor, he couldn't bring the boat in by himself in the storm."

Barb sipped her wine thoughtfully. "Is there any evidence that might have happened?"

"Well, if that is Blaze in the Lorain morgue, he must have

been separated from the boat. He wasn't found anywhere near Lanny and the wreckage. And Waldron thought he saw a bruise on his head."

Barb set her wineglass down on the coffee table. "A bruise?"

Keaton recalled the sloughing skin on the body's face and head. "I couldn't see it. But Waldron has had lots more experience than I do. And the pathologist said he'd check it out."

"Poor Blaze. If that's really what happened, he could be an innocent victim in all of this."

"I don't see how."

"Well, there's no way of knowing who actually drove the hit-and-run car. That man, that Raptor, assumed it was Lanny, because Lanny was driving when he pulled them over. So he would have approached Lanny for hush money, and Lanny would have taken the problem to Blaze."

"But Blaze must have been culpable somehow, because he still felt guilty enough to pay the blackmail."

"But it's such a different picture if Lanny was driving, engineered the blackmail, and then finally killed Blaze. It changes everything. Don't you see?"

"No. Not at this stage of the game."

"Oh, it changes quite a bit. The way you've described it, Blaze becomes a victim. Voters love victims. It wouldn't surprise me if the story might make some of those negative baseball writers change their Hall of Fame votes from no to yeas next time out."

Keaton had become acquainted with many different sides of Blaze Stender's persona, but "victim" wasn't a word that fit any of them. "That's quite a stretch, Barb. No matter how you spin the story, Blaze has still been cheating on his taxes for over twenty years. The IRS loves victims too. They must. They make so many of them."

Barb bit her lower lip. "If it wasn't for that, I almost wouldn't mind if you did tell the whole story."

"The body in the morgue is almost certainly Blaze. The story will have to come out. You'd better resign yourself to that fact."

"But why does it have to come out now? Or at all? I mean, what's changed, really? Just a day ago, everyone thought Blaze Stender had died in a boating accident. In another day, they'll know for certain he died in a boating accident."

"If it was an accident, I might agree with you. But there's a chance Blaze was dead before he hit the water. That's murder."

"How can they tell for sure what killed him if he's been in the water for such a long time?"

Keaton couldn't rid himself of the image of the sloughing skin. "The body took quite a beating from the water. But the pathologist thought he could at least narrow down the possibilities."

Barb dipped her head and massaged both eyelids with her fingertips. "Oh, God. I don't want to think about it. It's exhausting." She put her hand on Keaton's arm. "And I'm exhausted. Would you mind sleeping in the guest room tonight, darling?"

"Of course not," Keaton said. "I'll need to leave early for Menckenburg anyhow. If we're in separate bedrooms, I can get out without waking you."

She rose and kissed him on the forehead. "I'll make it up to you next time you're here."

Barb was still asleep when Keaton left the next morning. Instead of driving straight to Menckenburg, he stopped at the Cleveland Public Library, where he worked on a memorial column for Blaze Stender, anticipating that a positive identification of his body would come soon. Then he visited the stacks and researched seasonal current patterns on the south shores of Lake Erie.

Before leaving town, he bought a new shirt at Lazarus and

dropped the shirt he'd borrowed from Barb off at the Cleveland PD office of Gerry Waldron.

A call from Waldron was waiting for Keaton when he finally got to the *Herald* office late in the afternoon.

"Coroner's office called around two," Waldron said. "Dental X-rays confirm that the body belongs to Blaze Stender."

"Can't say I'm surprised," Keaton said. "What about the cause of death?"

"Pathologist's not sure. Head took a pretty good blow, but that could have come from the current bashing it against rocks, ice, or the Vermillion pier. Lots of abrasions on the head, elbows, and knees consistent with that kind of current movement. There's water in the lungs, but some of that would happen anytime a body's been in the water that long. Anyhow, Blaze might have been hit on the head before he went into the lake, but there's no way of knowing for sure. Most likely, it's death by drowning. The coroner's getting up a press conference to announce that conclusion in time to make the evening news and the morning papers."

"Timing is everything in life."

"At least in Johnnie Crain's life."

"I did a little research," Keaton said. "Currents at the time of the accident were more likely to take the body east to Ashtabula than west to Vermillion, but that's not certain either."

"Got a body under water that long, things get messy."

"Guess the rest of the inquiry will take a little longer."

"I'll get back to you as soon as I know anything."

Keaton called Barb as soon as Waldron hung up. "I just heard," he said as soon as she answered.

"Well, we pretty much knew it was Blaze as soon as we saw the belt buckle."

"I'm sorry."

"It was a help having you here. When will I see you again?"

"I should be able to make it up this weekend. Look for me on Friday."

"I can hardly wait."

Keaton was shutting down his computer before leaving on Friday when he got another call from Waldron.

"Well, you were right about the shirt," the detective said. "It's pretty much what you thought."

"So now we know," Keaton said. "What are we going to do about it?"

Chapter Twenty-Three:
We the Jury

KEATON'S KORNER

The many local fans of Blaze Stender took a double hit last week. First, the popular former pitcher fell just short of the seventy-five-percent vote needed for election to the Baseball Hall of Fame. Next, his body was found under the ice near the Vermillion pier, dashing any faint hopes that he might have escaped death in last September's tragic boating accident.

When the Herald *first published news of that accident, well-wishers filled my office with e-mails and letters praising Blaze and forwarded a flood of cards, gifts, and flowers to his home in University Heights. With the discovery of Blaze's body, the outpouring of grief and good wishes has started again, and his widow has asked that, instead of flowers, readers send contributions to the Tommy Fund, the center for research into Down's syndrome founded by Blaze to commemorate the untimely death of his own son.*

The Tommy Fund is just one of Blaze's many bequests to his family and the fans that loved him. He left an indelible mark on the baseball diamond and the many lives he touched.

Barb met Keaton at her door Friday night wearing a frilly white apron over a black satin cocktail dress with a slit up the side that was a little beyond suggestive but stopped just short of obscene.

"I was expecting you a little earlier," she said, taking the bottle of cabernet he offered.

"Sorry. Couldn't get away." He didn't want to tell her he'd stopped off at the police department to visit Detective Waldron.

Barb led him inside as she inspected the label on the wine bottle. "Nice. I've got a roast in the oven. I'll check on it and open this bottle in the kitchen. Don't want to risk another shirt."

Keaton shook his head and snapped his thumb and middle finger together without producing any sound. "I forgot to bring back Blaze's shirt."

Barb waved him off. "Don't worry about it."

"I meant to bring it. I did take it to the laundry."

"You're welcome to keep it. It wasn't that bad a fit." She gestured toward the couch. "Just sit and relax. I'll go open the wine."

Keaton sat on one end of the couch, facing the glowing fireplace. An assortment of lit candles lined the mantel and dotted the coffee table in front of him.

Barb returned with a tray holding the opened bottle of cabernet and two wineglasses that she set between the candles on the coffee table. She gave Keaton an eyeful of cleavage as she bent to fill the glasses. Then she straightened, did a discreet bump and grind while unfastening her apron, which she twirled around her head before letting it fly through the door to the dining room.

"Wow," Keaton said. "What's gotten into you?"

"I just felt I shortchanged you the last time you were here. I'm afraid I wasn't very good company."

"You had a lot on your mind."

She sat next to him on the couch, and they clinked glasses. "So tonight I'm giving you my full attention." She took a sip of wine. "Also, I should admit that I've got a favor to ask."

"After that buildup, how could I refuse?"

"You know I fought against holding a memorial service for

Blaze after the accident. I guess I kept hoping he'd turn up alive. Now that they've found his body, though, it's time to hold that service. And I'd like you to speak at it."

"I'd be honored."

"I think you knew him as well as anyone."

Much too well, Keaton thought. He'd have to work to avoid any mention of tax dodging, hit-and-run accidents, philandering, card cheating, steroid use, and God knows what else.

"What are you thinking?" Barb asked.

Keaton tapped his forehead with his index finger. "You gave me an assignment and my reporter's mind was searching for a suitable lead."

Barb set her wineglass on the coffee table and nibbled his earlobe. "Forget that. I'm your assignment for tonight." She kissed him hard on the mouth, then drew back. "What's the matter?"

Keaton shook his head. "I don't know. I just can't shake the image of Blaze on that gurney in the morgue."

Barb took his hand in hers. "I shouldn't have asked you to view the body."

"Better me than you." Keaton took a deep breath and exhaled slowly. "There was this crease alongside his head. As if he'd been struck by something."

"Do you think Lanny Morton might have hit him?"

Keaton shrugged. "No way of knowing. He'd been in the lake so long, the coroner couldn't pinpoint the precise cause of death. There was water in his lungs, and the blow on his head might have come just from being knocked around by the currents."

Barb closed her eyes and sighed. "I don't want to think about it."

Keaton covered her hands with his own. "I'm sorry I brought it up. But I can't get it out of my mind. And there's a lot that just doesn't make any sense."

"Like what?"

"Well, like the shirt Blaze was wearing."

"What about it?"

"It had a laundry mark from a dry cleaner's in Put-In-Bay."

Barb shrugged. "Nothing unusual about that. We rented cottages there several summers. Always right on the lake."

"This laundry mark was a fresh modern one. A bar code stapled to the shirttail."

"So?"

"So the laundry's records show they last cleaned the shirt ten weeks ago. A couple of weeks after Blaze's accident."

Barb hesitated, wrinkling her brow as if the information was difficult to process. After a long pause, she said, "If it's the laundry I'm thinking of, it's a small mom-and-pop operation. They must be mistaken about the date."

"It's Mom, Pop, and a computer. Mom seemed certain. And she had computer records."

Barb pulled her hand free of Keaton's. "You've been pretty busy since I saw you last."

"Just doing my job as a reporter." Actually, Waldron had done the job, but Keaton didn't want to bring his name into the conversation.

"Are you saying Blaze faked his death? I don't see how you can possibly say that. You helped to identify his body."

"I saw the body after it came out of the water." Keaton leaned forward and held Barb's gaze. "I don't know when it went in."

"Surely the coroner can tell how long Blaze's body was in the water."

"Not really. It's tough to do during the winter. They might be able to tell the difference in summer months, but the difference between two and three months during the winter, when the bacteria aren't working, won't register." The coroner had compared the process to storing meat in a freezer, but Keaton chose not to pass along that analogy.

Barb shook her head. "I don't understand."

"I think you do. In fact, I think you must."

Barb just stared at him.

Keaton decided to take the plunge. "Why'd you do it, Barb?"

"Why'd I do what?"

"All of it, I guess. Any of it. Starting with the boat accident. You must have helped Blaze fake his death. Picked him up after he rigged the *Three Strikes* to run into the breakwater. You're an accomplished sailor. You had access to Dale Lewis's boat. You're the only one Blaze would have trusted to help him."

Barb looked at Keaton as if he were an actor who was suddenly spouting dialogue from a different play. "Where is all this coming from?"

"I think I understand what happened. I just don't understand why. Did Blaze only want to get out from under his debts? Did he think killing Morton would turn off the blackmail spigot?"

"Blaze didn't fake his death. He died in the water. You identified his body."

"He may have died in the water. But not when the *Three Strikes* wrecked."

"I can't believe it. You're getting all this from a waterlogged shirt and a Podunk laundry? You're behaving more like a fiction writer than a reporter."

"I'm getting a lot of it from the shirt. And not merely from the laundry mark. After the *Three Strikes* went aground, you asked me to go to the morgue to identify the body everyone thought was Blaze. But when I asked you, you said you had no idea what kind of clothes Blaze would have been wearing."

"And I didn't." Barb shook her head. "And the body was Lanny Morton's anyhow."

"But when I asked you the same question this week on the

way to the Lorain County morgue, you pegged his wardrobe exactly. Jeans and a Pendleton shirt."

"I had some time to think about it."

"But you didn't see Blaze take the boat out. And the people who did said he was wearing a hooded jacket, not a slicker."

"He could have changed. Or it could have been Morton they saw."

"Morton wasn't wearing a hooded jacket when they found him."

"This is crazy. Your theory rests on what somebody says they saw from the dock, my faulty memory, and a waterlogged laundry tag. None of these things could ever stand up in court."

"Maybe not. But it sure forms a compelling pattern. Blaze faked his death. You helped him. But then something must have gone wrong. What went wrong, Barb?"

"How should I know? Why are you doing this? I thought you cared for me."

"I do care for you. God help me. But I have to know what's going on."

"What does it look like?" Barb spread her hands wide, taking in the candles, the fireplace, and the bottle of wine on the coffee table. "I'll tell you what's going on. I planned a nice intimate dinner. And now you're wrecking the evening with these wild accusations."

Keaton shook his head. "They're not so wild. It's the only way I can make sense of it."

"But what you're saying doesn't make any sense. Why would Blaze fake his own death?"

"To get a fresh start. You'd have the insurance money. And he'd be free of the blackmailer who had been hounding him."

"But where would he live? He was a public figure. People recognized him wherever he went."

"He lived in Put-In-Bay for at least a month without being

301

recognized. And he was known there. Nobody at the laundry could remember him."

"They couldn't remember him because he wasn't there."

"Somebody dropped that shirt off at the laundry. And Blaze was wearing the shirt when they fished him out of Lake Erie."

Barb's eyes teared over. She rested her left hand on Keaton's thigh. "Let it drop. Please, can't you? If you love me you'll let it drop."

"I can't let it drop. You're asking me to cover up a murder."

"What murder?"

"Lanny Morton's, for starters."

Barb's hand tightened on Keaton's thigh. "Lanny died in a boating accident. Same as Blaze."

"But it wasn't the same accident. Blaze didn't die in the accident that killed Lanny. He was still alive in Put-In-Bay for at least a month after they found Lanny's body." Keaton shifted his leg out of Barb's reach. "If you helped Blaze fake that accident, you're guilty of Lanny's murder."

"Stop it. Just stop it. Please." Barb's shoulders slumped and she exhaled an extended sigh. "You're right. I helped Blaze fake his death. But I didn't know Lanny would be on board. That was just the first of Blaze's little surprises."

"One of those surprises must have been the shooting in your driveway. It was Blaze who shot at me, wasn't it? That's the only thing that makes sense. Did he do it because he didn't want the hit-and-run story to get out? Or because he didn't want us sleeping together?"

"Who knows what he was thinking. He was over the edge by that time. Thought he could get away with anything. 'Off the grid,' that's what he called it. Said no one could catch him because he didn't exist. Surely you don't believe I had anything to do with the driveway shooting."

"Of course not. He could have hit you as easily as me. But

that doesn't explain Lanny Morton's body. Blaze wasn't off the grid when he killed Lanny. What did he have to say about that?"

"He said he'd just found out Lanny was skimming the blackmail money."

"From his call to Raptor in Oklahoma."

"Yes. He invited Lanny onto the boat. They argued a lot and drank even more. Lanny passed out, and Blaze left him on board the *Three Strikes* when he sent the boat into the breakwater."

Barb moved her head back and forth slowly as if her neck hurt. "But I didn't know Lanny was on board until they found the body. I never would have agreed to help if I'd known he was on board."

She turned toward Keaton and laced her hands together behind his neck. "Everyone thinks Blaze died with Lanny. Nobody needs to know what really happened. Can't we just leave it at that?"

Keaton pried Barb's arms from around his neck. "The hit-and-run story will have to come out, Barb. As soon as they find Raptor's killer. And the killing's almost certainly tied up with the blackmail scheme."

"They'll never find Raptor's killer."

Something in the way Barb said "never" made Keaton's flesh tingle. "Why not? Did Blaze kill Raptor? Is that one of the things he got away with when he was off the grid?"

Barb shook her head. "No. He didn't kill Raptor. Someone beat him to it."

"Jenkins, then. Jenkins beat him to it. And Blaze killed Jenkins. That's why the police haven't been able to locate him."

Barb gave a half nod that left her talking into her lap. "Yes, Blaze boasted that he'd taken Jenkins off the grid. For good."

"The police haven't been able to find out who killed Raptor. How could Blaze have known?"

"Your trip to Oklahoma stirred up several hornets' nests.

After you came back, I told Blaze what you'd learned there. He went wild. Blamed Raptor and Jenkins for all his troubles. He stole a car and drove to Oklahoma. Raptor was already dead, but Blaze confronted Jenkins."

"But Jenkins wasn't a part of Raptor's blackmail scheme. Why would Blaze kill him?"

"Raptor kept track of your investigation when you were in Oklahoma. He figured out Jenkins's role in the Weber girl's death the same way you did. Only he did something about it. He tried to blackmail Jenkins."

Keaton produced something between a laugh and a cough. "Got to admire the man's initiative. One blackmail victim dies and he finds another mark without missing a beat. But how do you know all this?"

"Jenkins confessed to Blaze. Under duress. It's my fault, really." Barb raised her head and looked at Keaton. "Or maybe yours. I told Blaze you'd never be able to keep the hit-and-run story quiet once the police found Raptor's killer. So he took it upon himself to find the killer before the police found him. He felt he had a score to settle with Jenkins anyhow, and when Jenkins confessed to killing Raptor, he signed his own death warrant."

"My God."

Barb returned her hand to Keaton's thigh. "But don't you see? The police will never find Raptor's killer. Blaze took care of that. He hid Jenkins's body and left a credit-card trail that leads nowhere. So the story never has to come out." She traced her index finger around Keaton's earlobe. "You and I are the only ones who know."

Keaton sucked in his breath. "Do you smell something burning?"

Barb moved her lips next to the finger that was toying with Keaton's earlobe. "It's only me, darling." Then she drew back, sniffed the air, and said, "Oh, my God. It's the roast." She leaped from the couch, grabbed her apron from the dining room floor, and disappeared into the kitchen.

A smoke detector screeched, and Keaton left the couch to see if he could help. Smoke billowed from the open oven as Barb stood on a chair to stab the overhead detector with a carving knife. When the detector fell open, she used the knife to pry the battery free and stop the beeping.

"Anything I can do?" Keaton asked.

Barb waved her hand to dispel the oven smoke. "Everything's under control now." She climbed down from the chair and applied the carving knife to the roast. "Go on back to the living room. I'll be in as soon as I check on this meat."

Keaton returned to the couch.

Barb followed after a few minutes, folding her apron into a tidy square. "I hope you like your meat well done."

She laid the folded apron on the edge of the coffee table and poured the last of the bottle of cabernet into their two glasses. "Dinner can wait. Let's let the roast cool while we finish this wine."

She kicked off her high-heeled pumps, hiked her skirt above her waist, did a quick shimmy, and a pair of black panties appeared on the floor beside her shoes. Stepping free of the panties, she slid onto the couch beside Keaton and raised her glass in a toast. "To us."

Keaton left his glass on the coffee table. "I don't see how you can be so offhand about all of this. Blaze might have been over the edge, but you're not. You're ignoring the final piece of the puzzle. You killed Blaze."

Barb smoothed the hem of her dress, which had settled at mid thigh. "Don't you see? I had to do it. For you. For us. There was no reasoning with him. No way of stopping him. If I hadn't stepped in, he would have killed you. He hadn't expected you to find out as much as you did about his private life."

"Blaze was my friend once, Barb. You can't expect me to forget that."

"I haven't forgotten that. He was my husband. But he'd changed, don't you see?"

"We all change."

"You and I have changed for the better. I love you. You love me. But Blaze just wasn't the same man. Not the man I married."

Keaton shrugged. "Actually, he probably didn't change as much as you think. It just took us a while to see him clearly."

"But nothing's gained by showing the world that side of him. And I haven't even told you the worst of it." Barb gulped down half her wine and set her glass on the table beside Keaton's. "We were on Dale Lewis's boat. Just off Put-In-Bay. He was drinking and laughing about how much he'd gotten away with. There was no stopping him. He threatened you. Threatened me. Said he'd get Rosemary Spinetti to help him. Even had the nerve to hint that he and his father had plotted Tommy's death. My God. That was the last straw."

She grasped the empty bottle of cabernet by the neck and slammed it into the palm of her left hand. "The last straw. I hit him with a wine bottle. As hard as I could. He was too drunk to duck."

She shook her head and shuddered. "He just slumped over the galley table. Dead weight. It was all I could do to drag him to the side of the boat and leverage him overboard."

She hefted the empty wine bottle. "Imagine that! A man who could kill his own son, my baby, just because he wasn't the perfect little version of himself that he wanted." Her face twisted with pain, then hardened into something darker. "I always thought his version of Tommy's death was a little off. But he was so charming. So sincere." Her voice trailed off, then picked up force and venom. "Imagine admitting he killed Tommy. Imagine threatening to kill you. He thought he was beyond reach." She returned the bottle to the table with such force it teetered and tipped onto its side. "Well, he wasn't."

She turned to Keaton. "But now, don't you see, none of this ever has to come out. Raptor's death can go unsolved. You and I are the only ones who know what really happened."

She hiked her skirt up and swung one leg over Keaton's lap, straddling him. "Everyone thinks Blaze drowned when the *Three Strikes* crashed. Even the coroner says so. It's perfect, don't you see?"

"You're asking me to be an accessory to murder."

She wound her arms around him and murmured into his neck. "No. No. Not an accessory. It's already done. All you have to do is keep quiet about what you know."

She ground against him. One hand snaked down the front of his trousers. "Do it for me. For us."

Keaton shook his head. "I can't do it, Barb."

She pulled back to look at him. Her hand stopped moving inside his pants. "Can't? Or won't?"

"What difference does it make?"

"You said you cared for me."

"I do. But you're asking too much."

"Not if you really love me. I saved your life. In some cultures, you'd belong to me."

"You killed Blaze. I can't be a party to that."

"Blaze was already listed as dead. I just made it official." Barb sighed and pulled her hand out of Keaton's pants. "You're not ready yet. I understand." She reached back and retrieved his glass of wine from the coffee table. "Let's finish our wine. We can talk more after dinner."

Keaton took the glass of wine. Barb leaned back to allow him to take a sip, then leaned forward and undid two of his shirt buttons. "Maybe I was going a little too fast."

Keaton moved her hand away from his buttons. "Fast or slow, before or after dinner, my answer won't change. The way I feel about you doesn't matter. I can't keep quiet about murder."

Barb swatted away Keaton's defending hand, undid a third button, and slipped her hand inside his shirt. She started to massage his chest, then stopped. "What the hell's this?"

She poked at the flat rectangular shape beneath Keaton's undershirt. "My God. You're wired for sound." She grabbed the rectangle through the undershirt and yanked it toward her.

Adhesive ripped and Keaton yelped. He jumped up, dumping Barb on her back on the coffee table and scattering the wine, her apron, and the lit candles on the floor. She rolled off the table, grabbed the empty wine bottle, and rose to her feet brandishing the bottle like a club.

Keaton backed away. "Drop the bottle, Barb. It won't work twice. I'm not drunk like Blaze was."

Barb drew short, tight circles in the air with the wine bottle. "It doesn't have to be this way. Can't we work this out somehow?"

"I don't see how. I'd have to spend my life keeping you away from wine bottles."

Barb stopped drawing threatening circles with the wine bottle and let it fall to her side. "The people listening to that thing on your chest. How far away are they?"

Detective Waldron appeared in the front doorway. "We're right here. Please put the bottle down, Mrs. Stender."

Barb retreated toward the kitchen, but a uniformed policewoman blocked her exit. She struggled briefly with the policewoman, then stopped, exhausted.

"What took you so long?" Keaton asked Waldron.

"You kept drawing more and more new information out of her," the detective said. "Besides, until the end there, it didn't sound as if you'd appreciate being interrupted."

Keaton fished the transmitter out of his undershirt. "Did you get it all?"

Waldron held up a pocket recorder. "Clear as a bell. Up until we heard a crash. That's when we decided to come in."

The policewoman read Barb her Miranda rights and then snapped handcuffs on her.

Barb held out her cuffed hands to Keaton. "Lloyd, how could you?"

"It wasn't that hard," Keaton said.

Barb flexed the wrist that had just been in Keaton's pants and was now in cuffs. "Yeah, I know. I could feel that."

Keaton watched the policewoman usher Barb out the front door. Then he emptied his lungs in an enormous sigh.

Waldron put his hand on Keaton's shoulder. "You did the right thing."

Keaton shook his head. "I'm not so sure."

Waldron bent down and lifted the edge of the apron that had been knocked to the floor. The blade of the carving knife gleamed in the light from the fireplace. "No doubt about it. You're lucky we came in when we did."

"Yeah. That's me. Lucky."

Waldron stood. "You'll feel differently when you've had some time to think about it. Why don't you let me drive you down to the station? We'll need a formal statement from you to wrap things up."

"I hope it won't take too long," Keaton said. "I've got a story to write."

ABOUT THE AUTHOR

John Billheimer, a native West Virginian, lives in Portola Valley, California. He holds an engineering PhD from Stanford University and is the author of the "funny, sometimes touching," Owen Allison mystery series set in Appalachia's coalfields. The *Drood Review* voted his first book, *The Contrary Blues,* one of the ten best mysteries of 1998. Four subsequent novels, *Highway Robbery, Dismal Mountain, Drybone Hollow,* and *Stonewall Jackson's Elbow,* explore a variety of Mountain State scams, scandals, and frauds. *A Player to Be Maimed Later* is the second book in a new series featuring sportswriter Lloyd Keaton, following *Field of Schemes.*

Billheimer has also written *Baseball and the Blame Game,* a nonfiction look at scapegoating in the major leagues. More information can be found at www.johnbillheimer.com.